THE MIDNIGHT MAN

A Selection of Titles from Paul Doherty

The Canterbury Tales Mysteries

AN ANCIENT EVIL
A TAPESTRY OF MURDERS
A TOURNAMENT OF MURDERS
GHOSTLY MURDERS
THE HANGMAN'S HYMN
A HAUNT OF MURDER
THE MIDNIGHT MAN *

The Brother Athelstan Mysteries

THE NIGHTINGALE GALLERY
THE HOUSE OF THE RED SLAYER
MURDER MOST HOLY
THE ANGER OF GOD
BY MURDER'S BRIGHT LIGHT
THE HOUSE OF CROWS
THE ASSASSIN'S RIDDLE
THE DEVIL'S DOMAIN
THE FIELD OF BLOOD
THE HOUSE OF SHADOWS
BLOODSTONE *

* available from Severn House

THE MIDNIGHT MAN

The Physician's Tale of Mystery and Murder as he goes
on a Pilgrimage from London to Canterbury

Paul Doherty

CRÈME de la CRIME

This first world edition published 2012
in Great Britain and the USA by
Crème de la Crime, an imprint of
SEVERN HOUSE PUBLISHERS LTD of
9–15 High Street, Sutton, Surrey, England, SM1 1DF.
Trade paperback edition first published
in Great Britain and the USA 2012 by
SEVERN HOUSE PUBLISHERS LTD.

British Library Cataloguing in Publication Data

Doherty, P. C.
    The midnight man.
    1. Great Britain--History--Plantagenets, 1154-1399--
    Fiction. 2. Detective and mystery stories.
    I. Title
    823.9'2-dc23

ISBN-13: 978-1-78029-026-3 (cased)
ISBN-13: 978-1-78029-528-2 (trade paper)

Typeset by Palimpsest Book Production Ltd.,
Falkirk, Stirlingshire, Scotland.

*To Sally Parry, in grateful thanks
for her outstanding support and work.*

PROLOGUE
Words Amongst the Pilgrims

Murder, Master Geoffrey Chaucer of the Custom House, London, reflected, and mystery were two invisible chains which seemed to link all his fellow pilgrims as they wandered down the old Roman road towards Canterbury. Strange, Chaucer continued his musing, that Becket, whose blissful bones these pilgrims hoped to venerate, was the victim of both murder *and* mystery. Did Henry truly order the killing of his archbishop during those Christmas days over two hundred years ago? Some claim it was the work of his Queen Eleanor . . .

'Master Chaucer, you like this tavern?'

Chaucer broke from his reverie and smiled at the physician sitting next to him. He then gazed around the taproom of The Strong One of Jacob, a spacious, well-endowed hostelry with its lush gardens and lofty stories of open galleries, each with their own narrow guest chambers. Chaucer pointed to the window-shutters, flung back to allow in the warm scent from the herbers. 'The day is fading,' he murmured. 'Darkness will fall and all these passageways and entrances will fill with dancing shadows.'

'And another macabre tale will be told.' The narrow-faced pardoner clawed at his straw-coloured hair, hanging lank as rats' tails, before moving to finger the host of relics dangling on a chain around his neck, or pinned to the great woollen cloak Chaucer truly believed the pardoner had filched from The Tabard in Southwark.

'Yes, another tale will be told,' Chaucer lisped, scratching his neatly clipped moustache and beard. He glanced at the physician sitting next to him at the communal table. The physician, who openly despised the pardoner, had turned his back on that peddler of untidy, unholy rubbish. A handsome man, the physician's face was oval-shaped and ruddy-coloured, the nose thin and sharp as a quill pen, deep laughter lines marking the full lips and clever grey eyes. He was clean-shaven, his silver-grey hair cropped close like that of a knight and, when he moved, his blood-red garments, slashed a bluish-green and lined with taffeta, gave off a pleasing perfume. Gold and silver rings glittered on his long fingers, their nails neatly pared and clean. A precise man, Chaucer concluded, in both dress and action, except for one nervous gesture: the physician kept fiddling with the Saint Joseph medal on a silver filigree chain around his neck. He followed Chaucer's gaze, tapped the medal and smiled.

'This, too, tells a story.' He gestured down the table at the pilgrims, bellies now full, chattering amongst themselves. 'We travelled well today,' he murmured. 'I mean, from Demonhurst. Thank God we'll not sleep out in the open tonight.' He paused as the miller made a grab at the buxom Wife of Bath who sat even more flushed-faced, wimple all askew. She opened her gap-toothed mouth and screamed so shrilly at her tormentor that it stilled all clamour. The miller withdrew, grabbed his bagpipes and blew a strident, wailing blast in reply. The knight, Sir Godfrey Evesden, warned the miller with an outstretched hand. Chaucer noticed how the knight, a self-confessed hunter of the Strigoi – blood-drinkers, even then did not fully turn his back on the monk; that dark shaven pate sat close, cowl pulled forward, hands pushed up the voluminous sleeves of his gown.

'He keeps a dagger there, I am sure,' Chaucer murmured to himself.

The yeoman, the knight's faithful retainer, sitting directly across the table from the bald-headed, wolf-toothed monk, his eyes staring like those of a mad March hare, drew his knife. The cowled, cloaked man of the dark, as Chaucer secretly called the monk, swiftly showed his hands in a gesture of peace. Minehost, the keeper of The Tabard, also sensed the tension surfacing amongst this motley group of pilgrims who seemed, in one way or another, related to each other. He abruptly rose to his feet from his chair at the top of the table, clapping his hands for silence.

'Fair gentlemen and ladies, *Domini atque Dominae*.' Minehost tipped his head at the murmur of praise for his use of Latin. 'The day is done and soon we are for the dark.' He let his words echo like the peal of a funeral bell. 'We have journeyed far, feasted well but, remember, we have decided that each of us tell a tale during our daily pilgrimage along the white, dusty shire roads.' He paused. 'At night, however, we tell a different tale, of murder, mystery and intrigue. We have promised visions of those who parade through hell carrying their severed heads like lanterns before them. We summon from the shadows those beings with skin like that of a boar and the face of a monkey.'

'You mean the summoner?' the miller shouted.

Up jumped the summoner, armed with a wooden trancher. The knight also sprang up, calling for his squire, who held Sir Godfrey's sword. Down went the summoner, slamming the trancher back on the common board, glaring around at the rest of the pilgrims, daring anyone to continue their sniggers at the miller's jibe. The franklin rose, combing his snow-white beard with the glittering fingers of one hand, the other resting on his silken purse with its ornate gold stitching. The purse was strapped to a beautiful Cordovan belt around the franklin's bulging belly, which intended his purse to stay there, not cut by some thief such as the summoner, who'd been eyeing it as lustfully as he had the Wife of Bath's shapely ankles in their gold-starred hose, ever since they'd left The Tabard in Southwark. The franklin rapped the table with the loving cup he always drank from.

'My friends,' he called over the whispers and murmurs, 'fellow pilgrims, I insist that, for your silence, I buy us all jugs of wine and firkins of ale.' The declaration was cheered with noisy banging on the table. 'On one condition.' The franklin grinned in a show of yellowing teeth. 'By the time I count to forty, the same number of days as our Lord's Lenten fast, one of you will have agreed to tell us a tale to tingle the spine and chill the blood.'

The franklin began counting. He'd reached twelve when the physician abruptly rose. Tall and dignified, he held up both hands. 'I will,' he declared. 'Indeed, I already see my story curling into our midst like black smoke or some ruthless phantasm waiting amongst the dead for Death to come.'

'What do you mean?' the pardoner cried.

'I have seen sights,' the physician replied, 'which haunt the soul for ever, poisoning life till life is done. There, my grim warning has your attention! So, hush now.'

The taproom did not seem so well lit now. Shadows moved. Timbers creaked. The weak fire in the stone-bound hearth crackled noisily, spitting sparks. Outside the darkness thickened. A brisk breeze stirred the branches of a tree to clatter against the bolted shutter, as if someone stood outside desperate to get in. So, as the light faded and night descended, the physician began his tale . . .

ooOOoo

The Physician's Tale

Part One

Brother Anselm, Carmelite friar and principal exorcist to the Archbishop of Canterbury, closed his eyes and breathed out slowly. He and his clerk, the novice Stephen of Winchester, were now alone. The doors to St Michael's, Candlewick in Dowgate Ward, London were closed and guarded by Parson Smollat and members of his parish council. All *flambeaux*, candles, cressets and tapers had been extinguished. They were alone in the darkness and already 'the presence', as Brother Anselm described it, was making itself felt. The usual mustiness had faded. The warmth of the spring day, still to be enjoyed in the gloomy cemetery beyond the corpse door, now disappeared. A horrid cold swept the nave of that ancient church, bringing with it the stinking stench of corruption, the horrid perfume of hell. The attack had already begun. Memories whirled through Anselm's mind like black fat flies. He thought about what he had witnessed in Norwich. The lady who'd fled with her lover monk: her brothers had caught up and killed both her and her priestly paramour. They'd castrated the monk then drowned both in a sack weighed down with rocks. Their souls had refused to move on into the light and judgement. They had clustered in that derelict watermill, sheltering like bats twittering in a cave, the horror and bloody terror of their deaths darting out like tongues of hellish flames to disturb and harm the living.

'Brother Anselm,' Stephen whispered, 'it's cold, and I'm frightened.'

Anselm started, freeing himself from the devilish distraction. 'Surely we shall see the Lord's goodness in the land of the living,' he intoned reassuringly. 'Take heart and hold firm. Hope in the Lord.'

Stephen threaded his Ave beads, fingers slippery with sweat. He tried to recite the Pater Noster but could not speak the words.

'*Qui est in coelis* – who art in heaven.' He stared into the gathering blackness. Anselm had warned him about this sticking cold, the unpleasant thoughts. More terrors would soon press in. Stephen's mouth and throat turned dry. He jumped as something brushed his face, soft yet menacing, like a fluttering hawk wing. He must remain vigilant, prayerful and remember everything so as to faithfully record it. He drew himself up on the stool next to the shriving chair in which Anselm sat. He was about to cross himself when his shoulder was poked. He whirled around, alarmed by the hissing whispers. Something crawled over his sandalled feet, cold and slithering – a viper, here? The novice moved his feet. Anselm did likewise. He gripped Stephen's arm and pressed reassuringly. 'Phantasms!' he murmured. 'Ignore them. More will come.'

As if in answer a dog howled, a flesh-tingling sound. Stephen was not sure whether the hound was in the church or beyond the corpse door. A black shape moved furtively between the drum-like pillars of the nave.

'Magister,' Stephen whispered, 'this is supposed to be a holy place, not the domain of demons.'

'So it is,' Anselm whispered back, 'but, as scripture proves, Satan even appeared to the Holy One himself. What I am certain of is . . .' Anselm broke off as candles in the chantry chapel immediately to his right flared into life, lit by some unseen hand. Stephen followed his master's gaze and shivered. The candles on their spigots were burning briskly, shoots of flames leaping up to illuminate the vivid wall painting just beneath the darkened window. The fresco recorded a vision of hell where the damned hung by their tongues from trees of fire. Others smouldered in furnaces, heaped with burning coals, roasted on spits or plunged head first into cauldrons of bubbling black oil. All around these gathered hordes of demons, serpents and monstrous beasts. Black dogs, armed with swords, stood guard over other damned souls being led to a gibbet which stretched over a plunging abyss. The candles were abruptly extinguished and the flames smothered. The whispering began again as a crowd of ghosts hustled close.

'Earth swallowed Abel's blood; it thirsts for more.' The voice was low and mocking.

'Aye,' Anselm replied sharply, 'and all those hallowed by receiving Christ's body before the great resurrection condemn you.'

The voice screamed and faded away. Anselm rose to his feet, Stephen likewise.

'In the name of the Father and of the Son and of the Holy Spirit.' Anselm began the rite of exorcism. He had assured Stephen, before being locked in this darkened church, that 'the scriptures say this type of demonic activity can only be driven out by prayer and fasting.'

They had certainly fasted. Stephen's empty stomach grumbled in protest. He forced himself to join in the prayers, even as the ghastly voices began to mimic what was said. The verses drifted back, distant echoes. Lights appeared, floating like those strange marsh fires above the fens of Ely. Were they, Stephen wondered, goblins, fairies, fireflies or the souls of the damned? Anselm was now chanting a psalm. The lights disappeared; the stench remained as if from some open sewer. A cold, as freezing as the north wind sweeping across the snowbound fields of Lincolnshire, chilled their bodies. Anselm had stopped his reciting. He just stood in the centre of the nave, hands hanging by his side.

'Magister, Magister?'

Anselm turned and grabbed Stephen's shoulder in a hard squeeze. 'I saw one once, Stephen – a knight. The cross-bolt bow had knit his gorget to his throat. Another had smashed into his nose. Others were being slaughtered, some eviscerated; they trod on their own entrails and vomited their own teeth. Some stood gazing speechlessly at where their arms should have been. Yet when I turn away, I see the pestilential horde, bodies covered with buboes, white and round like shining shillings. These turn into burning candles in their flesh; they erupt like the seeds of black peas, broken fragments of brittle sea coal, dark black berries . . .'

'Magister, Magister?' Stephen freed himself from his master's grip. He seized Anselm's freezing cold hands, even as he was aware of sinister shades gathering like bats, their silent wings wafting putrid air towards them. 'Magister?' Stephen could not see Anselm's face through the gloom but he felt his master's hands grow warm. Anselm gave a great sigh, turned and promptly fainted into Stephen's arms. The novice, sweat-soaked, lowered his body down to the cold paving stones. Stephen knelt by his master, aware of the darksmen, as Anselm called them, the night-walkers pressing in. Anselm stirred, groaned and struggled to sit. 'Don't be alarmed,' he whispered. 'Let us see . . .'

Anselm staggered to his feet and walked down the nave. He was calling out questions, pausing and listening to replies. The darkness thinned. The ancient mustiness of the church returned. No longer was it cold. No voices echoed. No lights flared. No darting shadows or flitting shapes. They had all faded, trailing away. Anselm stood in the centre of the nave, hands clasped, staring up at the elaborately carved rood screen. He stepped forward as if to go up into the sanctuary but paused and looked over his shoulder. 'Stephen,' Anselm murmured, 'it's over. Unlock the doors.'

A short while later Anselm, Stephen and others assembled in the great solar of Sir William Higden's stately mansion which overlooked St Michael's, Candlewick. Anselm had washed his hands and face. He'd drank a full loving cup of water and eaten a platter of diced meat, beef garnished with a spicy vegetable sauce. Stephen had also eaten and drunk, perhaps more wine than he should have done. The excitement of the evening had diminished. The novice stared around the opulent chamber, such a contrast to the stark simplicity of the cells at the House of the Carmelites, the White Friars. The solar was luxuriously furnished. Oaken panelling gleamed against the walls; above this the delicately plastered walls were decorated with gorgeous cloths, embroideries and tapestries. The tiled floor was carpeted with dark turkey cloths while the full glory of the solar was illuminated by an array of fiery candles and flaring cressets. Stephen felt the strong arms of his leather-backed chair and stared at the other items of polished furniture: the dressers, tables and shelves displaying a magnificent array of silver and gold cups, mazers, platters and dishes. Stephen glanced at Anselm. The exorcist slouched in his chair at the top of the table picking at strips of dried fruit, his bony face creased with tiredness. Anselm, Stephen reflected, looked what he was, a priest used to the tangled warfare between the visible and the invisible. Anselm had a streak of gentleness carefully hidden behind his hard-featured face, hooded eyes, aquiline nose and bloodless, thin lips. He was clean-shaven, his black-silver hair closely cut to reveal the tonsure as well as proclaim the austerity of this former knight who'd once fought and killed under the snarling, gold leopards of England.

The others grouped around the table were subdued. Parson Smollat, neat and fussy, his rosy cheeks now full-red from the claret he'd generously supped, his piggy eyes ever darting, his clean little face screwed up in concentration as he listened to the conversations swirling about him. Simon the sexton was no different. A smug little man with a streak of vanity betrayed by the way he let his scrawny, silver-grey hair tumble down to his shoulders. Curate Amalric was different. A scion of a noble Somerset family, or so he often proclaimed, Amalric disdained what he dismissed as 'courtly fancy' and dressed simply in a long black robe, heavily stained with food, wine and other unmentionables. Amalric, head and face completely shaved, was bony and angular – so much so that the curate reminded Stephen of a skeleton.

'You want more claret?'

Stephen glanced down at the other end of the table where their host, Sir William Higden, sat enthroned, holding up the wine jug, gazing expectantly around at his guests. A plump city merchant knighted by the King, dressed in a beautiful quilted jerkin of dark murrey, Sir William was trying to remain cheerful despite what was happening in his parish church of which he was the lord, holding its advowson, the right to appoint the parson and other clerics. Sir William's podgy face under its mop of thinning reddish hair gleamed with oil.

'More wine, sirs, surely?'

Sir William's question was politely refused. Amalric gazed longingly into the far corner where the flame of the hour candle was slowly sinking to the next ring – compline time.

'Are you sure?' Sir William's face was now drained of all good humour: his small black eyes hard as pebbles, no longer wrinkled in a smile. The merchant knight put the wine jug down. He played with the medallion on the chain around his

neck then started to slip on and off the rings decorating his
podgy fingers. A strange man, Stephen reflected, Sir William
had fought strenuously for King Edward in France before
amassing a fortune in the wool trade. He had raised loans for
the King who'd rewarded him with a knighthood and a secure
place in the Commons where, of course, Sir William could
defend the Crown's rights. A warrior turned merchant, Sir
William's stately mansion overlooked the sprawling cemetery
of St Michael's, Candlewick. He was a lord who took a keen
interest in his local church and all things parochial. He now
used the wine jug to bang on the table and still the desultory
conversation. He was about to speak but paused at a knock on
the door. This swung open immediately and Sir Miles
Beauchamp, Chief Clerk in the Chancery of the Secret Seal,
swept into the room. Beauchamp arrogantly surveyed them all
as he undid the clasps of his heavy, dark blue cloak; he swung
this off, tossing it over an old chair just within the doorway.

'Gentlemen, kind sirs, good evening.' Beauchamp undid his
war belt carefully, folding it around the two blood-red scabbards
carrying sword and dagger. He placed this carefully on the cloak
and pulled down the quilted jerkin so its high collar showed
off the snow-white cambric shirt beneath, the tight-fitting waist
and padded shoulders emphasizing Beauchamp's slim figure.
The royal clerk walked the length of the table, studying each
of them carefully. Dressed in black, the silver spurs on his
high-heeled boots clinking at every step, Beauchamp carried
himself as if his person was sacred and his very presence of
crucial importance. Just past his thirtieth summer, Beauchamp
was a clerk greatly favoured by the old King. He looked and
dressed like a fop with his be-ringed fingers, tight-fitting hose
and languid ways, almost womanish with his handsome features,
blond hair coifed and pricked like any court lady. Beauchamp
could be dismissed as one of those decadent minions whom the
preachers thundered against with cutting references to the secret
sin of Sodom.

Brother Anselm, however, after he and Stephen had met
Beauchamp earlier in the evening, had warned the young novice:
'*Cacullus non facit monachum* – the cowl does not make the
monk. Sir Miles is not what he appears. In truth, he is a

ferocious warrior much trusted by the Crown and a true ladies' man. Indeed,' Anselm smiled, a rare occurrence which transformed his face, 'he reminds me of myself before.' The smile then faded. 'He reminds me, that's all,' and he had refused to elaborate further.

Sir Miles stopped at the end of the table, lazy blue eyes studying both Carmelites. Stephen noticed the slight cast in the clerk's right eye, which enhanced rather than retracted from Beauchamp's good looks. He smiled faintly at both, nodded and sauntered back to slide easily into the chair to the right of Sir William.

The merchant spread his hands. 'Welcome, Sir Miles. I am sorry you could not be with us for the exorcism, which—'

'I am not finished,' Anselm abruptly interrupted. 'I must leave. I have to because I want to, not because I am being forced to. Stephen and I,' Anselm glanced at his companion, 'must go back.'

The exorcist rose so swiftly he took the rest by surprise. Amalric the curate threw his hands up in horror. Simon the sexton flapped his arms like a spring sparrow caught in a net.

'You cannot.' Sir William half-rose but then sat down as Sir Miles gently pressed the back of his hand.

'I have eaten and I have prayed,' Anselm replied. 'God will give me the strength.' He leaned down, snatched up the leather satchel resting against the leg of the table and thrust it into Stephen's hand.

Sir William made to object again but Beauchamp rose languidly to his feet. 'The priest desires to go. If our exorcist wishes to run one more tilt in this demonic tournament so be it, I shall join him.'

Anselm half-raised his hand, as if to protest.

'I shall go,' Beauchamp declared, 'or no one goes.'

They left the solar, going across the spacious entrance hall with its monumental fireplace surmounted by a giant hood, its pure stone studded with diamonds to defend against poison and magical incantation as well as gleaming topaz, a sure protection against sudden death. Just in case neither of these worked, above the fireplace hung the Cross of San Damiano, much beloved by Saint Francis, while triptychs on either side

displayed in brilliant colours dramatic scenes from the life of
St Christopher. The rest of the walls were hidden by painted
cloths brought to life by the darting light of candle and taper;
the windows were glazed while Persian carpets and woven
mats covered the paved floor. A servant standing by the main
door handed them their cloaks. Outside the April night had
turned dark and cold. One of Higden's retainers, a large, thick-
set man holding a torch, led them across the rich gardens
Stephen had glimpsed earlier, out through a small postern door
and across to the huge, brooding lychgate of St Michael's.
They entered the broad, rambling cemetery. In daylight hours
it stretched quiet and still, a mass of wooden crosses and
weather-beaten stones, a wild garden with shady yew trees
planted to fend off wandering cattle. Here and there clumps
of flowers, violets, lavender, peonies and lilies planted years
ago by some enterprising parson or his woman. Now night
cloaked everything in darkness. For Stephen this ancient burial
place, God's acre or not, seemed a domain of brooding menace
dominated by the sheer stone mass of the old Norman church.
Some of its glazed windows caught the light; others, covered
by stretched oiled pig's bladders, simply gazed sightlessly out
into the darkness.

'Look!' The retainer pointed to the top of the soaring tower.
'No light! The beacon fire has been extinguished.'

'But I relit it,' Simon the sexton declared hoarsely. 'The
beacon was firmly packed, and there's been no rain.'

'I am tired of this.' The retainer turned and came back.

Sir William stepped forward to urge him on but Anselm
placed a restraining hand on the merchant's arm.

'You are tired of what, my friend?' Anselm asked. He took
the torch and raised it high. 'What's your name?'

Stephen stared at the man, his burly, unshaven face all pocked
and marked, furry eyebrows either side of a fat drinker's nose,
with the jutting lips and protuberant jaw of a mastiff.

'Bardolph.' The man's voice was grating. 'My name is
Bardolph, Brother. I serve the parish as a gravedigger and
corpse-mover. My wife and I also own a small alehouse nearby.
We used to sell ale here in the churchyard after Mass on
Sundays and holy days. Now, because of this, there are no fees

for digging, no fees for corpse-moving and no fees for ale stoups.'

'I had no choice.' Parson Smollat stepped forward. 'The eerie happenings here, God save us.' He breathed out noisily. 'Sir William wants that, don't you, Sir William?'

'I certainly do. The cemetery will be closed until these matters are settled.'

'This is our parish church.' Bardolph wouldn't give way.

'Enough!' Sir William declared. 'Bardolph, this can be discussed elsewhere.'

'God will resolve all these problems,' Anselm offered.

'Then I hope He does so soon.' Bardolph grasped the torch and stomped off up the path.

They were about to follow when a loud banging echoed from the church. Anselm ordered everyone to go on. They did, following the pool of light thrown by the fluttering torch up to the narrow corpse door. The path turned and twisted between the stark, fading memorials of the dead. Briar, bramble and bush snaked out to catch the ankle or snare the cloak. The ominous banging continued. Simon explained how it might be the door leading down to the crypt, the charnel house where the gleaming white bones and skulls of the long dead were stored. Bardolph, holding the torch, began to tremble, the flame shaking and juddering. Stephen could even hear the man's teeth chattering. Beauchamp seized the torch and dismissed Bardolph back to the house.

'We are in the realm of the rat and rot,' Beauchamp turned, face all smiling, 'of corruption and decay. If you have the words, you can even summon up each soul buried here and ask them if they're damned or not.'

'Walk on,' Anselm insisted. 'The dead gather here but so do a horde of angry, hostile spirits.'

'Or,' Beauchamp, still trying to make light of it, lifted the torch and stood blocking the narrow path, 'I remember the story of a man who, every time he passed a cemetery, recited the *De Profundis* for the departed. One night, as he did so, he was attacked by robbers but was saved by the dead who rose up, each holding the tool they'd used in their lifetime to defend him vigorously.'

'Not here,' Anselm whispered hoarsely. 'This is not the place for your mockery. I am an exorcist – ghosts gather here. I can hear their faint chatter. Listen!'

'Nothing!' Beauchamp retorted.

'Exactly,' Anselm replied. 'Can you hear anything? Where's the snouting fox, the furtive rat, the floating, ghost-winged owl?'

Beauchamp stared around, lowering the torch. 'True, true,' he conceded. 'There's nothing but silence.'

'And the dead.' Stephen spoke before he could stop himself. The novice pushed his hands up the sleeve of his gown. He knew he could see and hear things others, like Beauchamp, could not. In spite of Beauchamp's mockery, this was happening. Strange lights had appeared. Sparks of flame leaped up only to sink into the blackness, followed by chattering, whispered conversation where one word could not be distinguished from the next. Across the cemetery shapes and shadows moved, darting shifts between the headstones. A hideous scream rang out.

Beauchamp cursed, fumbling with the torch. 'Now I hear,' he declared. 'Let us . . .'

Anselm didn't wait but, clutching his leather satchel in one hand, the other on Stephen's shoulder, stepped round the royal clerk and marched swiftly through the darkness. Simon hurried behind, jangling his keys. They reached the narrow door with its rusty iron studs. Simon unlocked and pushed back the creaking door. Anselm, Beauchamp and Stephen entered. The royal clerk lit one of the sconce torches just inside. Immediately a cold wind swept by them; the torch flickered and died. Higden and the rest hastily retreated.

'You should also go,' Anselm warned Beauchamp. The clerk just shrugged. Anselm walked into the church and pulled across a bench into the centre of the nave. He sat down with Stephen on his right. Once again the exorcist began the ritual. 'Oh, God, come to our aid . . .'

Stephen and Beauchamp murmured the responses. The novice began to tremble. Anselm grasped his hand and squeezed it. Beauchamp was at a loss, aware of the cold, the rank stench, though he could not see the faces which swarmed out of the gloom, white and drawn, eyes black holes of fire, hair like trailing wisps of mist.

'You see them, Stephen?'

'Aye, Magister.'

'What?' Beauchamp whispered.

Anselm ignored him as he concentrated on the gathering malevolence. The dire memories those terrors of the night summoned up swept in to distract his mind and chill his soul. Anselm was back as a soldier in that French city the English had stormed, its streets full of wild animals feeding on human flesh. Drunken ribauds, armed to the teeth, looting and raping as they moved like a horde of demons through the fallen town. Old women dragging out corpses from houses filled with fire and smoke. Packs of rats, bellies full, snouts stained with a bloody froth. Corpses stacked like firewood in the middle of squares. The black smoke of funeral pyres winding everywhere. The screams and yells of souls in their last extremity. The gallows breaking under the weight of cadavers while corpses crammed the wells and polluted the streams. Anselm forgot the rite and began to mouth the memories which plagued him.

'Magister!'

Anselm heeded the cry. He began to recite the Credo as he stared at the haunting, nightmare faces massing close. Beside him, Stephen could take no more. He fell to his knees, head bowed, hands clenched in prayer. Beauchamp, cloak tight about him, drew his sword and half-raised it. Anselm pressed on the clerk's arm until he lowered the blade.

'By the grace of God,' he whispered at the wraiths which surged all around him. 'By the grace of God, in the name of that same God, by the grace of the Lord Jesus Christ, who are you? Why are you here? Why do you haunt this place? In the Lord's name, tell me, here in the House of God and at the very gate of heaven.' Anselm closed his eyes and prayed. Neither he nor Stephen knew if the phantasms spoke or whether their own souls echoed the desperate pleas for forgiveness, for justice.

'Against whom?' Anselm begged. 'Take comfort. I shall light tapers and sing Masses for the repose of your souls. Tell me, who are you? Why are you here?'

'Thrust out!' a voice hissed close to Stephen. 'Thrust out, our souls winkled out of their shells; now we swim amongst the dark ones.'

'Except for me!' A man's voice, mocking and strident, called out. 'Taken, plucked from my rightful place but then . . .' The voice faded like the rest.

Stephen strained to hear but it was like listening to the murmured conversation of a crowd passing beneath a window. He caught some words and phrases, some in English, others in French or a patois he couldn't understand. Stephen opened his eyes. 'They're going,' he murmured. He felt the press around him ease. The cold faded. The stench seeped away, turning back to the general mustiness of that old church. Stephen sat back on the bench. Beauchamp began to softly whistle the tune of a song.

'What happened . . .?' A clatter and clash stilled the clerk's question. Beauchamp jumped to his feet as around the church kneeling rods, stools, benches and other furniture were violently overturned.

'They are leaving,' Anselm explained. 'They vent their temper at not being believed or not being helped. They are withdrawing for a while but I think they'll return.'

'But why are they here?' Beauchamp insisted.

'In a little while . . .' Anselm sighed. 'Sir Miles, that will have to wait. For the time being, we are finished here . . .'

Sir William Higden gathered all his guests into his dining parlour, a fine pink-washed room with a gleaming oaken table. A mantled hearth, the carved face of a dragon in its centre, warmed the chamber, while on the walls either side of it hung tapestries celebrating David's victory over Goliath. Green, supple rushes, tossed with herbs and sharp garden spices, covered the floor and sweetened the air as they were crushed underfoot. A partition to the petty kitchen had been removed. A cook, assisted by two sleepy-eyed servitors, prepared bowls of diced chicken smothered in mushrooms, cream and garlic sauce. Sir William had broached his finest cask of wine sent from Bordeaux four years earlier. Goblets were filled, except for Anselm's – he never drank. The exorcist had once confided to Stephen that if he started to drink the delicious juice of the grape he'd never stop.

When the food had been served and blessed, the kitchen shutters replaced, the fire built up and the doors closed over,

Beauchamp raised his goblet in toast towards Anselm, who replied by lifting his beaker of water.

'Well,' the royal clerk dabbed his lips with a napkin, 'Brother Anselm, I have business with you. However,' he shrugged, 'that can wait. Why did you go back to the church?'

'I had to,' Anselm retorted. 'An important principle. An exorcist never lets himself be driven out, though God only knows the truth behind all this.'

'I began it,' Parson Smollat put his horn spoon down, 'or rather, I noticed it first, both me and my good friend, Simon.'

The sexton nodded in agreement.

'Tell them all,' Sir William urged, 'from the beginning.'

'I was provided with the benefice here,' Parson Smollat began, 'two years ago by the grace and favour of Sir William, who has the right of advowson to Saint Michael's, Candlewick.'

'As well as other parish officials,' Simon, his spotty face flushed with claret, quickly added.

'Saint Michael's is an ancient church,' the parson continued, 'built during the time of William the Norman. You can see that from its nave – the thick, clumsy pillars have none of the beauty of Westminster or La Chapelle. The great tower is built on the side and has been strengthened and extended by successive generations. To the north-east of the church lie the sacristy and store rooms, and there is a cellar and a crypt which serve as our charnel house. The cemetery itself is sprawling, the soil very coarse, difficult to cultivate. The dead have been buried there for at least three hundred years. During the day, despite my protestations, the people used to flock there to trade. Well,' Smollat's fat face creased in embarrassment, 'it depends on what they were trading. Prostitutes, tinkers and hawkers. During summertime the cemetery is the trysting place of lovers of either sex or both. At night, well, sorcerers, wizards, warlocks and practitioners of the dark arts creep in to sacrifice black cockerels and offer their blood to the full moon.' The parson's voice grew weary. 'I did my best. The parish is, or was, a busy, thriving community – baptisms, shrivings, weddings, funerals, ale-tastings. We observe the liturgical feasts, especially Michaelmas, the solemnity of the great Archangel. We have a fine statue to him.' The parson paused as the door opened. A woman came in, round as a dumpling with cherry-red cheeks, a smiling mouth and eyes bright as a sparrow. She was garbed in a blue dress with a silver cord around her plump waist. A thick white veil covered her black hair, streaked with slivers of silver, and over her arm she carried a heavy cloak.

'My housekeeper, Isolda,' Parson Smollat explained. The woman bobbed a curtsey to the assembled guests. 'She came with me tonight,' the parson continued. 'Isolda, what do you want?'

'Shall I stay, Parson Smollat, or do you want me to go?'

'It's best if you left.'

'Ask one of my men to act as Lucifer,' Sir William joked, 'light-bearer.' He answered the woman's puzzled look. 'One of them will see you safely across to the priest's house.'

Isolda again bobbed a curtsey. Stephen noticed the smiling glance she threw Parson Smollat as she made her farewells to the rest of the guests.

'God be with you,' Anselm called out.

'And you too, Brother.' Isolda gazed hard at the exorcist then left.

'Very good, very good,' Beauchamp softly declared once the door closed behind Isolda, 'but why are we really here?'

Stephen glanced at the parson. A good man, he thought, but weak and reluctant to grasp the tangled root of the evil festering here. Despite the warmth, the wine, the sturdy furniture and brightly painted wall cloths, the evil, the bleak despair, the heinous malice Stephen had experienced in that church had followed them here. It lurked watching in the shadows, away from the light. Some malevolent ghost or hell-born creature was dragging itself through the murk across that great barrier between the visible and invisible. The exorcist was also alert; he fingered his Ave beads, the other hand touching the small wooden tau cross on a cord around his neck. Stephen recalled one of Anselm's sayings: 'Thistles of the souls bring forth sin and despair. Satan and his demons can only feast on what we offer them'. What was at stake here? Stephen broke from his reverie as Parson Smollat pointed to the red cross with trefoiled ends painted on a shield which hung on the wall above the mantled hearth. Next to it a second shield displayed the Agnus Dei, a white lamb with a nimbus of gold showing three red rays.

The lamb held a scarlet cross against a field of deep azure and a banner which had a silver staff with a gilt crown on top.

'For all our weaknesses and stupid sins,' Parson Smollat confessed, 'I thought we were a godly community shielded against evil, protected by the Lord and his great henchman, Archangel Michael.' Parson Smollat took a deep breath. 'All that changed last year around the Feast of All Souls. You know,' he swallowed hard, 'that the eve of All Saints, thirty-first of October, Saint Walpurgis, is one of the most solemn black feasts of the sorcerers and other practitioners of the dark arts. I was absent that evening, when our cemetery was invaded by a warlock well-served by the knights of hell, the one who calls himself "The Midnight Man".'

'I've heard of him,' Anselm broke in. 'One day I would like to meet him.'

'One day you shall!' Beauchamp retorted. 'You can shrive him just before he's burnt as a warlock at Smithfield.'

Anselm turned in his chair and stared at the subtle clerk. 'God,' he whispered, 'has ordained all our ends. Pray God we are not consumed by his fire in the second death.'

Beauchamp's smile faded. He looked sharply at Anselm, then indicated that Parson Smollat should continue.

'As I said,' Anselm would not be outfaced, 'I would like to meet the Midnight Man – he claims to be constantly attended by a spirit dressed in a flesh-coloured tunic under a dark robe. I wonder,' he mused, 'why warlocks and sorcerers place such great emphasis on petty demons like that?'

'I do not know any of this, nor does anyone here.' Parson Smollat sniffed. 'Nor do I know what went wrong, what horrid sights and hideous manifestations made their presence felt. Murderous chants, snatches and war cries were heard amongst the howling of a pack of wild dogs which invaded the cemetery and drove off a herd of pigs, snouting around the dead. Apparitions were glimpsed, ghouls and night-stalkers. Menacing shadows with strange lights were also seen.' Parson Smollat crossed himself. 'All I know is that sooty souls, their evil minds fastened in wicked sins, came into our cemetery and sang their own devilish vespers. They opened the very doors of hell. According to rumour and, it is only rumour, the Midnight Man and all his devilish crew were so terrified at what they'd provoked, they fled.' The parson mopped his fleshy face with a napkin. 'I should have been content with that. The rogues and villains fled but, no sooner had the Feast of All Souls come and gone, than the hauntings began.'

'At first they were minor matters.' The sexton took up the story while the parson wetted his throat. 'Tombstones were tumbled. Crosses were knocked over, then those who crept into the cemetery after dark, the night-lovers, stopped coming, eager to avoid the place.'

'Why?' Beauchamp asked.

'They talked of prowlers, sinister shapes and threatening shades snaking around the tombs. Cries and strident screams were heard. Strange lights and tongues of flames licking the darkness.'

'The same also appeared in the church,' Parson Smollat intervened.

'Frightful.' Curate Almaric spoke up, clawing at his hair. 'I heard similar tales when I was a boy at my father's manor . . .'

'Well, yes,' Parson Smollat glared at his curate, 'but we're talking about our church where tables and benches were over-thrown. Triptychs pulled down from the walls. Cruets and thuribles smashed in the sacristy. A tun of wine was shattered.' Parson Smollat paused to gulp more claret.

'Even at Mass,' Sir William Higden declared mournfully, 'I was there. Candle spigots dashed to the ground. The pyx chain sent swinging. Foul smells, horrid sounds.'

'All the same, I thought ghosts and demons could not haunt a hallowed place?' Beauchamp asked.

'Not true.' Anselm tapped the table. 'Christ was taunted by demons. Read the scriptures: devils thronged around him, even if it was to beg for mercy. Evil can open up the gates of hell. Demons swarm up, drawn by feelings of hate, resentment, malevolence, wickedness and malicious evil. Like soldiers laying siege they seek paths into our souls, drawbridges across the great void which separates us from them.'

'Like an enemy horde attacking a castle?' Beauchamp asked.

'Precisely. The demon lords, the restless spirits, pound on our doors and clatter like the wind against the shutters of our souls. Some castles can be taken by direct assault, others

by siege or attack from afar with catapults, mangonels and
the siege towers of hell. Sometimes the attack is very violent; the
soul can be devastated by fire and sword as deadly as any
kingdom being put to the torch. For most of us, thank God,'
Anselm crossed himself, 'it's just a quiet, desperate struggle.'
He paused. 'No one is safe; holy men and women suffer the
most vicious assaults. Look at Saint Anthony of the Desert,
Benedict or the great Francis of Assisi.'

'But why here? Why now?' Almaric protested.

'I don't know. I am trying to discover why. Isn't that the
reason you asked for me?'

'True, true.' Parson Smollat's fingers went to his mouth. He
acted like a frightened child, staring down at Anselm. 'I thought
that tonight . . .'

'What did happen?' Beauchamp had dropped his world-weary
airs: he was harsh, accusatory. 'Did you fail, exorcist?'

Stephen glanced expectantly at Anselm. He, too, was deeply
curious about what he had seen and heard. Why had old memories come floating back? Why had his master, the man he
reverenced as the magister, appeared so lost? The rest of the
company were also attentive, waiting for the exorcist's reply.

'I did not fail,' Anselm declared, 'but neither did I succeed.
However, I am not a cozener, a cheat. I do not draw pentangles
and circles. True, I would like to meet the Midnight Man and
discover his tricks but,' Anselm drew himself up, his voice
forceful and carrying as it was when he delivered a homily to
a crowd in Cheapside, or harangued a group of fops in their
brocaded fineries, their palfreys, saddled and harnessed, glittering with gold and silver, 'what I do is not some sleight of
hand. Let me assure you: we are not only dealing with ghosts
and relics of the past, but something very evil.' Anselm breathed
in deeply. 'Let me explain – what is a ghost? We have the
Lord's own words that ghosts do exist. When he walked on the
water his disciples thought he was a ghost. After his resurrection Christ had to assure them that he could eat and drink and
was no phantasm.' Anselm paused, listening to the gathering
sounds of the night. 'No one,' he continued softly, 'knows what
truly happens to a soul after death.' He joined his hands together.
'Perhaps it's like a child being born. There is confusion, chaos.

Perhaps the immediate aftermath of death can be like someone caught at a lonely crossroads not knowing why they are there, where they are going or even who they are. Awareness in the soul after death dawns, I am sure, slowly, according to the way we have lived. Most souls take their chosen path; some, God alone knows why, do not – they linger. They believe they have unfinished business so delay by possessing a house, a church – even another soul. They press for their business to be completed.' He paused. Anslem now had their full attention. 'I believe that is what's happening here but,' he held up a warning hand and his voice thrilled, 'even more, these spirits are in the grip of some malignancy which has fastened tight about them. It blocks their path – why? I do not know. I suspect the practices of the Midnight Man did not help. He invoked something which now prowls your cemetery and church like a ravenous wolf.'

'Why don't these souls tell you?' Beauchamp asked.

'They cannot,' Anslem retorted. 'Only God's grace conveys knowledge of what is truly beyond the veil. Think of us as looking through the bars of a prison door. We can see the captives within. We can watch their torment. They may even know we watch. We sympathize with them but they cannot truly explain why they are there, who they are or what they are doing. We are witnessing souls twisting in pain and torment. The noises, the lights, the horrid stench, the rank odours are simply manifestations.'

Anslem stared hard at a painted cloth on the far wall celebrating the legend of the Lady of the Lake. He sat as if fascinated by the snow-white hand breaking free from the dark green water bathed in a setting sun to grasp the great jewel-encrusted sword Excalibur.

'And?' Beauchamp asked gently.

'Something else is also there – retainers of the apostate angel, hell's dark robber.'

'What are you saying?' Sir William insisted.

'The Midnight Man, in his foolish blundering, drew in the rankest lords of the air. However,' Anslem's voice grew sharper, 'some great evil,' he pointed in the direction of the church, 'has definitely occurred there. No,' he hushed their protests, 'let me assure you of that. I have great experience, God forgive me, of hauntings, ghosts and exorcisms. I tell you all, such spiritual manifestations have their suppurating roots firmly in human wickedness. Let me explain. Once,' Anselm paused, his head down. 'Once,' he repeated, 'I was summoned to an old manor house. I shall not give you the name but it stood in the Romney marshes, a forbidding, gloomy place built of stone, wood and plaster. It was much decayed, a desolate habitation abandoned after the great pestilence. The nearby village was also an abode of ghosts.' Anselm shrugged. 'No life, no work. Once a thriving community, the angel of devastation had swept through as it had so many places. A sheer nothingness brooded over it. No crops, cattle or sheep. The trackways around it lay abandoned as traders and tinkers saw little profit in going there. Now, the King, freshly returned from France, wished to reward one of his young knights. He granted him that manor and all the land attached to it. This young paladin received his chancery writ to take up possession.' Anselm waved a hand. 'He also married a young noblewoman. Both knight and lady moved into their new home.'

'Romney?' Beauchamp abruptly asked. 'Why, Sir Thomas de—'

'Please,' Anselm interjected, 'I beg you – such matters are best kept secret. I promised.'

Beauchamp pulled a face, shrugged then sat back cradling his goblet, watching Anselm intently.

'The knight and his beloved bride occupied this manor on Romney marsh. Retainers and servants were hired, ditches dug, fields cleared, the house and outbuildings were repaired.' Anselm sipped at his beaker of water. 'Few of the retainers stayed. The house was declared accursed. Like you, Sir William, the knight appealed for help . . .'

'Not really,' Beauchamp interrupted.

'Sir William, you do want our help, yes?'

The merchant knight murmured his agreement.

'But there was more,' the royal clerk insisted. 'The King's Justices of Oyer and Terminer have just completed their circuit through the London wards. They received many petitions that the hauntings at Saint Michael's be investigated. Similar pleas were sent to the Archbishop of Canterbury and the King's council.'

'I encouraged these,' Higden declared. 'Didn't I, Smollat?' He turned to the parson, who nodded vigorously even as he stifled a yawn.

'The same,' Anselm continued, 'occurred with this hapless knight. I was asked to visit the manor and exorcize whatever lurked there.' He stretched out and grabbed Stephen by the arm. 'This was before my young friend here joined me.'

Stephen smiled at the word 'friend'.

'When I arrived at Romney,' Anselm continued, 'the manor house was gloomy, a place bereft of joy. I walked its chambers, store rooms and galleries, its cellars and outhouses. The very walls exuded a deep sadness, a horrid despair. Ghosts truly gathered there. It was one of those arid places where demons loved to lurk, well away from the light. I celebrated Mass in its small chapel and felt a malevolent presence just beyond the door, a rank horde of venomous spirits mouthing their own foul curses as they controlled who or whatever was also there. I searched that manor, and the more I did the deeper the darkness grew. A heavy pall of misery stifled my own spirit – never more so than in a narrow chamber, a dusty room with peeling plaster and dirty boards. Cobwebs cloaked every corner and niche; its lancet window was divided by a thick, rusting iron bar. I grasped this and stared out into the weed-filled kitchen yard. As I did I heard a voice.' Anselm shook his head. 'Let me explain. When I say I hear a voice, or see anything supernal, as God is my witness, I am never certain if it's within or without me.'

'And this voice?' Almaric asked.

'A woman's voice.'

'And she said?'

'"Help me, for the love of God, help me! Let me be free. Let me move into the light. Break the chains which bind me to him." I asked her who she was and what she meant.'

'And?' Almaric asked.

'The door behind me opened and shut with a crash. I heard a scream, something brushed my face – the ice-cold fingers of some ghostly hand – then it was gone. I stayed and searched that manor. The more I did, the more I returned to that morbid chamber at the back of the house and the long, gloomy paved passageway leading down to the kitchen and buttery.'

'Did you attempt an exorcism, as you did here?' Sir William asked.

'I attempted, and I failed. I could hear a woman's voice but some hell-lurker, a darkness-dweller, always intervened. I blessed and sanctified. I also prayed that the Lord would send me an angel of light.' Anselm gave a rare smile. 'Angels come in many forms and guises. Near the manor stood a hermitage, an ancient, small dovecote hidden in a dense clump of trees. The land around it was so marshy and treacherous, the hermitage could only be approached carefully. I tried to speak to the old man who lived there, locked in his fasting and prayers. I failed but one morning he came to see me, a true ancient with his white hair and beard. He asked to be shriven. I cannot reveal what he told me except that afterwards he agreed to help me lift the paving stones of the passageway stretching from the kitchen to that godforsaken prison chamber.'

'Why?' Beauchamp asked.

'Let me explain without breaking the seal of confession,' Anselm retorted. He glanced quickly at Stephen. 'I certainly could have used your help there. I, the manor lord, his henchman and even his lady helped. The henchman had to retreat, as did the knight's wife.'

'Why? Why?' Almaric sat like a rabbit petrified by a stoat.

'Evil swept that gallery like the winds of hell. Full of hideous terrors, rank smells, fearful faces, curses and obscenities. Sometimes it turned hot as if a blast of wind blew from the seething deserts of Outremer, only to turn so cold we could scarcely grasp the picks and poles we used.' Anselm lifted the Ave beads wrapped around his left hand. 'I prayed and sprinkled holy water. I insisted that the candles in front of the cross on the table set up in the passageway stay alight. At last we found it – a pit beneath the paving stones containing the skeleton of a woman. We could tell that from the remnants of her robe and sandals. She lay in an oiled sheet drenched in pine juice with no cross, pyx holder or Ave beads; instead, between her legs, laid the severed head of a man.' Anselm stilled their gasps and exclamations. 'The head and face had been preserved though these were shrunken and ghastly. Severed cleanly at the neck, the head had been soaked in brine and tarred like

those of traitors polled on London Bridge. I blessed these gruesome remnants. I thanked the hermit. I could now question him
outside the seal of the sacrament, and he confessed the most
macabre tale. Years earlier, before the great pestilence, the manor
lord who lived there married a local woman of outstanding
beauty. He loved her to obsession but, during the King's early
wars against the Scots, this knight was called away by the
commissioners of array. He obeyed the writ, fought valiantly
along the Scottish march then returned to his manor . . .'

'To find she had been unfaithful?' Beauchamp asked swiftly.

'Yes, she had fallen in love with the steward of the manor,
a man she'd known since childhood. Other servants betrayed
her secret trysts. Her husband caught her. He had the steward
decapitated, his severed head pickled and preserved.'

'And his wife?'

'She was condemned to a living hell. She was confined to
that ghastly cell, walled up like a recluse. Every night her
husband and chosen servants entered her cell and prepared the
table for supper. Three chairs: one for him, one for her and a
third for her dead lover. Every evening the food would be served,
brought from the kitchen, along with the severed head which
would be placed opposite her. The manor lord insisted that she
eat and drink with him. Never once would he utter a word to
her or answer any of her pleas, except to point to the ghastly
remnants of her former lover.'

'Surely,' Stephen asked, horrified by the story, 'the other
servants would object?'

'No.' Anselm tapped the table. 'The knight was both feared
and loved, well-respected by the King; and his wife had been
found playing the two-backed beast while he had been honouring
his oath to the Crown. She had betrayed him and been caught
red-handed. God forgive them but no mercy or compassion was
shown to her.' Anselm drank from his beaker. 'By then the
vengeance was making itself felt throughout the kingdom. The
great pestilence had emerged in Dorset. All the terrors of the
underworld emerged. The village and manor on Romney Marsh
was devastated by the Angel of Death. Entire families fled.
Apparently, according to the hermit, only the manor lord, his
wretched wife and a few servants remained. Nevertheless, the

torture continued until one day she managed to get a length of rope. She hanged herself and her husband buried her in that passageway; the final insult was her dead lover's severed head being placed between her legs. The husband was later swept away by the plague. The manor house and village were deserted.'

'Except for the ghosts?'

'Aye, Sir William, evil ghosts, supported by their kind as well as those two unfortunates who had loved unwisely.'

'And what did you do?' the sexton asked.

Anselm sat listening to the cries of some night bird in the gardens beyond, a lonely sound answered by the creaking of this stately, three-storey mansion.

'I arranged a Christian burial for the remains in consecrated ground. The new lord of the manor and his lady vowed to go on pilgrimage to Our Lady of Walsingham as well as Saint Swithun's Well. I offered Mass in reparation as well as a requiem for the dead. I blessed that house, hallowed the chamber and,' Anselm lifted his hands, 'as God be my witness, peace returned.'

'And you think the same has happened here?' Sir William demanded.

'Yes, I do. The secret rites of the Midnight Man disturbed something, opened the door to spiritual forces, venomous and vindictive, but they must have a nestling place here. Something wicked and hideously evil has been committed in and around that church.'

Parson Smollat gulped his wine and stared askance at Sir William.

'I was granted the advowson of this church three years ago after my wife died,' Sir William declared. 'I could not abide to continue to live in my house in Cheapside where my wife had lingered with a wasting disease. I moved here. A year later I was pleased to appoint Parson Thomas Smollat as the parson but,' his voice faltered, 'well, that's all I know.' He almost gasped before continuing: 'I cannot tell you what the cause of all this is.'

'I have studied the recent history of the church,' Parson Smollat offered. 'Certainly there have been murders in the cemetery, drunkards with flashing knives, while during the great plague a huge burial pit was dug in the cemetery . . .'

'It cannot be any of these,' Anselm observed.

'But what you're claiming,' Beauchamp declared, 'is that all the hauntings and ghostly manifestations at Saint Michael's are rooted in human activity? Some bubbling iniquity, some unresolved sin?'

'Yes,' Anselm got to his feet, 'that is what I am claiming. A mortal sin, an act which has killed God's life in souls. I did not succeed tonight because I could not find the root.' He beckoned at Stephen. 'Now, Sir William, I believe we have lodgings here?'

'Magister,' Beauchamp also got to his feet, 'as I said, I have other business with you. Messages from the council but,' he smiled, 'you have worked long and hard. I shall have words with you tomorrow, if not here then at White Friars.'

Anselm shrugged, picked up his pannier and moved to the door.

'Tell me,' Sir William called out, 'did you learn anything tonight during your exorcism?'

'No,' Anselm retorted. 'Young women, perhaps, who died in great distress except for one voice, a man's, strong, rather mocking, loudly complaining at being dragged away though what that means I cannot say. Now, Sir William, if you could show us to our chambers . . .'

ooOOoo

Words Amongst the Pilgrims

The physician stopped speaking. He drank generously from his wine cup while studying, as if for the first time, two painted cloths hanging against the wall to the left of the great mantled hearth. The first showed a creature with a beast's snout, ears like a pig, a human body and legs with hooves. This grotesque had a long tail curled up behind it and was watching an ape riding face to tail on a galloping goat. On the ape's left wrist perched an owl, while the ape's right hand was raised in mock benediction. Next to this painting was an

Agnus Dei; the lamb held the Cross of the Resurrection while blood from the lamb's side seeped into a waiting chalice. The rest of the pilgrims watched the physician, wondering why he had paused so abruptly.

'A fearsome tale.' The yeoman spoke. 'Do these paintings, my friend, remind you of something?'

'Yes and no,' the physician replied. 'Not of my story – more about the contrast of good and evil in man.' The real reason why the physician had paused was the Wife of Bath who – her fat, cheery face even redder from the wine – sat staring, her mouth gaping.

'I know of both Sir William and Sir Miles,' the knight declared. 'I came across both in my hunt. Have you, Brother?' The knight pointed directly at the monk who, cowl pushed up, now retreated deeper into the shadows which thronged the taproom. The darkness had certainly deepened, while the flames of the candelabra danced in the strengthening breeze, seeping through window-shutters or beneath closed doors.

'My friend.' The monk's voice was rich, mockery charging every word with double meaning. 'My friend,' he repeated, 'why should what you hunt – the Strigoi, so I understand – trouble themselves with the dead or those who try to speak to them? I have never been to Saint Michael's, Candlewick, though I have heard about its ripe, full whores . . .'

'And I've heard the same,' the friar intervened, his brown face and bald head greasy with sweat. 'I've preached at the cross nearby. I heard the most terrifying stories about . . .'

'Then hush, friend.' The physician smiled. 'Let me tell my tale as it unfolds.'

'Oh, I shall,' the friar replied. 'I knew the White Friar Anselm, a peaceful, powerful man of deep prayer and austere life.'

'Unlike other friars we know,' the miller scoffed.

'He came to our convent once,' the prioress intervened. Like the rest, she wanted the physician to continue. She had to know the end and not have it spoilt by childish squabbling amongst her companions. 'Yes, Brother Anselm came to our convent,' she repeated, 'because of a shocking haunting. Our cloisters were walked by the ghost of a young novice who hanged herself from an iron bracket there. She simply slipped a noose around her pretty white neck and stepped off the ledge. Weeks afterwards her ghost could be both seen and heard sobbing uncontrollably. They say,' the prioress said, now forgetting her usually exquisite courtesy and glaring venomously at the friar, 'that she fell enamoured of a wandering preacher, a troubadour, really a friar in disguise, hot and lecherous like a sparrow. I think . . .'

'I saw a painting once,' the friar cheekily replied, 'of an ass playing a harp.'

'What was that?' The prioress' voice rose to a screech.

'Gentle pilgrims,' Master Chaucer quickly intervened. The physician had quietly disappeared.

'He's gone out.' The softly spoken ploughman pointed to the taproom door, which hung slightly open.

Chaucer rose swiftly and went out into the moon-washed garden. The air was heavy with the smell of the late spring flowers and the fragrance from the herbers. Water splashed from a fountain, carved in the shape of a pineapple, into an ornamental pool lit by flaring cresset torches, lashed to poles on either side. Chaucer heard the cries and exclamations from the pilgrims in the tavern as they demanded the tale continue. A figure stepped out of the shadows, a slattern bearing a tub smelling richly of crushed roses, violets, bay leaves, fennel, mint and other aromatics. Chaucer immediately recognized them as a sure protection against any contagion in the air.

The slattern stopped before him, her pale, skinny face under the hair cap eager to please. She indicated behind her. 'The physician, as soon as he arrived, advised the tavern master to keep the air fresh. Anyway, your physician is back there with his friend.' She slipped by him. Chaucer followed her back in and sat down, pretending to fuss over the wine jug. Eventually the physician returned, clapping his hands and apologizing to his fellow pilgrims, distracting them all except Master Chaucer. He glimpsed the scabby-faced summoner also slip back in from the garden, silent and stealthily as any hunting stoat. Chaucer chewed his lip. He wondered if the summoner, who acted the shifty nip or foist, was only playing a part. The physician, however, eyes all bright, lifted his goblet in toast to the company and returned to his tale.

ooOOoo

The Physician's Tale

'Saint Michael, defend us on the day of battle. Do thou leader of the heavenly host, thrust down to hell Satan and all his horde who wander the world for the ruin of souls.'

Stephen, kneeling beside Anselm, answered, 'Amen.' He rose and followed the exorcist from the chapel across the nave, under the great, elaborately carved rood screen and up the main sanctuary steps into the sacristy. He helped his master divest and returned to ensure all was cleared from the chantry chapel of St Joseph. Afterwards he followed his master, clothed in the brown and white of the Carmelites, as he strolled around St Michael's, Candlewick. They had both slept well in the comfortable chambers provided by Sir William. They'd risen before dawn, washed and dressed, packed their panniers and moved across to the church, where a sleepy-eyed Stephen had helped Anselm prepare for the dawn Mass. As usual, Stephen had acted as Anselm's altar server; now he was famished, eager to break his fast. Anselm, however, was keen to catch what he called 'the essence of this place', so Stephen leisurely followed him around the ancient church. In the grey light of the April dawn St Michael's did not look so forbidding: it appeared clean, swept and tidy, with benches and stools neatly arranged. The sanctuary was laid out in strict accordance with canon law: pulpit, lectern, ambo and offertory table. The pyx hung on a thick brass chain, a fluttering red sanctuary lamp dangling beside it. The windows were filled with horn or oiled pig's bladders; a few were glazed and some of these brilliantly decorated with the heads of angels or saints, the face of Christ with a nimbus of gold and, of course, depictions of St Michael the Archangel in various guises: as a nobleman, judge, even a knight in armour. In the corner of the chantry chapel dedicated to St Michael stood a life-size statue of the Archangel, cleverly carved and brilliantly painted with the royal colours of blue, scarlet and gold. Anselm stopped before this and pointed to where the painted stone had crumbled; the hilt of the Archangel's sword was cracked, while the heraldic devices on St Michael's great oval shield were clearly battered.

'Sir William told us the statue had been tipped over.' He gestured at the candle stand of heavy iron. 'That, too. What force, Stephen, could move them?' He glanced around. 'Ah, well, it's so different now, I mean, from when we were here last night – look!' He pointed at the light pouring through the windows, now turning gold in the glow of the rising sun. Stephen agreed. St Michael's now seemed no different from any London parish church – St Mary Le Bow, St Nicholas or St Martin. Anselm walked round. He lit a taper in the Lady chapel, inspected the different inscriptions and went into the Galilee porch. He paused to examine the bell which hung just inside the door. Any man, fleeing from the law, who sought shelter would enter here, ring the bell then hasten up into the sanctuary and grasp the horn or side of the altar, as Joab had done in the Old Testament when fleeing from the killers dispatched by King David. Anselm studied both door and bell closely then walked across to the empty sanctuary recess where he crouched, tapping the palliasse; a fleeing man would use this during his forty-day stay in the church.

'Magister?'

'During the exorcism last night, Stephen, a male voice, different from the rest, spoke about being dragged from here. I wonder who it was?'

'Magister, last night during the exorcism you seemed distracted. What truly happened?'

Anselm rose to his feet and peered down the church. 'Something quite common, Stephen.' Anselm rubbed his forehead. 'During an exorcism I do suffer tricks of the mind,' he confessed. 'I do not know whether they are just phantasms born from what is happening or the ploy of an evil spirit. But, rest assured,' he added grimly, 'they're certainly here. Indeed, I think of Ecclesiasticus, chapter twenty-nine, verse thirty-three: "There are spirits who thirst for vengeance and in all their fiery fury inflict grievous torment". Do they, I ask myself, conjure up visions of sin from the past to dull my soul, chill my heart, darken my mind and so frustrate my soul? Grinning, mouldering skulls, snatches of violence, the smoke and stains of past offences?' Anselm stared down at Stephen. 'Augustine claims our sins run like foxes through our souls while God, for his own secret purposes, sends in his hounds to hunt them down. In times of distress these foxes manifest themselves.'

'Even if you have confessed and been shriven?'

'Sometimes the foxes are only driven off – they slink away and lurk waiting in the undergrowth.' He patted Stephen on the shoulder. 'All I can do is ask God, if I'm in His grace, to keep me there and, if I'm not, to put me there. My sins may be absolved, Stephen, but that doesn't mean I haven't lost my appetite for them.' He gestured around. 'There's certainly a banquet going on here, an unseen, diabolic feast. Evil spirits summoned up by the Midnight Man have, and are, feasting like hungry hounds on the rank despair which seeps through this church. Anyway, go round, look for anything untoward.'

Anselm walked across the sanctuary. Stephen went down the steps into the sombre nave. He entered the chantry chapel of St Joseph and admired the cleverly carved statue of Christ's protector as well as the paintings depicting scenes from the carpenter's life. He turned left and stopped before the tombs of former parsons, read their inscriptions, then walked on. The light was dim except where the painted glass caught the flash of the sun. Nonetheless Stephen now felt a prickling fear: he was not alone. He glanced up and caught the twisted smile of some gargoyle carved at the top of a pillar or the corner of a sill. He recalled the legend of how such babewyns could spring to life and crawl down the pillar to taunt and trip the unwary. Stephen stopped before a wall painting describing the death of Holofernes in the Book of Judith. The artist had created a vivid scene in the fallen tyrant's pavilion. Judith the heroine clutched a great two-handed sword. The tyrant's corpse lay sprawled amongst his precious cloths and treasures; his severed head had rolled away and stared out from the corner of the painting. Not a dead gaze, the eyes held a ghastly glare, as if the head still lived and was aware of its ignominious situation. The more Stephen stared at the painting the more those eyes seemed to pulsate with a vindictive life. He walked on to another fresco, undoubtedly the work of the same itinerant painter. Here the artist proclaimed his own vision of hell: a great city high and wide under a sky of fiery bronze, cut through by a turbid, blood-black stream boarded by trees with thorns as sharp as daggers. Flames leapt up to greet black snowflakes and pelting grey rain. Fruit, bloated and rotten with noxious potions, gave sustenance to savage dogs. Lungeing vipers and all kinds of loathsome insects crawled. Demons swarmed like bees, thick and plentiful from the hives of hell. Dragons swam the fiery heavens while beneath the soil of hell other monsters reared their ugly heads, fighting to break through. Stephen glimpsed the tags written beneath the painting. '"Within its darkness dwell",' the novice translated, '"regions of misery and gloom".' He heard his master cough and turned. Immediately a fierce chill seized him. Anselm was staring up at an iron bracket fixed to a wall in the far aisle on which lantern horns could be hung. The exorcist was not alone. Figures clustered around him: a blond-haired man dressed in a shabby jerkin, followed closely by young women with long dirty hair, ragged clothes, pitted skin and horrid faces. Stephen shut his eyes and cried out: 'Magister!' When he looked again, Anselm was standing by him.

'What is it? Stephen?'

'Magister, nothing.'

'Nonsense!' Anselm pushed his face close. 'You saw something, didn't you?'

Stephen nodded and described what he'd glimpsed.

'I felt it,' Anselm murmured, staring at a shaft of window light. 'Even now, Stephen, at day time, they make their presence felt, but come . . .'

They left by the corpse door going out into the cemetery. At first Stephen considered it to be a different place from the night before. The weak sun's glowing warmth soothed his fears. The tumbled headstones and crosses didn't seem so threatening. The ancient yew trees were just solid reminders of how things were rather than threatening shapes through the darkness. The wild grass and flowers exuded a sense of the ordinary. The air was sweet with different scents. Beyond the cemetery wall surged the noise of the ward coming to life: the clatter of carts, the

clop of horse hooves and the first cries of tradesmen. Anselm
insisted on walking the length and breadth of that unkempt
cemetery. They went round the church, Anselm peering up at
cornices, sills, ledges and buttresses. He seemed fascinated by
the sun sparkling the glass and pointed out the carved faces of
gargoyles with their gaping mouths, through which the rain
water would pour. Anselm patted the grey stone wall of the
square tower built to the right of the main door. He stepped
back, shading his eyes as he stared up at the sheer height of
this soaring donjon. He then walked on, stopping to rattle the
latch of the narrow door to the sacristy, though that had been
firmly locked the night before.

'Magister?'

'Nothing.' Anselm walked back into the sunlight. 'Do you
sense or feel anything strange, Stephen?'

'No, but . . .'

'Too silent, eh?' Anselm nodded. 'I also have a feeling of
being watched.' A rustling behind them made Anselm turn.

He strolled back up the low bank through the long grass,
pushing aside the tangle of briar and bramble bush. Despite the
disturbance there was no muffled pigeon cooing, no chattering
jay or raucous gang of sparrows fluttering here and there, no
swooping swallow or blackbird singing its heart out. Anselm
seemed intent on finding something. Stephen hurried after him.
He'd almost caught up with his master when a figure loomed
up from behind an ancient, moss-covered tombstone. Stephen
stifled a cry of surprise.

Anselm grabbed the stranger's shoulder and pulled him closer.
'Who are you?'

The stranger was tall and burly. His black hair hung in lank
strips, his bushy moustache and beard almost hiding the sunburnt
face. He broke free of the exorcist and held up a wickedly
pointed harvest sickle.

'Don't threaten us,' Anselm warned.

'And don't seize me!' the stranger rasped back. 'I am Owain
Gascelyn, hired by Sir William to tidy this cemetery, if I am
not harassed by demons, haunted by ghosts, plagued by warlocks
or grabbed by exorcists.'

Gascelyn was the same height as Anselm, two yards at least,

thick-set and well built, dark eyes bright. He was dressed like a labourer in a smock, leggings and scuffed boots, but his voice was cultured and, in his angry protest, he'd moved fluently from English to Norman French and then into Latin, describing Anselm as 'Exorcisimus'. Anselm, taken by surprise, stepped back, studying the man from head to toe.

'A labourer, a gardener with a Welsh first name and a Gascon surname, fluent in both French and Latin! Greetings and blessings to you, Brother! Excuse my surprise but I thought we were being watched . . .'

'As you were.' Gascelyn stepped closer, scrutinizing Anselm and Stephen.

The novice stared back; for some reason this man frightened him. Why was that? Stephen wondered. Because he emanated the same violence Stephen's father had, and still did? Gascelyn had thrown the sickle down but his fingers played with the Welsh stabbing dagger in its sheath on his broad belt.

'Who are you, really?' Anselm asked. 'No, let me guess. Despite your appearance you're educated, undoubtedly in some cathedral school then in the halls of either Oxford or Cambridge.' He leaned forward and gently poked the man's chest. 'I know who you are, I know what you are. You're a mailed clerk, aren't you? A scribe who arms for battle? One who is also prepared to dirty his hands? Sir William's man, yes? Ostensibly you're here to clear this tangled mess now winter's past but, in fact, you're here to guard and to search, perhaps?'

Gascelyn grinned in a display of white broken teeth. 'I am he,' he replied. 'And Sir William told me about you, Brother Anselm. You are correct. Since All Souls past and the depredations of the Midnight Man, I guard this cemetery. I am,' he joked, 'the *Custos Mortuorum* – the Keeper of the Dead. I warn off those night-walkers who might lurk here once twilight falls.' Gascelyn grinned lopsidedly. 'Not to mention the whores with their customers, the gallants with their lemans and the roaring boys with their doxies.'

'And what have you seen?'

'Nothing,' Gascelyn replied. 'Word has gone out, seeping along the alleyways, runnels and lanes of Candlewick, that this truly is God's acre. Nothing more exciting happens here than a hunting cat, or that tribe of stoats nesting in the far wall. Come,' he picked up the sickle, 'I'll show you my kingdom.'

Gascelyn led them off along the narrow, beaten trackway, pushing aside bramble and briar. He explained how most of the cemetery was full, pointing to the mounds of milk-white bones thrusting up out of the coarse soil. On one occasion he surprised a mangy, yellow-coated mongrel from the alleyways, nosing at a broken skull. Gascelyn hurled a stone and the dog fled through the long grass, barking noisily. Gascelyn showed them where the great burial pit had been dug, its soil still loose due to the lime and other elements used. Only the occasional sturdy shrub now grew in this great waste ringed by bushes and gorse. It also served as the Poor Man's Lot, the burial place for strangers as well as *Haceldema* – the Field of Blood, where victims of violence or those hanged along the nearby banks of the Thames were buried. Nearby stood a simple wooden shed: two walls and a roof like any city laystall. Anselm and Stephen walked over to this. The inside was gloomy and reeked of putrefaction. Three corpses lay there, wrapped in filthy canvas shrouds lashed tightly with thick, tarred rope. Gascelyn explained how all three were the cadavers of beggars found dead in the surrounding streets. Anselm recited the requiem and blessed the remains. Gascelyn thanked him, adding how all three corpses would be later buried in the great burial pit as the soil was looser and easy to dig.

Stephen felt the place was stifling hot. 'A brooding evil hangs here,' he whispered.

'Though that can be for the good,' Gascelyn offered. 'It keeps the undesirables away.'

He then answered questions about himself as the exorcist led them out of this dingy shed: how he was the son of a Welsh woman and a Gascon knight who'd served in the King's wars against the French. How he'd been educated as a clerk, entered Sir William's retinue and seen military service with his lord both in France and along the Scottish march.

'And so you're Sir William's sworn man by night and day, in peace and war?'

'I've not taken an oath of fealty, but yes.'

'Were the Midnight Man's revelries held on the site of the

great burial pit?' Stephen asked, abruptly trying to shake off a deepening unease.

'Yes, I believe they were.'

'A place of desolation and devastation where any abomination could flourish,' Anselm declared. 'I felt it. I am sure my friend Stephen did also. This is a sad and sombre place.'

Gascelyn never replied but plodded on, Anselm and Stephen close behind. The novice just wished they could leave. At first sight this cemetery had seemed a true place of the dead yet the longer they walked, pushing aside nettles and thorns, their feet cracking fallen twigs, the more this cemetery transformed into a living, ominous place breathing out its own malign spirit. The silence was unsettling. The desolation hung like a veil hiding darker, more sinister forces. Now and again Stephen glimpsed the forbidding church tower and the mass of its leaded roof black against the late spring sky. Stephen took a deep breath. A voice whispered to his right, though when he turned only a bush moved in the morning breeze. Stephen turned away then spluttered at the gust of corruption which caught his mouth and nostrils. He stumbled.

Anselm caught his arm. 'Be on your guard,' he whispered, 'for the devil is like a prowling lion seeking whom he may devour.' Anselm winked at Stephen and called out to Gaceslyn that they'd seen enough, though he'd like to visit the death house which stood some distance from the church, shaded by a clump of yew trees.

'My manor,' Gascelyn called back, 'my fortress – come and see.'

The death house was a spacious, rather grand building of smart red brick on a grey stone base, its roof tiled with blue slate. The windows were covered in oil-strengthened linen; the framework and heavy shutters, like the door, were of sturdy wood and painted a gleaming black.

'Sir William had this refurbished,' Gascelyn explained. 'He intends to renovate the church and make the cemetery worthy of the name "God's acre".'

'When?' Anselm asked.

'Once May has come and gone. Stone masons and painters, glaziers as well as labourers by the score have been indentured.'

Gascelyn waved around. 'Some will camp here, others in tenements Sir William has bought down near Queenhithe. That's why he's asked me to guard this place. So,' he shrugged, 'the death house is my dwelling place.'

He lifted the latch and led them inside. Stephen was surprised. The death house was unlike any he had ever seen. Its walls were smoothly plastered and painted a lovely lilac pink; the floor, of evenly cut paving stones, was ankle-deep in lush supple rushes strewn with scented herbs. Capped braziers stood beneath the two windows. The bed in the far corner was neat and compact and covered with a beautiful gold counterpane sprinkled with red shields. The long mortuary table stood against one wall with the parish coffin on top, half-hidden by a thick woollen black fleece embroidered with silver tassels, while pots of flowers ranged beneath this.

At the other end of the room stood a chancery table, a high leather-backed chair and two quilted stools. The room also had a long chest with coffers and caskets neatly stacked on top. Pegs on the back of the door were used to hang cloaks as well as Gascelyn's gold-stitched war belt with its decorated scabbards for the finely hilted sword and dagger.

'I sleep well.' Gascelyn gestured round. 'Isolda the parson's woman brings me cooked food.' He paused as he heard voices. 'Indeed, I think that is Parson Smollat and his lady now. They'll be going in for the Jesus Mass – wait here.'

Gascelyn left the death house. Anselm walked round and sat on the edge of the bed, Stephen on a stool. The novice glimpsed a book bound in calfskin, fastened by a silver chain on the chancery table. He rose, walked over and opened the book of hours. He read the first entry, a line from the introit for Easter Sunday: 'I have risen as I said.' Stephen admired the silver-jewelled illumination. The 'R', the first letter of '*Resurrexi*', was covered in red-gold ivy and silver acanthus leaves. In the top of the 'R' a chalice, in the lower half a milk-white host above the Holy Grail. Stephen was about to read on when he heard a girl's voice whisper, 'Eleanora.' He glanced at Anselm, who'd risen to his feet and was staring at the long mortuary table. The room had grown very cold; a faint perfume tickled their sense of smell. After a few heartbeats the sound of a lute could be heard, then the music faded but the rushes beneath the table shifted and a small puff of dust rose.

'Someone is dancing!' Stephen exclaimed. 'Someone is dancing!'

The rushes ceased moving. No more dust whirled. A harsh sound echoed through the death house like a cry suddenly stifled.

'Is there anything wrong?' Gascelyn stood, blocking the doorway. He came in. 'You heard it, didn't you?'

Stephen glimpsed the desperate, haunted look in the man's harsh face. Gascelyn stood hands on hips, staring down where the rushes had moved. He kicked these with the toe of his boot. 'Perhaps,' he confessed, 'I don't sleep too well. I've seen it, I've heard things. I wish Sir William would release me from this.' He lifted his head. 'Well, is there anything else, Brother Anselm?'

The exorcist simply sketched a blessing in the air, then he and Stephen left.

'Magister, shouldn't we ask what causes that?'

Anselm stopped and stared at him. The exorcist's long, bony face was pale, the sharp, deep-set eyes like those of a falcon, lips tightly drawn, square chin set stubbornly. Stephen recognized that look. Anselm was troubled – deeply troubled – because he was confused. The exorcist had confessed as much as soon as they'd risen that morning, and apparently his mood had not changed. Anselm ran a finger down the stubble on his chin then scratched his head. He opened his mouth to speak but then shrugged and walked into the shade of a yew tree, beckoning at Stephen to follow.

'Night-time, Stephen,' Anselm leaned down like a magister in the schools, 'night-time,' he repeated, 'is the devil's dark book, or so authorities like Caesarius the Cistercian would have us believe. He described Satan as a tall, lank man of sooty and livid complexion, very emaciated, with protuberant fiery eyes, breathing ghastly horrors from his gloomy person. In another place Caesarius describes Satan as a blackened, disfigured angel with great bat-like wings, a bony, hairy body, with horns on his head, a hooked nose and long pointed ears, his hands and feet armed like eagle's talons.'

'And you, Magister?'

'I regard that as pure nonsense – foolishness! Satan is a powerful angel. He is pure intelligence and will. He pulsates with hate against God and man. He does not creep under the cover of darkness or feast on fire. He is arrogant. Dawn or dusk makes no difference to him. Filthy dungeon or opulent palace does not exist for him, only his enemy.'

'God, Magister?'

'No, Stephen. Us, the children of God. Satan never accepted God's creation and rose in rebellion, which lasts from everlasting to everlasting. Satan, Stephen, is no respecter of person or place. He waxes fat in the sombre shadows of vaulted cathedrals, behind the stout pillars and recesses of its choirs. He draws power in the silent cloisters from the secret thoughts and feelings of the good brothers. You'll find Satan on the ramparts of castles, breathing pride into the lords of war. He can also be found in the lonely corpse where the sorcerer hums his deadly vespers and casts his foul spells. He lurks in the furrow and fans the hatred of peasants who plough the earth for those who own it. He also lurks here, Stephen, feasting on some filthy nastiness. What that is remains a mystery which must be resolved. In the end we must make him fast and drive him out. So, let us collect our satchel and panniers from the church – we will return to White Friars.'

They stepped out of the yew trees and paused. The corpse door swung open. Parson Smollat and Isolda came out. Isolda was about to walk away, then abruptly strode back and kissed the parson full on the mouth.

'Lord, save us,' Anselm whispered. 'So our good parson, like us all, is moved by the lusts of the flesh. Quick, Stephen, collect our baggage and away we go.'

Thankfully Parson Smollat was in the sacristy and didn't see Stephen enter the church. He collected the panniers he had left in the Galilee porch and hurried to join Anselm, who was standing under the cavernous lychgate.

'Should we not bid farewell to Sir William or Sir Miles?'

'We'll return soon enough,' Anselm replied. 'While Sir Miles, believe me, will seek us out.'

They left the precincts of the church, going past All Hallows and into the trading area of Eastcheap. Stephen, lost in his own thoughts, felt his sleeve being plucked. He turned, stared at the young woman brazenly walking beside him and was immediately struck by her: soft and feminine, yet a truly determined young woman. Her skin had a golden, healthy hue; her thick, auburn hair, bound in two plaits, was almost covered by a blue veil. This trailed from a small cap on top of her head, then wrapped around her soft throat like a wimple. She wore a woollen fur coat decorated with silver leaves over a dark clean kirtle, with stout leather shoes on her feet. One of these was loose so she gripped Stephen's arm to steady herself as she put this right.

'Mistress?'

Anselm, a little further ahead, turned and came back.

'Mistress?' Stephen flustered, staring into the young woman's beautiful grey eyes. 'What business do you have with me?'

'None, Brother.' She smiled cheekily. 'I am sorry. I'm Alice Palmer. My father owns the tavern The Unicorn on the corner of Eel-Pie Lane close to Saint Michael's church.'

'I know it,' Anselm replied above the noise of the crowd around him. 'What is that to us?'

'A scullion, one of our maids, Margotta Sumerhull, has been missing for weeks. Sometimes she'd go to pray before the Lady altar at Saint Michael's. I've asked Parson Smollat.' She smiled, moving a wisp of hair from her face. 'My father has also petitioned Sir William but neither can help. Margotta could be wild. Anyway,' she shrugged, 'we've heard of you, about the strange happenings at Saint Michael's, as well as the presence of a King's man – Sir Miles Beauchamp. We know him. He lives nearby. Sometimes he visits our tavern. Perhaps you would be kind enough to support our petition?'

'We shall do what we can.' Stephen stood fascinated by that beautiful smile. The young woman grabbed his arm, kissed him full on the lips and fled into the crowd. Stephen's fingers slowly went to his mouth. Anselm, smiling, shook him gently.

'A woman's kiss,' the exorcist murmured, 'one of God's great gifts. Count yourself lucky, Stephen, and let's move on.' They hastened through the crowds. 'The world and its retinue,' Anselm murmured, 'have gathered to buy and sell.' Stephen kept close to his master. The busy, frenetic atmosphere of the city, hungry for trade, was overwhelming. Carts and sumpter ponies laden with Italian spices, Gascon wine, Spanish leather, Hainault linen and lace as well as timber, iron and rope from the frozen northern kingdoms, forced their way through. The clatter of all these competed with the constant din of chickens, pigs, cows, oxen and geese loaded on, or pulling, heavy wheeled carts and tumbrils. The air was riven by the crack of the whip, the neighing of horses and constant yapping of alleyway dogs. From the cramped alleyways and runnels leading on to the broad thoroughfares of Poultry and Cheapside swarmed London's other city: the hidden world of the wandering musicians, rogues, cozeners, naps and foists, charlatans and coney catchers, all bedecked in their motley, garish rags and eager for prey. A sweaty tribe, which reeked of every foul odour, these swarmed around the hundreds of market stalls, pitting their wits against the bailiffs and beadles who constantly patrolled the markets. The officials had already caught one miscreant, a toper, his nose as brilliantly red as a full-blown rose; arrested for foisting, he was being led off to stand in the cage on the top of the tun which housed the conduit for Cheapside.

The crowd surged, broke and met again. Apprentice boys hopped like frogs, shouting for custom. Fur-gowned burgesses, arm-in-arm with their richly dressed spouses, rubbed shoulders with fish-wives hurling obscenities at each other over a cohort of men-at-arms marching down to the Tower. A market beadle proclaimed the names of two whores missing from their brothel. A juggler leading a mule decorated with cymbals stopped to ask two Franciscans in their earth-coloured, rope-girdled robes for their blessing, only to be screamed at by a group of fops, in their elegant cloaks and soft Spanish leather boots, for blocking the way. Underfoot the thoroughfare was littered with all forms of dirt and refuse. Gong-carts were attempting to clear the mess but were unable to get through. The street air, fragranced by freshly-baked bread and platters of spiced meats, turned slightly rancid as the stench curled in from the workshops of the tanners, fullers and smithies.

The two Carmelites entered the Shambles. Butchers and their boys, bloodied from head to toe, were busy slaughtering cattle.

In a flutter of plumage birds of every kind: quail, pheasant, chicken and duck had their necks wrung, their throats slashed, before being tossed to the sitting women to be plucked and doused in scalding, salted water before being hooked above the stalls. The cobbles glittered in the bloody juices from all this carnage. Dogs, cats and kites fought for globules of flesh, fat and entrails. The air reeked of blood, iron and dung. Anselm hurried past on to the great concourse before the forbidding mass of Newgate prison, its crenellated towers soaring either side of the grim, iron-studded gates. An execution party was assembling. The death cart rolled out, crammed with manacled prisoners bound for the Elms at Smithfield or the Forks by Tyburn stream. Immediately the waiting crowd surged forward as friends and relatives fought to make a sombre farewell. Some prisoners screamed their messages; a few were so drunk they lay unconscious against the sides of the cart. Mounted archers beat back the mob with whips and sticks while the sheriffs, resplendent in their ermine-lined red robes, shouted for order. Anselm and Stephen waited until the execution party moved off, then pushed their way through a crowd thronging around a Dominican garbed in the distinctive black and white of that order.

'Beware,' the trumpet-voiced preacher declared, 'beware, you adulterers! In hell you shall be bound to stakes in a fiery pool; each will have to face his mistress similarly bound. And that is not all, oh no! Demons will lash your private parts with wire. You traders who cheated the poor, your fate will be sealed in a red-hot leaden casket in Satan's own black castle. You gluttons who stuffed your gaping mouths . . .'

'I don't think this concerns us,' Anselm murmured. 'Never mind gluttony! I'm starving.'

They passed through the old city walls, turning left into the maze of alleys leading down to Fleet Street and the House of the Carmelites, the White Friars. Stephen tried to hide his nervousness. These runnels were a labyrinth of iniquity. Here lurked the sanctuary men, the wolfsheads, the utlegati and the proscribed wanted by this sheriff or that. Here the knife, the garrotte or the club were drawn at the drop of a dice or the turn of a counter. Narrow, evil-smelling lanes, the walls on either side coated with a messy slime, the ground under foot squelched with the dirt and refuse thrown out by those who lived in the rat castles on either side. Now and again a candle glowed against the perpetual darkness. A *flambeau* burnt under a crucifix which did not hold the figure of Christ but Dismas the Good Thief. Shadow people, nighthawks and darksmen flittered through the murk. Anselm and Stephen were watched then dismissed.

'Friars, white-garbed!' The cry went out. Doors slammed, shutters clinked. Anselm and Stephen hurried on. The figures who confronted them seemed to merge out of the gloom: three women, street-walkers, their hair dyed different stripes of colour, their feet bare and their loose-fitting gowns open at the neck and chest to expose nipples painted a bright orange. The women blocked their way. At first Stephen thought they were drunk but, as he grew more accustomed to the dim light from the lantern horn the woman in the middle held, cold dread seized him. All three stared, hard-faced and glassy-eyed. Creatures from beyond the edge of darkness.

'Out of our way!' Anselm ordered.

'Preacher! Peddling preacher! Interfering mumble-mouth! Another shaven pate comes with his cub to confront and oppose,' the woman opposite Stephen snarled, bringing the long stabbing knife out of the folds of her gown to glitter in the juddering light. 'Who are you?' the woman jibed mockingly.

'Anselm the do-gooder,' one of her companions replied. 'Mind you, he's seen enough hot blood gurgle and splash. So, who set you up as a prophet in Israel? Why have you come to meddle?'

'To spoil our little games with your stupid chuntering,' her snarling friend jeered. 'You whoreson bastard! Why have you come into our domain? You, Anselm, a filthy sinner with your dirty thoughts and foul moods.'

'And you, Stephen of Winchester,' the third woman took up the litany of insults, 'a friar, are you – why? No vocation, surely? Fleeing your father?' The voice was harsh, mocking and ugly.

Stephen, mouth dry, was aware of other dark shapes creeping

along the walls on either side – scuttling shadows, as if a horde of hairless rats were swarming around.

Anselm stepped forward. 'In the name of the Lord Jesus, by what are you called?'

'The hordes of hell greet you,' one of the women retorted.

'And the power of heaven responds.' Anselm grasped the tau crucifix. 'In His name . . .'

One of the women darted forward, dagger blade snaking towards Stephen, but Anselm knocked her aside with his satchel even as he cried. '*Deus vult, Deus vult* – God wills it, God wills it.'

The third woman lunged with the club she was hiding by her side. Anselm punched her full in the face. She staggered back. The attack faded. The sinister scrabbling along the alleyways disappeared. The darkness thinned. All three women dropped what they were carrying and withdrew, looking fearfully down at their hands then up at the exorcist, faces vacant, eyes staring, mouths gaping. They backed away, then turned and fled. Anselm leaned against the wall, trying to catch his breath.

'Magister, what were those?'

'*Succubi*,' Anselm replied, 'the demons we tried to exorcize last night. They swarm like flies seeking entrances to souls. Well, they found an open door to those three ladies.' He blew his cheeks out. 'They came to threaten, even to kill. God knows.' He sketched a blessing above Stephen's head. 'And what did they tell us? That we are sinners? Well, we know that already! I am also very hungry and our refectory awaits . . .'

Stephen knelt on the prie-dieu before the Lady altar in the Church of the White Friars. The Angelus bell had sounded. Stephen had listened to its peals, recalling the ancient tradition that tolling church bells were a sure defence against demons and diabolic attack. He stared around the lovely shrine. The three walls of the chapel were painted a deep blue. The silver borders at top and bottom were decorated by resplendent, bejewelled gold *fleur de lys* with a gleaming ruby at the base of the middle stalk of every flower. The chapel ceiling was of a fainter blue; it depicted a scene from the Apocalypse, of the Virgin about to give birth while confronting a scarlet, seven-headed dragon. The floor of the Lady chapel was tiled in a glossy stone, which sparkled in the pool of taper light fixed from silver spigots in front of the magnificent statue. The sculptor had carved the Virgin in the brilliant likeness of a young court maiden, her dark hair half-hidden beneath a gold-edged, gauze white veil, her body clothed in a sheer silk gown under a robe of imperial purple edged with gold. The Virgin's feet, encased in diamond-studded sandals, crushed the head of a writhing serpent. Stephen, however, as always, was fascinated by the face: not pious or holy but wreathed in a warm, welcoming smile. Such a look, Stephen had come to realize, was all he could remember of his beloved mother bending over him, her face full of concern, a lock of hair out of place – then she had gone. All that remained was a stern father, an esteemed physician who had no time for his son's flights of fancy.

Now in safety, Stephen's mind drifted back to the events at St Michael's and the assault in that eerie, smelly alleyway. Was this what he really wanted? Anselm he liked, respected and even loved, but this constant battle with the lords of the air, the barons and earls of hell? Stephen drew deep breaths to calm himself. Anselm had taught him to do this while repeating the Jesus prayer. Anselm maintained this would lead Stephen to meditation and contemplation but, invariably, it always put him to sleep. He was shaken awake by a servitor, face all anxious.

'Brother Stephen, Brother Stephen, I've been looking for you everywhere! Master Anselm and Sir Miles Beauchamp are waiting for you in the parlour.'

Still heavy-eyed with sleep, Stephen was ushered into the elegant chamber overlooking the main courtyard of the friary. A spacious but austere room dominated by a gaunt, crucified Christ and an embroidered cloth telling the story of the Virgin's miraculous appearance on Mount Carmel. Sir Miles and Anselm were sitting opposite each other at the oval table, which ran down the centre of the room. Shafts of afternoon light, in which a host of dust motes danced, pierced the glass windows high on the outside wall. Anselm beckoned him to sit on his left and returned to watching Sir Miles. The clerk, as elegant as ever in his blue quilted jerkin and matching hose, was sifting through a sheaf of documents on the table before him. He looked as if he had stepped out of the royal presence chamber: hair neatly combed, jewels sparking on his fingers. Stephen caught sight of the chancery ring emblazoned with the royal arms which could demand entrance to any building as well as insist on the allegiance of those who lived there. Beauchamp had slung his thick war cloak over the prior's chair at the head of the table and looped his sword belt around the chair's high post.

Stephen, embarrassed by the brooding silence, apologized once again, explaining where he'd been and how he had fallen asleep. Anselm brushed him gently on the arm. Sir Miles kept shuffling the pile of manuscripts before him. Stephen glimpsed red and purple seals and wondered what the Clerk of the Secret Chancery would want with them.

'I apologize.' Sir Miles lifted his head and smiled dazzlingly at both of them. 'Master Anselm, I apologize for dragging you from your meeting with Father Guardian, and you, Brother Stephen, from your prayerful sleep. Yet,' he pulled a face, '*tempus fugit* and, cometh the hour, cometh the man.' He abruptly pushed back the stool on which he was sitting and got to his feet. He thrust the parchments back into a leather pannier, strapped on his war belt and slung the heavy cloak about his shoulder. 'You have eaten and rested?'

'We have eaten,' Anselm replied sharply, 'but not rested.'

'You must come.' Sir Miles was no longer smiling. 'I, or rather my master, has permission from your masters to take you to Westminster. By the time we reach there the light will be fading.'

'The abbey or the palace?' Anselm asked.

'Why, Magister, the abbey.'

'But that has been shut, closed by interdict since the murders there.'

'To others, yes.' Sir Miles shrugged. 'To me and mine, no. Now, Brothers, I suggest you go cloaked and hooded. Bring what you have to.'

Within the hour Anselm and Stephen clambered into the royal barge waiting by the narrow quayside near the friary river gate. A dozen royal archers escorted it. Four served as oarsmen either side; the rest clustered in the prow behind the jutting, gilt-edged lion head. The archers wore dark brown fustian under brilliantly coloured *surcotes* boasting the golden leopards of England and the silver *fleur de lys* of France. They looked sinister, deep cowls hiding both head and face, and they moved to the clatter of weapons and a reeking, sweaty stench. Once Sir Miles and the two Carmelites were seated in the leather-canopied stern, the order was given to cast off and, with the cries of the serjeant ringing out, they moved swiftly midstream, the oarsmen on either side bending and pulling in unison. Now and again the serjeant would blow a hunting horn, a powerful braying call warning all other craft to pull aside and recognize the royal pennant snapping prominently in its clasps on the lion-headed prow. The weather was calm; the stiff spring breeze had subsided. The barge moved serenely, cutting through the water, rising and falling now and again as it met a surge in the choppy tide.

Sir Miles opened a small fosser lined with costly samite and brought out linen parcels of fresh bread, diced ham and shredded cheese which they could open on their laps. All three ate in silence, then Sir Miles, winking at Stephen, put the linen cloths back into the fosser and drew out a loving cup which he filled from a stoppered wineskin. He took a generous sip himself then circulated the cup. Anselm just sniffed and handed it to Stephen. Once it was drained, Sir Miles smiled across at the two friars.

'I am sure we'll eat at Westminster, yet an empty belly can also attract demons – yes, Magister Anselm?'

The exorcist made the sign of the cross in the air as a gesture of thanks. Sir Miles busied himself with the fosser while Stephen peered out over the river. Anselm called it a true road of ghosts; he had told him some heart-chilling tales about the dead, doomed to float there like tendrils of mist. How the drowned, the victims of murders or suicide, gather in ghastly choir to sing their own haunting plain chant. Great evil was also perpetrated by those who lived in the marshes or along the tide-washed river bank – creatures of the dark who emerged after sunset to prey on lonely craft or use false beacons to lure wherries stacked high with produce into some night-shrouded ambush.

'An interesting meeting yesterday. What did you make of our company?'

Stephen glanced across at Beauchamp, now muffled in his cloak.

'Brother Anselm, Stephen, I know a great deal about you. What do you know about them?'

'Only what you tell us,' Anselm retorted sharply, 'and, by the way, we know very little about you.'

Beauchamp laughed softly. 'Sir William Higden,' the royal clerk declared, 'is much beloved by the Crown – a warrior who has seen service in France and along the Scottish march; a merchant who has proved himself most generous to our king. Sir William truly loves the church of Saint Michael's, Candlewick. He has lavish plans to pull it down, rebuild it and put that cemetery to better purpose.'

'He lives by himself?' Anselm asked, steadying himself as the barge met with a swell. A seagull, strident in its shrieking, swooped low over them.

'His wife died; he is childless. He regards Saint Michael's parish as his adopted son. He wishes to build something magnificent there.'

'And Parson Smollat?'

'A London priest of good reputation, he has served a number of parishes.'

'And Isolda, his woman?'

'You mean his kinswoman,' the clerk grinned, 'or so common rumour has it. The rest,' Beauchamp moved swiftly on, 'are what they appear. Simon the sexton had held that position for a number of years.'

'You seem well-acquainted with Saint Michael's?'

'I'm sorry.' Sir Miles put on his elegant, gold-edged gauntlet. 'I should have told you. I live in the parish. I have a house in Ferrier Lane on the other side of Saint Michael's. As for the others, Almaric the curate is a butterfly who constantly moves and never settles. A man of good family, Almaric was apprenticed in his youth as a carpenter. From the little I know he enjoyed a fine reputation as a craftsman but left when God called him' – Sir Miles steadied himself as the barge shuddered slightly – 'to be a priest. He served as a chaplain in the commissions of array both at home and abroad. Sir William's man, both body and soul. He is perhaps not the devoutest of priests or the most assiduous of scholars, yet a good man.' Beauchamp paused as the serjeant of archers rapped out an order to the oarsmen. The barge shifted slightly in a swell shimmering under the glow of the late afternoon sun.

'And Gascelyn the *Custos Mortuorum* – the dweller in the haunted death house?'

Beauchamp glanced away as if distracted. 'So,' he turned back, 'Gascelyn told you?'

'He let us see it.'

Beauchamp pulled a face. 'Gascelyn is Sir William's squire by day and night, in peace and war. A man hot against witches and warlocks. In Bordeaux he served as man-at-arms for the Dominicans, the Inquisition, in their fight against sorcerers. Oh, yes, Sir William couldn't have a better man or stronger guard.'

'And the Midnight Man?' Anselm's voice remained sharp.

'I know what you do, Magister.' Beauchamp's voice was low, as if abruptly fearful that the oarsmen might overhear.

'And that is very little,' Anselm retorted, 'except by reputation. They say he is a lord of the night, an enemy of the sun, the close companion and friend of the darkness. A being who rejoices at the cries of the screech-owl and the barking of dogs in the ungodly hours. They say he wanders among tombs and sups on human blood.' Anselm crossed himself. 'These are only legends, stories to frighten. In the end, however, the Midnight Man has a reputation as a great magus.' He paused. 'Or a great sham. Nevertheless, one whom the King's Council, not to mention the tribunals of Holy Mother Church, would love to question.'

Beauchamp lifted his hand for silence as the barge moved in towards the quayside at Westminster. Stephen glimpsed the soaring turrets of both abbey and palace, the lights sparkling on windows, gilded crosses and cornices. Anselm was now threading his beads and Stephen recalled how the exorcist had a great fear of water. The barge serjeant blew hard on the hunting horn. The barge thrust against the tide and swept into the landing at King's Steps. Beauchamp led them out, up the steps, under an archway guarded by men-at-arms and into the palace precincts. A busy place thronged with sweat-stained clerks, ostlers and scriveners, busy lawyers in their ermine-lined cloaks

and judges in their scarlet silks. They pushed by officials from
the Exchequer, the chancery or the many courts which sat next
to the great hall nearby: King's Bench, Common Pleas and
others. They passed the Jewel Tower and went down a hollow,
vaulted passageway. They reached New Palace Yard, thronged
with plaintiffs and pleaders, men-at-arms and a horde of clerks,
scriveners and ink-stained officials from the different depart-
ments of the royal household, be it the Buttery or the Wardrobe.
The day was drawing on and all these royal servants were now
eager to eat and drink at the different cook shops set up in the
yard by the itinerant food-sellers with their movable grills, ovens
and charcoal braziers. The air was heavy with roast meat, richly
spiced and salted to curb hunger and quicken the thirst, so the
ale-sellers and wine-tipplers could do an even more prosperous
trade. The chatter and clatter were deafening. Everyone seemed
to be in a hurry and eager to impress with their business.
Stephen, trailing behind Beauchamp and Anselm, noticed how,
when the royal clerk passed, gossip died and people hastily
drew aside, glancing away as if unwilling to catch Beauchamp's
gaze. In turn, the royal clerk neither looked to the right nor left
but swept on towards the heavily guarded abbey gates. A knight
banneret of the royal household hurried up and, under
Beauchamp's instructions, he opened the gate and allowed them
through into the abbey grounds.

Stephen had been there before but, as always, he was struck
by the sheer magnificence of the abbey: a breathtaking vision
of stone with its many walls and sides, turrets and towers, chapels
radiating out like jewelled stems, all supported by a double tier
of lofty buttresses. To the far right rose the spires of the parish
church of St Margaret of Antioch, and between this and the
abbey ranged the domestic granges, courtyards, gardens,
orchards, carp ponds, vineyards, mills, guest houses and other
outbuildings. Just as they entered the precincts the abbey bells
began to toll the next hour of divine office. However, the black-
garbed monks of St Benedict now streaming out of the cloisters
where they'd washed and prepared themselves, did not hurry to
their abbey church but along the path leading to St Margaret's.

'Of course,' Anselm murmured, 'the abbey church is closed
because of the slayings.'

'And will be for some time.' Beauchamp waved them along
to the red-tiled guest house, a magnificent building of Reigate
stone with glass-filled windows. The guest master, an old,
wrinkled-faced monk, greeted them warmly. He asked no questions but took them along a corridor, the walls whitewashed
and gleaming, the paving stones sprinkled with herb dust. He
stopped before a door, pushed it open and motioned them in.
The stark, austere chamber lacked any ornamentation except
for a crucifix nailed above a painted cloth displaying the IHS
symbol. In each corner stood a narrow cot bed draped with a
counterpane displaying the abbey's coat of arms, a blue shield
bearing a gold cross with silver *fleur de lys* and five golden
doves. In the centre of the chamber stood a square table with
stools on each side – this had been set up for dining with
tranchers, napkins, knives, horn spoons and pewter goblets for
water and wine. Two large jugs carved in the likeness of a dove
stood on a side table beneath the light-filled, latchet window.
Next to this was a squat lavarium with stoups of rose water,
towels and pieces of precious Castilian soap in a copper dish.
The guest master explained how the garderobe and latrines were
in a special shed outside. He then hurriedly assured Beauchamp
that all was prepared. They only had to ask for anything. Food
would be served as soon as divine office finished and the abbey
kitchens were ready.

Beauchamp, throwing cloak and sword belt on to a peg against
the wall, courteously thanked him, then shut the door firmly
behind the guest master, drawing across the bolts and turning
the key.

'Sir Miles,' Anselm sat down on one of the beds, 'Father
Guardian told me that His Grace the King demanded my
presence here. He talked of the need for an exorcism in the
ancient crypt beneath the abbey, of the recent terrible crimes
here . . .?'

Beauchamp pulled the latchet window shut and walked
slowly over to the table. He picked up a taper and, taking a
flame from the solitary candle burning on its six-pronged
spigot, carefully lit the other five. 'Let there be light,' he
whispered.

'Let there be light indeed,' Anselm replied, pausing as the

melodious plain chant from St Margaret's carried across on the evening breeze:

'*They rise up, the kings of this world.*

Princes conspire against the Lord and his Anointed . . .'

Anselm nodded in agreement, then whispered the next lines from the same psalm:

'*You break them with your rod of iron.*

You shatter them like a potter's jar.'

'All in God's good time,' Beauchamp added in a tone so eloquent in its disbelief of the very words he'd spoken.

'Be careful, Beauchamp. Remember, the Lord comes like a thief in the night.'

'And I shall render to God what is God's,' the clerk replied blithely. 'But, for the moment, I must give, or I must return to Caesar, what is Caesar's.'

'What do you mean?'

Beauchamp, clutching a chancery pannier, sat down at the table, pushing aside the trancher and goblets. He drew out sheets of parchment as well as two velvet pouches bearing the royal coats of arms and tied at the neck with red twine. He undid these and gently shook out the contents. The first was a Saracen ivory-hilted dagger bound with fine copper wire, its curved blade of the finest Toledo steel. From the hilt and blade, Stephen guessed it was of considerable age: both were blotched and stained though they could easily be refurbished. Stephen then gasped loudly at the contents of the second pouch: a beautiful, pure gold cross studded with the most precious rubies and amethysts; even to the untrained eye the cross was a most costly item. It dazzled in the light, assuming a life of its own, as if some power within was making itself felt. Anselm, usually so reticent about anything, also exclaimed in amazement. He and Stephen handled the precious item, about six inches long and the same across. Although small the cross weighed heavy, Stephen lifted it up, staring at the sparking jewels, noting the intricate Celtic design.

'Beautiful,' Anselm whispered. 'Angelic! The work of God's own goldsmith.'

'The Cross of Neath,' Beauchamp explained, plucking the relic from Stephen's hand. He then picked up the Saracen dagger.

'Eleanor's knife.' He smiled at their look of puzzlement. Stephen felt a deep unease as soon as he had touched both precious items.

'I will be succinct.' Beauchamp put the items back in their pouches. 'On the Octave of Candlemas last in the middle of February of this year, Adam Rishanger, a petty goldsmith, tried to flee the kingdom. He had sold most of his paltry possessions and went down to Queenhithe where a cog out of Bordeaux waited to take him to foreign parts. On the quayside Rishanger became involved in vicious dagger play with three masked assailants. Rishanger, with the help of some sailors, drove his attackers off. The captain of the cog, however, was reluctant to allow Rishanger on board, so our goldsmith fled down river. He was pursued. He managed to reach the King's steps and sought sanctuary in the abbey, clinging on to the corner of the Confessor's tomb. But his assailants followed him in. A lay brother who tried to intervene was killed – a blow to the heart, close to the rood screen. The assassins then seized Rishanger, stabbed him to death and fled. The abbey was put under interdict and closed, as you have said, and will remain so until the Lord Abbot decrees that reparation has been done and the church reconsecrated.'

'And the killers?'

'Fled, disappeared. You must have heard about this hideous affray?'

'Of course,' Anselm acknowledged. 'I thought it was just a sign of the times.'

'Yes and no,' Beauchamp replied. 'What was not made public,' he tapped the pouches, 'was that Rishanger's killers did not have time to linger long after the murder; they fled, leaving their victim in a widening puddle of blood. Some of the good brothers tended to him. As they did, they found a sack Rishanger had pushed into one of the recesses beneath the Confessor's tomb. Inside were these precious items.'

'Plunder from some robbery?'

'True, Brother Anselm, though a robbery which took place over seventy years ago.'

'What?'

'In the April of 1303, during the reign of the present King's grandfather, the Hammer of the Scots, Edward I.' Beauchamp paused, as if listening to the faint plain chant from St Margaret's. 'Now, as you may know, the abbey is the royal mausoleum of the Plantagenet family. It also used to be the royal treasury. The Crown Jewels and all the King's personal wealth and precious items were stored in the crypt, at least until that robbery. Afterwards the crypt was abandoned. It, too, has a tale to tell, but that must wait for a while.' Beauchamp paused to collect his thoughts. 'In April 1303, around the feast of Saint Mark, a failed London merchant, Richard Puddlicot, seeking revenge against the King and eager for plunder, broke into the crypt.'

'What?' Anselm exclaimed. 'I deal with magic and things supernal. I've seen the crypt: it's an underground fortress, a bastion!'

'I know,' Beauchamp conceded. 'The abbot at the time, Wenlock, was being blackmailed by two of his leading monks, Sub-Prior Alexander of Pershore and his sacristan, the monk in charge of securing the abbey and keeping it safe, Adam Warfeld. These two reprobates enjoyed an unsavoury reputation with certain ladies of the town. They conspired with Puddlicot, who sowed fast-growing hempen seeds in the monks' cemetery close to the six windows of the crypt, which are on ground level. They set up a watch and hired a stonemason, John of Saint Albans who, as you will see, worked on the furthest window. They gained entry and passed up the treasure.'

'But they were caught?'

'Yes, Stephen, they eventually were. Some of the monks enjoyed a long stay in the Tower. A royal clerk, John Drokensford, who later became Bishop of Bath and Wells, rounded up the ring leaders and their coven.'

'Including Puddlicot . . .?'

'Including Puddlicot. Drokensford then began to hunt for the missing treasure. Some he found, a great deal he did not. No one has ever discovered the rest of the horde, which included items precious to the royal household. This Saracen dagger was once wielded against the present King's grandfather when he was on crusade in Outremer. A sect known as the Assassins despatched a killer who entered the royal pavilion and actually struck the King with a poisoned blade.'

'The same as you've just shown us?'

'Yes, Stephen. The King was wounded but his beloved wife, Queen Eleanor, or so the story has it, sucked the poison from the cut. In thanksgiving Edward dedicated the dagger to the Confessor and had it placed in his treasure house. The Cross of Neath is also symbolic. Once owned by the Princes of Wales, Edward crushed and killed these and seized their most sacred relic, the Cross of Neath, for his own use. Both these sacred items disappeared during the robbery of 1303. They were never seen again until the Octave of Candlemas past.'

'How did Rishanger come to have them?' Anselm asked. 'And what has that got to do with us or the business at Saint Michael's?'

Beauchamp drew a deep breath. 'My apologies,' he murmured, 'for the secrecy. I wish to finish before the good brothers complete their chanting. We searched Rishanger's house, which also lies in the parish of Saint Michael's, Candlewick, within the ward of Dowgate. It was stripped clean. Rishanger had also drawn all his gold and silver from his bankers in Lombard Street. He intended to flee the realm with these items. Rishanger never married. He had a mistress, Beatrice Lampeter – a courtesan, a woman of notorious reputation. She, too, had apparently disappeared, but we found her mutilated corpse, her eyes removed, buried in the garden behind Rishanger's house. Brother Anselm, you know how the removal of the eyes of a corpse is a curse intended to blight the soul after death. We suspect Rishanger killed Beatrice to keep her mouth shut. We also discovered amulets, inverted crosses, wax figurines, a pentangle.' Beauchamp shrugged. 'All the instruments of a warlock. Now,' Beauchamp kept his head down, 'the city, the court, even the church, houses those who secretly practice the black rites. Rishanger must have belonged to one of these covens. He certainly hated Sir William Higden.'

'Why do you say that?'

'According to witnesses, Rishanger once approached Sir William with a scheme to fashion the philosopher's stone. Higden threw him out of his house. When we discovered Rishanger's secret cache we also found a wax figure, allegedly of Sir William, wrapped in a scrap of parchment which contained the filthiest curses against the King's good friend. Sir William also believed Rishanger was one of those who frequented Saint

Michael's graveyard. He and others of that devilish crew were witches and sorcerers.'

'But the treasure?'

'To be brief, Rishanger may have been an associate of the Midnight Man and his coven. We know how that warlock held his satanic ceremonies here in the monks' cemetery, as well as that disastrous attempt at Saint Michael's.'

'How do you know this?' Anselm retorted.

'For the moment,' Beauchamp held up a hand, 'I ask you to be patient. Now, it's alleged that ghosts throng close about Westminster. An abbey has stood here when all the land around it was described as the Island of Thorns. Generations of monks have lived and died here. Many good, some indifferent, a few downright evil. Stories are rife about this or that haunting. However, recently, frightening phantasms have begun to trouble the monks: screams, cries, ghostly figures, the banging of doors.'

'Throughout the abbey?'

'No, just around the pyx chamber and the chapter house, as well as the crypt which lies beneath.'

'And?' Anselm shook his head. 'Your statements, master clerk, are like beads, but what is the string which holds them all together?'

'Rishanger lodged near Saint Michael's, Candlewick. The Midnight Man performed his rites there. He did the same here at Westminster. We ask ourselves: did he raise ghosts to question them about where the hidden treasure from Puddlicot's robbery lay hidden? Did the Midnight Man disturb what you call the spirits, malevolent or not, human or not, to achieve this?' Beauchamp paused, staring hard at the exorcist. 'Some would dismiss all you do, Brother Anselm, as arrant nonsense, yet you and I, we have seen the disturbances at Saint Michael's. Others also have – Sir William Higden is certainly very concerned. More importantly,' Beauchamp picked up the leather pouches, 'how did a petty goldsmith find such precious treasures over seventy years after they were stolen? Rishanger must have been part of some coven – hence his pursuit, his taking sanctuary and consequent murder. Finally, Rishanger's acquisition of such treasure must have been fairly recent. I reckon it was discovered early this year, perhaps in January?'

'I follow your logic,' Anselm retorted. 'It must have been very recent. Rishanger secured possession of those items. He was overwhelmed by their riches. He did not care about the others in his coven. He sells everything he has; in a twisted way he imitated the man in Christ's parable who finds treasure in a field so he sells everything he has in order to purchase that field. Rishanger was determined to keep such treasures – certainly the Cross of Neath. If he had sold it to the bankers in Marseilles, Genoa or Florence he would have been able to live like Croesus for the rest of his life.'

'His Grace the King must be greatly concerned,' Stephen declared, immediately blushing at Beauchamp's cold, hard stare.

Then the clerk relaxed, smiled and leaned across to touch Stephen lightly on the cheek. 'We'll make a courtier of you yet, Stephen. You have said it! That's why we are really here. Of course,' Beauchamp emphasized, 'the Royal Council is concerned at the hauntings both here and at Saint Michael's. The King, however, in a word, wants that treasure – the precious horde of his warrior grandfather. Look, my dear friars, our King is at war. The Commons sit at Westminster only an arrow flight away. They demand this and that before they vote taxes to the King.' Beauchamp sighed. 'That's before we try to collect such taxes. Now I have seen the list, kept in the remembrance chamber at the Tower, of all the treasures Puddlicot stole but were never returned. Pouches of precious stones, bags of jewellery, gold and silver coins, gold bars by the casket. A King's ransom, my dear friars – pure, unadulterated bullion. If it's here, our King wants it.'

'So we have been brought to Westminster not only to exorcize a ghost but to question it?'

'Perhaps,' Beauchamp murmured, 'you will also discover that His Grace has persuaded our Lord Abbot here at Westminster that the monks' cemetery is crammed with mouldering corpses, so it is time to open the graves and remove the bones to their ossuary or charnel house.'

'A good excuse to search the grounds,' Anselm countered. 'You, like the Midnight Man, believe that Puddlicot may have buried his plunder here?'

'I do, but –' Sir Miles paused at a knock on the door.

Two servitors entered carrying food and drink: bowls of beef broth, dishes of diced quail spiced with ginger, pots of mixed vegetables, freshly-baked manchet loaves as well as goblets of wine. Once they had served the food and left, Anselm recited the Benedicite and they ate in silence.

Stephen now and again watched Sir Miles eat with all the delicacy of a born courtier, even as the clerk sat lost in thought. Eventually Anselm coughed and took a sip of water.

Beauchamp lifted his head. 'Brother?'

'You don't believe in any of this, do you? Do you even believe in the good Lord, Sir Miles? I mean, sitting here, if not as friends then at least as comrades, I must know. It matters as to why you brought us here. It certainly influences what happens at Saint Michael's. If someone is present who doesn't really believe, that can affect an exorcism.'

'You are not from the Inquisition?' Sir Miles joked, a lopsided smile on his face. 'You will not lodge my name with them?'

'I regard you as a friend.'

Beauchamp pulled a face and dabbed his lips with a napkin. 'Let me explain,' he replied, 'you are wrong about me. I struggle very hard to believe after all I have seen, heard and felt in my life. No, no,' he shook a hand, 'I am not talking about the present ills of the church, be it the priest who is lecherous or,' Beauchamp grinned, 'the friar who might be even more so. God knows we are all sinners, born weak. No, I remember being in one of the King's *chevauchées* in France. I led a posse of mounted archers into a village south of Rouen. Marauding mercenaries had just swept through.' Beauchamp blinked, clearing his throat. 'I shall never forget what I saw.' His voice fell to a whisper. 'Corpses stripped, bellies ripped from crotch to throat, men, women and children. The village priest had been hung upside down in his own church; he'd been castrated. Children, babes in arms, lay with their skulls shattered like eggs. I found it difficult to accept a loving God would allow that. So,' he picked up his goblet, 'if that is life here on earth, is it any different beyond the veil? Isn't that what you investigate?' He glanced sharply at Stephen. 'Of course, you're the innocent. You believe different, that we really haven't lost Eden?'

'You know he does,' Anselm retorted. 'You are the Keeper of the King's Secrets. You must have heard the gossip, the tittle-tattle, and read the reports? You know more about Stephen and myself than we do about you.'

'You want to be a Carmelite?' Beauchamp gestured at Stephen. 'Do you really? Are you one because of your father, or in spite of him?'

Stephen felt a flush of anger. He ignored Anselm's swift intake of breath and moved his arm from the exorcist's reassuring grasp. Something about Beauchamp, as with Gascelyn, reminded Stephen of his own father. He felt the furies gather.

'I became a Carmelite . . .'

Beauchamp abruptly stretched across the table and squeezed Stephen's hand. 'I am sorry,' he soothed placatingly. 'I know you are the son of a famous, well-respected physician of Winchester.'

'One who was also famous for being free with both his fist and his cane?'

'You are also a young man who had visions from an early age, or so they say?'

'I'm not sure,' Stephen replied hotly, 'I was an only child.' He blinked away the tears of anger. 'My mother,' his voice faltered, 'died young. I remember seeing her, as well as other people who had died. When the church bells tolled, voices whispered to me. Faces and shapes appeared in the dead of night. I would also glimpse them in puffs of incense smoke.' Stephen paused. 'My father thought I was moon-touched, fey-spirited. He sent me to the White Friars, the Carmelites at Aylesford. He claimed that I would never follow his profession, which dealt with facts. Do you know something, Beauchamp? The more he pressed me the more intense the visions became. I was glad to be free of him, to hide, to shelter at Aylesford.'

'And I,' Anselm intervened, 'took him under my wing.' The exorcist smiled across at the novice. 'Cherished him as I would the apple of my eye.'

'Or as your own son,' Beauchamp cut in, 'the one you lost?'

'Aye,' Anselm pulled at his sleeves and stared down the table, 'the one I lost with his little sister and my beautiful Katerina. You know about the great pestilence sweeping in like the

Doomsday angel? In a matter of days my entire family was wiped out. Perhaps I went mad; I certainly lost my wits. To me the world, the very air, became dank. Nothing but visions of death, a yawning darkness. Out of this emerged an old woman with wild hair and glaring eyes wielding a broad-bladed scythe, and behind her a horde of hellish skeletons garbed in moth-gnawed shrouds, their bare-boned faces grinning with malice. Vipers curled in their ribs, clawed hands grasped the heads of the dying. Demons clustered like flies. I became insane with grief. Satan, like a huge raven, constantly floated above me. I fled into deep forest. I met shapes, shadows, spectres, wraiths – all the undead. I entered that misty underworld between life and the kingdom of the hereafter. I visited the dungeons of the dead and confronted the furies which scourge, the key-dangling janitors of hell. I had visions of the black lake, the rivers of flame, the fearsome battlements of Hades.' Anselm breathed out. 'Others would dismiss it all as nonsense. Nevertheless, I have seen the storm hags ride the winds and heard their calls from the deep, wet greenness of the woods. The dead danced around me. After a time the visions faded but the ghosts remained: those souls who do not wish to pass on.' Anselm rubbed his face. 'Eventually I came out of my grief. I bathed, I fasted, and I found my vocation as a Carmelite priest. I also realized,' he added tartly, 'that the dead will not leave me alone. Accordingly my superiors, so-called astute men, decided to use my unwanted gift. Yet,' he added wistfully, 'I still commit treason against my own vocation. I sometimes wonder what might have been: sitting in an orchard perfumed with apple blossom, hand in hand with my beloved wife, watching our children play . . . but, of course, these, too, are ghosts.' Anselm put his face in his hands. For a brief while he sobbed quietly, then fell silent.

Beauchamp glanced at Stephen, who put a finger to his lips and shook his head.

'If you want to know what I believe . . .' Anselm dried the tears from his seamed cheeks. 'If you want to repeat the question that people always ask me about death, we human beings suffer two deaths. The body dies, it corrupts. The soul, the spirit, goes forth. However, once it does, a challenge is mounted by those forces hostile to God and man. Each adult soul is confronted. Some are reluctant to face the challenge. They pause, they wait. They don't want to give up their lives on Earth. They cower, dragged down by sin, by unresolved acts and hopes. They are reluctant to go into the blinding light which burns all clear so they can make their decision for all eternity. Their world is my world. I try to reassure such souls. I try to release them from the traps. I urge, I pray for them to move on.' Anselm rose and moved across to the shuttered window. He opened this and stared out. A bell began to clang, a solemn salutation to the gathering dark.

'It's time, isn't it? You brought us here, Beauchamp. Let us see what the twilight brings.'

They left the guest house and entered the monks' cemetery, a stretch of wild grass, flowers and shrubs bending slowly under an impetuous breeze. Above them the gathering clouds promised rain: the sky was grey and lowering, shrouding the cemetery in a more sinister aspect. They re-entered the gardens of the dead, row after row of battered crosses and crumbling headstones, hummocks and mounds long overgrown. All this was being disturbed as Beauchamp had described. Graves were being opened, rotting shrouds ripped, mouldy coffins and caskets shattered. The skulls and bones of long-dead monks were being piled into carts, tumbrils and wheelbarrows all intended for the charnel house. The workers had stopped for the day but the mounds of white glistening bones and heaps of skulls with gaping jaws were unnerving. A huge crow perched on a skull, claws slipping as if that bird of ill omen wished to grasp and carry it away. Stephen fingered his Ave beads even as Anselm took out his own from the pouch on his waist cord. The dead truly hung close. Faint voices carried on the wind. Whispered conversation, softly murmured prayers and traces of plain chanting. Shapes and shadows assumed a life of their own. Wisps of mist hovered then moved swiftly out of sight. The undergrowth became alive with strange scuttlings. Twigs snapped as if others walked beside or behind them. Steven glanced at Beauchamp. The clerk seemed unmoved by all this, walking purposefully, cloak thrown back, hand resting on the hilt of his sword.

They entered the shadowy precincts of the great abbey church. Stephen glanced up and flinched at a massive gargoyle face glaring down at him from a cornice, a fierce dragon with scaly bat-like wings and a monstrous head, its clawed feet brought up as if ready to spring. Other stone faces glowered at him from pillars, sills, corners and ledges: grinning apes, fierce lions or rearing centaurs. A lay brother met them at the west door. As they turned into the cloisters, Stephen glimpsed the windows of the crypt; the lay brother, mumbling to himself, led them straight to that underground chamber. He unlocked an oaken door; black with age and studded with iron, it creaked open. The flaring sconce torch just inside leapt in the draught as if fiercely greeting them. The monk took this from its holder and handed it to Anselm.

'Brother,' his face creased in a fearful smile, 'everything is ready below. This is as far as I go. The cloisters are empty. Father Abbot wishes it so but,' he pointed towards the nearby pyx chamber, 'if you need help there is a bell. As I said, the cloisters are empty, at least of the living.' The lay brother bowed and padded off into the darkness.

'Sir Miles.' Anselm raised the torch a little higher to throw light on that enigmatic royal clerk, standing deliberately in the darkness. Stephen couldn't decide if the clerk was fearful or just a cynical observer of all that was happening.

'Sir Miles,' Anselm repeated, 'you need come no further. We will be safe.'

'I could stay and keep watch with you?'

'No, if need be we will ask.' Anselm sketched a blessing in the air. 'You will stay where?'

'In the guest house.' The clerk smiled and walked away in a clatter of high-heeled boots and the jingle of silver-edged spurs.

'*Et tenebrae facta*,' Anselm whispered, watching him go, 'and darkness fell. Come, Stephen.'

They moved on to the spiral staircase. Anselm closed the door behind them. They continued down, clutching the wall. Anselm paused. 'The steps here are wooden,' he explained. 'Another protection when the jewels were stored here. These steps were usually taken away to create a wide gap, a sure hindrance, or trap, for any would-be thief.'

They stepped on to the wooden casings which bent sharply under their weight. Stephen fought to control his fear. The wooden boards also created a noisy clatter which seemed to fill the iron-stoned, sombre stairwell. They continued down, the fiery cressets making the shadow dance. The air grew chilly and slightly musty. Stephen sensed they were not alone. Shadows flittered before them along the winding staircase. A gossiping voice rose and fell. Something brushed the back of Stephen's hand. He was gently jostled and slipped a foot. He steadied himself and thought of Alice, her face summer-warm, full lips firm against his, and he desperately wished to be with her. He would love to be sitting in a garden or some cheery taproom staring into those laughing eyes. Instead he was here in this ice-cold tomb, ghosts bustling around him, the crypt opening up like some greedy mouth ready to devour him.

'Leave us!' a voice spat.

Stephen paused at the clang of iron against stone, as if someone below was picking at the walls or floor.

'Ignore it, Stephen,' Anselm warned.

They reached the bottom. Torches, candles and oil lamps glowed. The crypt, buried deep beneath the chapter house above, was octagonal in shape, about four yards in width. The only natural light was provided by six windows set at ground level with chamfered jambs and square heads. Deep recesses swept up to the windows, the jambs being set back at least two yards from the inner wall. Each had a segmented pointed arch and could only be reached by that narrow sloping gulley. The windows were heavily barred, iron rods embedded in the stone sill along the bottom of each window and set in the square head at the top. The floor was tiled. The concave ceiling, a gloomy vault, was supported by thick ribs of stone radiating from a massive rounded pillar in the centre of the crypt. Stephen slowly walked around this. The pillar, with a moulded base and capital, was about three feet in circumference and fashioned out of red square brick. Stephen crouched and inspected one section closely. He realized that some of these bricks could be removed to reveal a hollow recess within. He got to his feet. Despite the candles, lantern horn and the faint glow from the brazier, the crypt was definitely cold. Even so, Beauchamp had prepared well. The crypt had been stripped of everything except for two stools, palliasses and a table with water and wine flagons, two pewter goblets and a platter of dried food. Anselm was staring at the windows; the shutters had been removed and the light pouring through was now greying as dusk settled.

'Seventeen feet thick,' Anselm murmured, 'that's what they say about these walls.' He pointed to the window on his far right. 'That's how Puddlicot got in; his stone mason chipped away at the sill. See, unlike the rest, it no longer has one. They then removed the iron bars, squeezed in and slid down the recess into the treasury. Some items were stored in the pillar; its removable bricks served as a strong box.' Anselm's account was so matter-of-fact that Stephen was startled violently by the pounding on the door leading to the stairwell. He hurriedly opened the door but there was no one. The pounding began again, this time against the door at the top of the steps, which Stephen had bolted behind them.

'Close the door!' Anselm shouted.

Stephen did so, pushing with all his strength, but some invisible presence, like a violent wind, seemed to be pressing against it. Anselm hastened to help. They slammed the door shut, pulling the bolts across. Anselm leaned against this, fighting a racking cough while wiping the sweat from his brow.

'So it begins.' He gasped and staggered across to pick up his psalter. He motioned Stephen to sit on the stool next to him as he intoned the opening verse of Vespers. 'Oh, Lord, come to our aid. Oh, Lord, make haste to help us. Our help is in the name of the Lord . . .'

Stephen glanced up and recoiled at the face, like an image in burnished steel swimming towards him, eyes all bloodshot, purple lips twisted in a cynical smile. Other figures, hideous in aspect, jostled in: hollowed, furrowed faces, eyes staring, mouths opening and closing. Stephen crossed himself. The faces seemed unaware of him but turned on each other as if in conversation. He could not hear though his mind caught sharply-whispered words such as 'treasure', 'pyx', 'charnel door'. The figures grew more distinct, taking on bodily shapes like steam twisting up from a bubbling cauldron. The visitants were garbed in the robes, girdles and sandals of Benedictine monks. Stephen could even make out their tonsures. One of them carried a massive key ring which he jangled, though no sound was heard.

'Monks,' Stephen declared, getting to his feet. 'Shapes of what once was.'

The hideous banging on the doors began again. Footsteps pounded on the stairwell. The door was tried, the latch clattering up and down; sounds at the windows made Stephen stare in horror. Dark shapes moved at the sixth window. Dust swirled down from the sill. A cold breeze smacked his face and Stephen gagged at a stench of corruption, the foulness from an open latrine. Anselm was reciting a Pater Noster. Stephen tried to join in. Candles guttered fiercely before snuffing out. The flames of the torches abruptly turned a light blue, flickered and died. Darkness filled the crypt. A hand clawed Stephen's shoulder, pulling him back even as the clatter outside, the banging on the doors, rose to a crescendo before lapsing into silence. The crypt lay eerily still except for the soft slither of footsteps. A brick in the pillar was pulled loose, crashing to the ground. Again, silence. Stephen sensed they were not alone. Something or someone stood in the blackness before him. Anselm began the prayer of exorcism. Despite the dark he found the stoup of holy water. Anselm incensed the threatening, clawing atmosphere closing in around them. Stephen recited the responses to the prayers until the formal act of identification was reached.

'By what name are you called?'

'Peregrinus.' The reply was low and throaty.

Stephen, as always, wasn't sure if the voice was real or an echo in his own mind.

'*Ego sum, peregrinus*,' the voice replied in Latin. 'I am a pilgrim.'

Stephen stepped back as a face, white and glaring, rushed through the darkness towards him. Ghosts swarmed, their voices mocking.

'You are a wanderer – why?' Anselm asked.

'No rest, no peace.' The voice was tired.

'Where have you been?'

'Here and there. I have met the jailers of the underworld. I have stood before its water black and bitter; around it lurk the ugly shapes of pestilence, fear, poverty, pain and death. I have sheltered under the great oak tree. I have been across the meadows of mayhem and misery where centaurs, gargoyles and harpies hunt lost souls like rabbits through the fiery grass. I have seen the dead flock and cluster, whispering like the dry murmuring of autumn leaves. I have wandered through the forest of the damned to confront the suicides. I have crossed the bridge of despair, over white-hot flame; I have glimpsed the iron towers of limbo and met the Furies who scourge the dead. I have encountered the Hydra with her yawning, poisonous mouth.' The voice sighed and faded.

Stephen recalled how ghosts, like the living, often describe their own nightly dreams. Anselm often argued that no more truth should be attached to them than the ravings of a delirious patient.

'Yes, yes,' Anselm retorted, 'but why do you not go into the light? Why dwell in darkness?'

'Judgement.'

'The Lord is merciful to the repentant.'

'I cannot,' the voice hissed. 'I will not,' it hurled back. 'I cannot rest. You know the injustice.'

'I know what?'

'We have met before, at the other church where the injustice was done.'

Anselm tensed. 'What other church? Saint Michael's, Candlewick? What injustice?'

'I cannot say,' the voice rasped. 'The guardians are here. You search for the treasure, like the rest?'

'Are you Puddlicot the thief? The executed felon?'

'The others asked the same.'

'Which others?'

'How can you describe a dream? Faces you see, all distorted, like gazing through running water? Give me peace; let me be buried. The sheer shame. How can I break free? Even Picard's prayers do not help.'

'Who is Picard? I adjure you to tell me the truth.'

'The guardians have come, swift and deadly. You cannot see them. They are here.' The voice crumbled into incoherent phrases, the occasional mumbled word. The clamour in the stairwell outside began again: the clatter of mailed feet followed by an incessant banging on the door, the latch rattling as if pressed by a mad man. Ice-cold draughts swept the crypt. The sound of dripping water grew as if a barrel was filling to the brim and splashing over. Spikes of fire appeared then faded. The blackness began to thin. The threat of impending danger receded. Anselm moved across to the table, searching for a tinder. After a few scrapes he forced a flame and lit the candles and cressets. The crypt flared into light. Stephen glanced fearfully at the pools of darkness. A disembodied hand appeared in one of these, long, white fingers curling as if searching for something, like the hand of a drowning man making one last desperate attempt to find something to cling on to, then it was gone.

'Stephen, look at the walls.'

He did so. Hand prints scorched the stone, the same on the table and pillar as if some being, cloaked in fire, had crept around the crypt desperate for an opening. Stephen watched these fade even as Anselm, sitting by the table, began to slice the bread and cheese.

'Eat, Stephen, drink.'

The novice did so though his belly rumbled. His throat felt dry, sore and sticky.

'Is it over, Magister?'

'It is never over, Stephen. Not until we free the nets and break the snares which keep these souls bound.'

'The snares?'

'Their own guilt, remorse and fear. Above all, the injustices done to them.'

'And the guardians?'

'Demons, Stephen, who prowl the wastelands between life and death, between heaven and hell.'

'He talked about Saint Michael's?'

Stephen bit into a piece of cheese and startled at the voice which bellowed: 'We've shut him up, forced his mouth closed.'

Stephen dropped the cheese and whirled around in terror. Something moved in the pool of darkness. Abruptly the noise outside began again; this was repeated by the pounding on the door opening on to the steps to the crypt.

'Enough is enough!' Anselm sprang to his feet. 'Why the door? I am sure it's the door, Stephen. God knows why. Is it seen as a barrier or a representation of guilt? Why?' Anselm opened the crypt door. He asked Stephen to bring the lantern horn and both began the arduous climb through the freezing stairwell. Every so often Anselm had to pause in a fit of coughing. They reached the wooden steps. An icy draught buffeted them. The wooden steps began to shake and, to Stephen's horror, slightly buckle, as if some unseen power beneath was striving to break free. He clutched his lantern horn, steadying himself against the wall as Anselm prayed. The wooden steps rattled but then settled. They reached the top and opened the ancient door. Stephen was glad to be free of the crypt. He welcomed the rich night air, the comforting sight of torches flickering in their holders. Anselm, angry at what had happened, strode up and down the hollow-stone passageway, peering into the darkness before coming back to examine the door. 'Nothing!' Anselm exclaimed. He sat down on a stone plinth.

'I'm satisfied about what we saw, heard and felt. I assure you Stephen, it was not of human origin.'

ooOOoo

Words Amongst the Pilgrims

The physician, who stood narrating his tale fluently and lucidly, now sat down, grasped the wine jug and filled his goblet to the brim.

'Is this a tale?' the pardoner jibed. 'Or the truth?'

'What is truth?' the physician quipped back.

'But these voices, shapes and shades?' The man of law spoke up.

'My friends,' the poor parson declared, 'listen to my advice. If God has his contemplatives and mystics so does Satan; he can immerse them in raptures. I've seen Satan,' he continued remorselessly, 'like a deformed bird winging through my own church. Once a parishioner of mine beheaded two old beldames. She later confessed how she'd been walking in Summer Meadow when a devil appeared to her in the form of a man, garbed and cowled. He handed her a scythe so she could do his bloody deed.

'And?' the man of law asked.

'She was hanged then burnt.'

'Satan stabs the heart with terror,' the prioress murmured, stretching out to clasp her chaplain's hand.

The conversation now descended into the pilgrim's personal experiences. Tales about gruesome demons with horns and tails, fire spurting from every orifice with harsh, horrifying voices. How demon ghosts had spindly bodies, bulging eyes, lipless mouths, horns, beaks and claws. Master Chaucer watched this carefully. Most of the pilgrims joined in, though the summoner sat stock-still, lost in his own dark memories. The knight, too, was silent, staring down at the table top, tapping it with his fingers. Master Chaucer had his own misgivings. The physician was sitting in his costly robes all serene, yet there was a tension here. Chaucer shivered. Wispy shapes swirled around the physician's head, which disappeared. Were these, Chaucer wondered, just his imaginings? Ghosts or traces of smoke from the chafing dishes and braziers? The taproom was decked out to be merry with its long table. Sweet-smelling hams, bacon and vegetables hung in nets from the smartly-painted rafter beams. The rushes on the floor were spring-green, glossy and powdered with herbs. Candlelight, lamplight and lantern horn all danced vigorously, yet there was something wrong. The physician's story had summoned up a dark cloud which housed its own macabre secrets. The friar looked not so merry now while the haberdasher, dyer, weaver and carpet-maker, so trim and fresh in all their livery, sat heads together, locked in hushed conversation. Next to them the cook, scratching his leg ulcer, listened in, his scabby head nodding vigorously.

'Master physician,' Minehost of The Tabard also sensed the unease, 'your tale is unsettling.'

'We've heard about this.' The fat-faced haberdasher, eyes all choleric, half-rose. 'Oh, yes, the great mystery at Saint Michael's, Candlewick.' He swallowed nervously. 'Hidden crimes, scandalous secrets . . .?'

'And I know of The Unicorn.' The cook spoke up. 'I've worked there. Master Robert Palmer and his daughter Alice . . .'

'Please,' the physician spread his hands, 'do not spoil my tale.'

'These ghosts and demons . . .' the bulbous-eyed manciple exclaimed. Thankfully his interjection forced the conversation back on to the personal experiences of ghosts, hauntings and visions of hell the pilgrims had either been told of or dreamed of. How the violent are boiled in blood while murderers turn into trees, their leaves and bark shredded and eaten by hog-faced harpies. The only exception was the Wife of Bath. She sat all flush-faced, slightly sweating. She did not join in the conversation but sat quietly, hands on her lap. She had taken out a pair of Ave beads and was threading these through her fingers, eyes glazed, lost in her own memories.

Minehost banged his tankard on the table. 'Enough!' he declared. 'The flame on the hour candle has eaten another ring. Master physician, your story, please?'

ooOOoo

The Physician's Tale

Part Three

'I can only tell you what I suspect.' Magister Anselm folded back the voluminous sleeves of his coarse, woollen white robe. 'Nothing is certain,' he added wistfully. 'Well, not in this vale of tears. No.' He shook his head at the murmur his words created and lapsed into silence.

The two Carmelites and the others had all assembled in Sir William Higden's council chamber next to his chancery office on the second floor of the merchant's manor in Candlewick. Sir William, Parson Smollat, Gascelyn, Amalric and Simon the sexton as well as the royal clerk, Beauchamp, who'd recently arrived from his own house in Ferrier Lane only a short walk away. Beauchamp sat opposite Stephen, the raindrops still glistening on his fair hair.

'You have reached certain conclusions, Brother Anselm,' Beauchamp urged. 'You must share them.'

'By Saint Joachim and Saint Anne that is true.' Anselm drank from his water goblet. 'Richard Puddlicot,' he began slowly, 'broke into the royal treasury in the crypt at Westminster in April 1303. He and his coven, which comprised most of London's notorious sanctuary men, outlaws and wolfheads, stole a King's fortune. They were not allowed to enjoy it. A royal clerk, Drokensford,' he glanced fleetingly at Beauchamp, 'hunted them down. Puddlicot, a married man who'd left his wife, was consorting with a woman of ill-repute – Joanne Picard. They lived in Hagbut Lane . . .'

'Lord, save us,' Sir William interjected, 'that's Rishanger's house, the goldsmith who tried to take sanctuary in the abbey and was murdered.'

'The same. I shall come back to him,' Anselm agreed. 'What is noteworthy is that Puddlicot, the great thief and violator, escaped from Drokensford's clutches and, Parson Smollat, took sanctuary in Saint Michael's, Candlewick.' Anselm's words created further cries and exclamations of surprise. 'It's true,' he confirmed. 'I have visited the crypt. I cannot say what happened there except that those involved in the great sacrilege decades ago still haunt that gloomy place. Little wonder! I also asked Sir Miles to bring from the memoranda rolls stored in the Tower all the records pertaining to Puddlicot. Our notorious felon was plucked by force from Saint Michael's, sanctuary or not.'

'But that is against church law!' Parson Smollat cried. 'Not to mention the statutes of Parliament?'

'Oh, at the time the Bishop of London and all the city clergy pleaded and protested but Drokensford had his way. Puddlicot was lodged in the Tower where he was tried before the King's justices. He tried to plead benefit of clergy, that he was a cleric – this was later proved to be a lie. He was condemned to hang on the gallows outside the main abbey gate. The King insisted that he be humiliated, so Puddlicot was pushed from the Tower to the Westminster gallows in a wheelbarrow. He was hanged, then his corpse suffered further indignities, being peeled and the skin nailed to the door leading down to the crypt.' Anselm paused at the exclamations this provoked.

'Our present King's grandfather,' the exorcist continued, 'was determined that the monks of Westminster never forgot their part in the sacrilegious theft. They had to pass that door with its grisly trophy every time they wound their way up to the chapter house.'

'And the skin remained there,' Almaric whispered fearfully.

'From what I learnt from the records, yes. It decomposed and merged with the wood. I went and re-examined that door; traces of human skin can still be detected.'

'So Puddlicot's ghost still walks?'

'Puddlicot, God rest him, was a great sinner. He left his wife to consort with a whore. He committed sacrilegious theft and died a violent death. I doubt if his corpse was given holy burial. Little wonder he haunts Westminster as well as here, at Saint Michael's, Candlewick in Dowgate ward.'

'You are sure?' Sir William swallowed hard.

'Puddlicot definitely lived in Dowgate, in Hagbut Lane. He and Joanne Picard were members of this parish.'

'Sir William is correct – that's where Adam Rishanger lived,' Almaric declared. 'Puddlicot was a thief and so was Rishanger . . .'

'A hateful soul.' Sir William spoke. 'A greedy madcap full of dark designs and sinister stratagems. He once approached me for money. He claimed he'd found a way to create the philosopher's stone and so transmute base metal into gold. Gascelyn threw him into the street.'

'Mad as a March hare,' the squire declared lugubriously.

'Rishanger rarely took the sacrament,' Parson Smollat observed. 'Rumours abound that after he was murdered treasure was found close to his corpse.'

'That is correct,' Beauchamp affirmed. He went on: 'Such a story spread across the city: a dagger and a pure gold cross,' then fell silent.

'But what,' Sir William pleaded, 'has this ancient robbery got to do with our troubles at Saint Michael's?'

Beauchamp gestured at Anselm. 'Brother, your thoughts?'

'*Primo*.' Anselm paused as if listening to the rain pattering against the window. 'Puddlicot hales from Saint Michael's, from whose sanctuary he was illegally dragged. He also haunts the abbey, the stage on which he lived and died a hideous death, sent into the dark, his soul drenched in sin. However, why Puddlicot's ghost has defied all attempts to prise him loose to continue his journey I am not sure. *Secundo*,' Anselm continued, 'ghosts surround us all like plaintiffs outside a court. They wait for their opportunity for a door to open; the demons do likewise. Our souls are like castles, constantly besieged by the lords of the air, the dark dwellers, malevolent wraiths and unsettled ghosts.'

'And a door has been opened?'

'Yes, Amalric, it certainly has. More than one gate or postern has been unlocked, unbolted and thrown wide open.'

'By whom?'

'Why, parson, the Midnight Man, which brings me to my third point – *tertio*: his macabre rites around All Souls, on Saint Walpurgis eve. What happened then? I truly don't know. Something went dreadfully wrong. I have questioned Sir Miles but . . .'

'All I have learnt,' Beauchamp explained, 'was from one of my spies in the city and, believe me, they are many. This gentleman, who rejoices in the name of Bolingbrok, heard rumours, nothing more, about a midnight ceremony where the Satanists summoned up powers they could not control, so they fled. I have searched – hungered – for more details.' He pulled a face. 'I have whistled sharply into the darkness but so far there has been no reply.'

'*Quarto*,' Anselm continued, 'somehow Rishanger, that petty goldsmith, found or was given two precious items from the long-lost treasure. Others, we don't know who, also discovered this. Rishanger tried to flee into exile but he was ambushed and later murdered. Now how – and where – did they come across this treasure? We don't know. Nor do we know if what Rishanger held was part of an even greater hoard, or who murdered him and his mistress Beatrice Lampeter, whose eyeless corpse was dug up in that garden at Hagbut Lane.' Anselm paused for breath. Stephen could hear the bubbles on his chest and wondered if his master was falling ill.

'*Quinto*,' Anselm continued, 'who is the Midnight Man? Is he still searching for the missing treasure which, according to the Exchequer records, still totals hundreds of thousands of pounds? *Sexto*, what has happened in Saint Michael's cemetery? Why has it led to an infestation of demons and ghosts? My friends, to conclude,' Anselm stared sadly around the assembled company, 'I believe some other grievous sin lurks deep within the layers of our existence. But what?' He pulled a face.

'Why did the Midnight Man choose Saint Michael's, Candlewick?' Beauchamp asked. 'My parish church, our parish church.'

'Because he knew about Puddlicot,' Stephen declared, 'which means that the warlock learned about Puddlicot's story, but from where? I mean, the robbery occurred decades ago.'

Anselm smiled at the novice. 'You are correct, Stephen. How did the Midnight Man know? Did he study the records? Yet I asked the clerk of the Tower muniment room. No one, apart from you, Sir Miles, has asked to study that schedule of documents.'

'I asked,' the clerk replied tersely, 'after the treasures were found near Rishanger's corpse.'

'Has any other such treasure been found in the city?' Sir William asked.

'No.' Beauchamp shook his head. 'The royal surveyors have been most scrupulous.' He paused as one of the window-shutters, loose from its clasp, banged noisily. Stephen, the nearest, rose. He pulled the shutter closed and stared back at the narrow face, eyes all bloodshot, mouth gaping, long hair straggling down, pushed up against the opaque, square window glass. Stephen caught his breath. The lips moved soundlessly, as if cursing him.

'Stephen?'

'Sorry, Magister.' Stephen glanced over his shoulder. Anselm was staring at him curiously.

'Sir William?'

'Yes?' The merchant knight glanced in surprise at the novice.

'Magister, my apologies, but that young woman, Alice Palmer, daughter of the tavern master at The Unicorn?'

'What about Alice?' Parson Smollat asked. 'Oh, she's approached you, hasn't she? About one of the slatterns at the tavern – a young woman called Margotta Sumerhull who has apparently disappeared?'

'Yes, yes, she has asked the same of me.' Sir William leaned back in his chair. 'Sir Miles, I appeal to you. How many young women in London just disappear?'

The royal clerk nodded. 'The chancery coffers and pouches are crammed with such enquiries.' Stephen caught the note of despair in the clerk's voice.

'I organized a search,' Sir William added. 'Ask Parson Smollat's parishioners. But to no avail. However,' Sir William rubbed his hands together, 'we have talked enough. My cooks have prepared brawn in mustard, some savoury *doucettes* made from the sweetest, freshest pork, all mixed in with honey and pepper.' He paused as Simon the sexton rose swiftly to his feet.

'Sir William, please excuse me.' Simon pointed to the hour candle standing in its ornate bronze holder on a corner table. 'God waits for no one. The archangel guild meet for their weekly devotions before the statue. I must ring the bells, open the doors . . .'

Sir William excused him and Simon hurried out. Anselm and Sir Miles began to collect their sheaves of manuscripts. Sir William rose and walked away, deep in conversation with Gascelyn and Amalric. Stephen stared around this comfortable chamber, its lime-washed walls above the highly polished, dark oak panelling, the lowered candelabra shedding a ring of glowing light. He rose and walked across to study the heraldic shields fastened on the wall. One boasted a silver pen with three gold books on a blue field depicting the insignia of St Hilary of Poitiers. Next to this the arms of St Thanus of Alexandria, the courtesan who converted to Christ, and beneath it a white scroll with the Latin tag: 'You who have made me, have mercy on me', written in black on a blue and violet field. Stephen studied these even as he guiltily recalled his meeting with Alice Palmer – her kiss so soft and warm, the faint trace of perfume about her. Excitement flushed his face. He only wished he could meet her again. What would it be like, he wondered, to court a young woman such as her? He tried to push aside the usual dark temptation of despondency. How refreshing it would be, Stephen wondered, to break from the shapes, shadows and glimmerings constantly on the border of both his vision and consciousness. He had rejoiced to be free of his father and his wealthy

Winchester mansion. The White Friars had welcomed him warmly, educated him as rigorously as any scholar in the schools of Oxford and Cambridge. Magister Anselm had proved to be both a brilliant teacher and a very close friend. Stephen had gone to him to be shrived, to confess these very temptations of the flesh as well as those of the spirit. He had asked Anselm if all the phenomena, phantasms and visions were really true? Hadn't Stephen's own father raged like a man possessed against such fancies? Was there a physical explanation? Anselm had surprisingly agreed. 'Most hauntings and so-called spiritual occurrences,' he had declared, 'are illusions, the result of some very cunning sleight of hand. But there are those which are true. Yet, even then I concede,' Anselm had kept repeating this as one of his sacred rules, 'such events or phenomena are always firmly rooted in the human will, in human wickedness, the devious perversity of the human heart.'

Stephen started from his reverie as he heard the Midnight Man being mentioned by Anselm. He walked back to the table where Sir Miles was explaining to the exorcist that neither officials of the Crown nor those of the Church, despite all their resources, could hunt down and trap that most elusive of warlocks. Beauchamp paused as the bells of St Michael's began to peal. They did for a while then abruptly paused, stilling all conversation in the chamber.

'What is the matter?' Sir William strode to the chamber door, flinging it open as the bells began to clang again but this time discordantly, sounding out the tocsin. Sir William, followed by his household, hurried out of the room, clattering down the stairs.

'We also should go.' Beauchamp strapped on his sword belt, beckoning to the two Carmelites to accompany him. By the time they reached the tiled entrance hall the servants had also been roused. They passed through the main doorway, down the steps across the rutted trackway to the lychgate. A crowd had gathered – a few going up the winding path to the main door of the church. Sir Miles ordered these to step aside. Stephen noticed how many of those in the cemetery wore a blue and gold livery with a great medallion celebrating St Michael's victory over Satan on a chain around their necks. The light was dimming;

the air fresh after the showers; the rain glinting on the grass and shrubs of the cemetery. As they hurried up the path Stephen noticed a group clustered to the right of the soaring bell tower. One or two were pointing up to the belfry where the tocsin still boomed out. Sir Miles strode off then hurried back, meeting them at the foot of the church steps. 'Bardolph the gravedigger,' he murmured. 'According to members of the guild, they heard the bells tolling and, as they approached the church, saw Bardolph's body fall from the tower bouncing like a pig's bladder on to the roof, spinning like a top to the ground.' Beauchamp crossed himself. 'Parson Smollat is administering the rites of the dead, and Almaric is with him. Let's find out . . .'

They hastened up the steps, through the doorway and left through the narrow entrance into the bell tower. Simon the sexton ceased pulling the two oiled, hempen ropes. He stood gasping for breath, almost oblivious to Sir William's constant questions. Gascelyn came clattering down the tower steps. 'Nothing,' he exclaimed. 'No one is there.'

'Simon,' Sir William gently touched the sexton's face with his gloved hand, 'Simon, what happened in this benighted church?'

'I er, came in,' Simon stammered. 'All was quiet.' He gestured around the bare-walled chamber furnished with a stool, table and a battered, iron-ribbed chest, its concave lid thrown back. 'I took out my gloves and the woollen clasp for the ropes. All was quiet. I prepared myself saying the usual prayer to Saint Michael.' He smiled, though his eyes were full of fear, his red-poxed face deeply flushed. 'Then one to Saint Gabriel and Saint Raphael – they are also archangels. Our two bells are named after them.'

'Yes, yes,' Sir William urged. 'And?'

'I began to pull, trying to establish a rhythm. I heard movement further up the stairwell. There are chambers above; they serve as lofts. I wondered whether children were playing there or if a beggar hid hoping for a warm night's sleep.' Simon scratched his thinning hair. 'I am sure I heard footsteps. Anyway, I began the peal. I heard screams, shouts and cries. A guild member came hurrying in saying that someone had fallen from the tower.'

Simon grasped the bell rope as if to give it another pull.

'Take him away,' Beauchamp ordered. 'Sir William, please tell the guild there will be no meeting here tonight.'

Stephen stared across the bleak bell chamber, its corners rich in cobwebs and drenched in dirt. He noticed the coils of rope, the pots of oil and grease, the empty buckets. Stephen left and walked into the nave. He stared down at the huge rood screen, above it the cross and on either side of that life-sized carvings of Our Lady and St John. The evening light pouring through the window was dappled and emphasized the darting shadows. Stephen peered closer. He glimpsed the red sanctuary light winking beside the pyx hanging on its chain. To the left tapers still glowed in the Lady chapel.

'This truly is,' he whispered, 'the walking place for wraiths, the domain of demons and a hall of beseeching ghosts.'

Was Christ really present here? Stephen reflected. Or was this church the mouth of hell yawning for its prey, breathing out terrors while the demons gathered like millions of grunting hogs?

'Stephen!' Anselm stood outside the bell chamber, beckoning him over even as Sir William and Gascelyn escorted a sobbing Simon to the main door where Beauchamp, half-hidden by the shadows, stood waiting. 'Stephen,' Anselm urged, 'come with me!' The novice hurried over. Anselm plucked him by the sleeve and led him back into the deserted bell tower. They climbed the steep spiral staircase. Anselm explained how the tower had been built over successive generations with one storey raised upon another. Stephen, breathless by the climb, could only grunt a reply. Now and again they stopped so that Anselm could rest. Once again Stephen heard the rasping deep in his master's chest.

At last they reached the first storey, prized open the wooden trapdoor and climbed into the deserted loft. The evening breeze pierced the window-shafts, whirling the dust and stirring the pungent odour from the bird droppings which coated the chamber. The air grew colder as they continued their climb. Stephen felt he was being followed. No candlelight or cresset flared in the winding stairwell. The blackness closed in, stifling and threatening. Now and again a bird, like some disembodied soul, flittered, a threatening blur across the lancet window. They reached other lofts, the stone staircase being replaced by wooden ladders leading up from one storey to the next. The breeze became more vigorous. Anselm was having trouble climbing. Stephen was wary. At any other time, Stephen, advised by Anselm, would have dismissed his feelings as wild imaginings, yet he was sure they were being closely watched. A brushing sensation against his cheek, a fluttering around his eyes and against his ears, a faint whispering as if people were gathered in the loft above chattering quietly amongst themselves. A voice abruptly called: 'Another is here!' followed by silence.

Anselm, despite his age and racking cough, clambered resolutely up the different ladders, the sweat drenching his face. At last they reached the belfry, a cavernous chamber. The windows in each wall were at least a yard high and the same across. The two great bells, Gabriel and Raphael, hung on a massive, oil-drenched beam separated by a huge half-wheel with cogs from which the ropes dangled through the gaps of the different storeys they'd entered. The belfry reeked of iron, cordage and a thick layer of bird droppings which covered everything, particularly the wooden parapet walk which ran around the belfry at least two feet beneath each of the oblong-shaped windows. Anselm, despite the rigours of the climb, the stench and the eerie call of the birds, ignored the sinister presence which had accompanied them. The exorcist asked Stephen to stand by the hatch through which they'd entered. Stephen was only too happy to obey. Staring through one of the windows, he realized how dizzingly high they had climbed. The darkened city stretching out below seemed a different world. Anselm, however, chattering to himself, impervious to everything else, walked hastily around the parapet, stopping at each of the windows to scrupulously study the stains on the floor beneath. 'Nothing!' he exclaimed. 'Come, Stephen!' He barely waited for the novice before grasping the rungs of the ladder reaching up to the trapdoor and on to the roof of the tower.

'Magister, must we?'

'I must, you must, we must.' Anselm stared down at him. 'We search for the root, young Stephen. I believe we are on the path leading to that; only then can we pull it up. Now, trust

in God.' He grinned. 'He will send his angels lest we dash our
foot against a stone.'

Breathing prayers to St Michael and all the heavenly host,
Stephen hitched his robe, thanked God for the firm, tough
sandals and followed Anselm up through the trapdoor to the
wind-blown roof of the tower. The strong breeze buffeted him.
Below spread a swathe of pinpricks of light; to his left Stephen
could glimpse the lofty tower of St Paul's in the gathering
murk. He stared around. The roof of the tower was slightly
concave so water would drain off through the gargoyle spouts.
Near the trapdoor stood a huge brazier crammed with kindling
which served as a beacon light. The floor of the tower was
covered in tightly-packed shale which provided firm grip. The
four sides of the tower, at least a yard high, were crennelated
with iron bars between each of the jutting crennelations.
Stephen stood near the brazier, grasping it firmly against the
buffeting wind. He never did like heights and this was truly
fearsome.

'Stephen.'

He reluctantly joined Anselm, who was kneeling before one
of the crennelations, examining the packed gravel. The exorcist
picked up pieces of fresh mud and then plucked coarse fibres
from the nearby brickwork.

'Bardolph's, I am sure of it. The mud is fresh and these fibres
are from a fustian jerkin or hose. But what was Bardolph doing
up here?' Anselm got to his feet. 'Come,' he urged, 'I can see
you prefer not to be so near heaven.'

Anselm smiled at his own joke but this faded as his gaze
caught something behind Stephen. The novice turned and stared
in chilling horror at the shape on the other side of the tower, a
pluming pillar of black smoke which did not move, even in the
gusty wind.

'Magister!' Stephen warned.

'Magister, Magister!' came the hissing, mocking echo.
'Magister this, Magister that! Anselm is no magister,' the voice
continued, 'he is nothing more than a dirty little mud worm.'

Stephen shivered against the cold horror pressing in around
him. Anselm staggered back towards the wall. The exorcist was
whispering the Jesus prayer: 'Jesus, son of the living God, have

mercy on us.' Abruptly the icy buffeting wind ceased but the pillar of blackness moved to hover over the closed trapdoor.

Anselm grabbed Stephen's arm and pulled him towards it. The air reeked of corruption. Stephen knelt to pull open the trapdoor. The freezing wind returned, pummelling them hard. Stephen desperately tried to pull back the trapdoor but it held fast as if bolted from the inside. Anselm, still reciting his prayer, knelt down to help. The reeking stench made them gag. The wind beat against them. Stephen glanced up. The plume of blackness descended. Stephen could not breathe. He recoiled with horror at the stricken face which chased towards him. He felt himself being pulled back. A slap on his face made him open his eyes. Anselm, soaked in sweat, crouched by the now open trapdoor.

'Stephen . . .' Anselm's exclamation was cut off as Raphael and Gabriel began to toll. Stephen felt the force of the reverberation. The floor of the tower shook like the deck of a ship hit by a huge wave.

'In God's name!' Anselm dragged Stephen towards the opening. The bells tolled fiercely as Anselm dragged Stephen on to the ladder. They hastened down. As they did the tolling ceased as abruptly as it had begun. They reached the bell chamber. The bells hung silently yet Stephen flinched at the oppressive atmosphere. He glimpsed a shifting shape. Some being, dark as night, fluttered around the bell chamber.

'Magister!'

'I know.' Anselm grasped his arm and pulled him on. 'Let us go down.'

They did so, carefully. Stephen noticed how Anselm would stop now and again to inspect the rungs on the ladder and the steps below.

By the time they had left the tower and entered God's acre, everyone had gone. They walked down the path, through the gate and across the now empty lane. Stephen glanced to the right and left. Householders had hung out lantern horns on the door-posts; these now glowed and glittered through the gathering gloom. A voice shouted. A child cried. Dogs barked but the sounds faded. Anselm was whispering verses from a psalm as they crossed the street and made their way to Higden's stately mansion. They were ushered up into the luxurious dining hall, a low-rafted chamber comfortable and warm with linen panelling and vividly painted triptychs on the wall. The merchant knight rose as they entered and ushered them both to their stools, shouting at the servants to serve the beef broth soup and slices of soft, buttered manchet loaves. Stephen, still shaken by what had happened on the tower, quietly admired Anselm's serenity as he swiftly blessed himself and began to question the rest about what they had discovered. Beauchamp remained engrossed, bending over his platter, intent on his dish, lifting the horn spoon as if quietly enjoying every mouthful. Parson Smollat wailed about how the church might have to be closed and purified. Sir William assured him that would not be necessary; he would inform the Bishop of London. After all, it was an accident.

'How do you know that?' Anselm asked, stilling the conversation. 'I mean, did anyone actually see Bardolph fall?'

'A guild member did.' Simon spoke up. 'He saw Bardolph drop like a bird, clear against the sky. He hit the slate roof, bounced, then fell into the cemetery.'

'And you were tolling the bells?'

'Yes. By the way, we heard them peal just now. Was it you?'

'No, it wasn't,' Anselm retorted. 'The bells tolled while we were on top of the tower. We thought . . .'

'Nobody there.' Amalric spoke up. 'We were . . .'

'All gathered here.' Beauchamp finished his broth, pushing away the bowl. 'We really did think it was you – I mean, the bells.'

'Sometimes that can happen,' Simon offered. 'The ropes which pull the bell wheel, if left hurriedly, slacken and drop. The wheels turn, the bells toll.'

'Never mind that.' Anselm tapped the table. 'What was Bardolph doing there? Why should he go up to the top of the tower?'

'I don't know,' Simon replied. 'As God is my witness, Brother Anselm, I truly don't.'

'Can anyone answer that?' Beauchamp insisted. He pointed at Anselm. 'What makes you ask, Brother? What have you found?'

'I am not too sure. Did anyone see Bardolph enter the church?'

'Nobody in this room,' Sir William declared. 'I have already established that.'

'Simon?' Anselm asked. 'You went in to peal the bells. You said you heard movement in the tower stairwell?'

'I am sure I did. I began the peal, then a guild member hurried in to tell me what had happened.'

'Bardolph definitely toppled from the top of the tower,' Anselm confirmed. 'A sheer fall?'

'His corpse is no better than a pulp of flesh,' Almaric observed mournfully. 'Not a bone unbroken. I had his corpse taken to the shabby alehouse he and his wife own in Hogled Lane. She's laid out the corpse and invited her friends to drink themselves sottish. Is he to be buried at Saint Michael's?'

'No,' Sir William retorted. 'Perhaps at Saint Martin's. I think it is more appropriate.'

'Did Bardolph ever climb to the top of the tower?' Anselm asked.

'No,' Parson Smollat replied between mouthfuls of meat.

'Did he talk about anything untoward before his death?'

'You heard what we all heard,' Parson Smollat replied, 'the night you attempted your exorcism. Bardolph explained how he fiercely resented what was happening at Saint Michael's: the disturbance to his routine, the lack of fees, not to mention that Sir William had asked Gascelyn to guard the cemetery. Brother Anselm, we knew very little about the man, except . . .' Parson Smollat glanced at Sir William and raised his eyes heavenwards.

'Except what?' Anselm pressed.

'Bardolph liked the ladies. Meet his widow,' Sir William declared. 'She will hardly mourn him. Bardolph bewailed his lack of fees but also felt he had been driven from what I can only call his rutting meadow.'

'He brought his whores into the cemetery,' Parson Smollat explained. 'During inclement weather into the old death house or, if the season was warm enough, they would lie amongst the gravestones. Bardolph would stretch out with this drab or that. He seemed to enjoy such lewdry. He ignored my strictures, saying he didn't give a fig.'

Anselm stared down at his platter. 'Dusk is falling,' he murmured. 'Soon the darkness will shroud us all. I cannot understand why Bardolph fell from that tower. Was he driven up there by some malignant spirit? Was he forced to commit suicide? God save him, because he went to God unshriven. You gave him the last rites?'

Parson Smollat nodded.

'Yes,' Anselm murmured. 'It is a terrible thing for any soul to fall into the hands of the living God.' The exorcist stared hard at Parson Smollat, who had retreated deeper into the shadows. 'Did Bardolph ever confide in you, parson?'

'Why, no. Why should he?'

'I thought he did.' Amalric, who'd drunk copiously, declared.

'No, no,' the parson became flustered, 'Bardolph was not the kind.'

'I thought I saw him in the shriving queue at the beginning of Lent, I am sure.' Almaric caught the annoyance in Parson Smollat's face. 'Anyway,' the curate shrugged, 'he has gone to God now.'

Stephen stared around the table. Sir William and Beauchamp sat lost in their own thoughts. Gascelyn murmured he should return to the cemetery but then made a plaintive plea about how long was he supposed to keep up supervision of that hell-haunted place? Sir William cut him short with an abrupt gesture of his hands. Servants came in to clear the platters. Anselm plucked at Stephen's sleeve, a sign they should leave. They bade farewell, collected their cloaks, panniers and satchels and made their way out. Darkness had fallen. The streets were emptying. This was lamp-lighting time, when shutters and doors were slammed shut. The only glow of gold was the flare between the chinks of wood or from the lanterns slung on door hooks. The rain had turned the dirt underneath to a squelchy mess. Shadows moved. Cries and shouts echoed eerily. They passed houses where doors were abruptly flung open to reveal scenes inside. It was like passing paintings on a church wall. A drunk collapsed inside a hallway; a corpse sheeted in white resting on a wheel-barrow ready to be moved elsewhere; a group of dicers gathered around a pool of light from a shabby table lamp, pinched faces intent on their game. Different smells and odours wafted out.

The sickening reek of raw meat being fried in cheap oil, the pungent aroma of rotting vegetables, the faint fragrance from incense pots; all these competed with the offensive odour of the slops being deposited on the streets from jakes' jars and urine bowls, as well as pails and buckets of filthy water.

'Magister, where are we going?'

Anselm pulled his cowl forward. 'Stephen, we shall be busy this eve of Saint Mark's. First, we shall visit Hogled Lane to pay our respects to Mistress Bardolph. Truth,' he peered through the dark, 'will break through eventually.' With that enigmatic remark the exorcist strode on. They took directions from a woman trimming a doorway lantern, turned up an alleyway and entered Hogled Lane, a mean, shabby runnel with a narrow, evil-smelling sewer channel along its centre. They found the alehouse, the sheaf of decaying greenery pushed into a crack above its doorway hung next to a peeling sign which proclaimed: The Burning Bush. The taproom inside was as bleak and squalid as the exterior, a low-ceilinged room with square open windows on the far wall. Bread, cheese and other perishables hung in nets from the rafters well away from the vermin which scuttled and squeaked between the ale barrels on either side. Under foot the dry rushes had snapped, split and corrupted to a mushy slime by those who had come in to pay their final respects to Master Bardolph. The dead man lay in his shroud, only his face exposed, on the long common table down the centre of the room. Cheap tallow candles ranged either side; these made Bardolph's face even more gruesome, while the small pots of smoking incense around the swathed feet did little to make the hot, close air any less offensive.

The assembled mourners moved like sinister ghouls through the gloom. They huddled in the dark either side of the candle-light watching the sin-eater, a gnarled old man with long dirty hair, moustache and beard. He wore a crown of ivy, his face was painted black, his eyelids and lips a deep scarlet hue. He muttered some chant as he moved along the corpse, picking up with painted lips the offerings of sin symbolized by pieces of bread and dried meat. Now and again he would stop and chew noisily, throwing his head back like a dog, clap his hands softly, gesture towards the ceiling and move on to the next piece.

Stephen expected Anselm to intervene but the exorcist just stood and watched. The old man's chanting grew louder. Greedily and noisily he devoured the sin offerings. Stephen did not like the ceremony; other beings were busy thronging in. Stephen could see, and he was sure Anselm also did, their swarthy, worn faces. These flocked close to his own, cheek by jowl, with pointed beards, glittering, dagger-like eyes, their chattering tongues crudely imitating the sin-eater's words. Stephen stared at the corpse; the more he did the stronger the visions grew: a road was opening up, long and dark, lit by a full moon and lined by shiny green cypresses, the moon-washed path glittered as the light sparkled on its polished pebbles. An owl, wings extended, passed like a ghost over the bedraggled figure staggering down the path. Stephen recognized the mud-splattered Bardolph. The dead gravedigger had lost his swagger and used the spade he carried as a crutch. As this hideous figure staggered closer, Stephen recoiled at the sight of Bardolph's eyes and mouth tightly stitched with black twine.

'Stephen!' Anselm shook him vigorously; the figure disappeared. The sin-eater had gobbled all the offerings. Someone was playing a lute. The mourners were drifting back to the casks where dirty-winged chickens roosted on their iron-hooped rims. A woman broke away from the rest and came towards them. She had a heavy, leathery face, hard eyes and a rat-trap mouth. She brusquely asked their business while she scratched her face, fingers glittering with tawdry rings. She forced a smile when Anselm courteously introduced himself and Stephen. She replied that she was Adele, Bardolph's relict or widow. Anselm leaned down and whispered in her ear. Her puffy arrogance and shrewish ways abruptly faded. She stared, mouth gaping, and gestured that they follow her into the buttery at the back of the alehouse.

'What did you say?' Stephen hissed.

'I told her that, unless she told the truth,' Anselm whispered, 'I had a vision of how, within a year and a day, she would join her husband in purgatory.' He nudged Stephen playfully. 'It always works; it still might.'

Adele took them into the buttery, a squalid room with chipped shelves, battered cups and tranchers, small casks and barrels.

'What do you want?' She sat down on a stool and nodded back at the taproom where raucous singing had begun. 'I have guests to cater for.'

'And a tidy profit to make on your husband's death, Mistress Adele? I will be brief. You do not seem to be the grieving widow?'

'That, Reverend Brother, is because I am not.' Adele wiped her nose on the back of her hand. 'I am no hypocrite. Bardolph was dead to me long before he was pushed from that tower.'

'Pushed?'

'Yes, Brother, pushed! What was Bardolph, a gravedigger and womanizer, doing on the top of Saint Michael's tower? Why go there?' She shook her head. 'I don't know.'

'Did he ever go there before?'

'Never. I tell you, Bardolph didn't like heights.'

'So why should someone push him? Did he have enemies?'

'Were you your husband's enemy?' Stephen asked.

'Bardolph had no time for me. We were indifferent to each other. He was only interested in his whores from that nugging house, The Oil of Gladness in Gullet Lane.'

'Nugging house?' Stephen asked.

'Brothel,' Anselm whispered.

'He was a mutton-monger.' Adele paused to listen to a cackle of laughter from the taproom. Stephen scrutinized this cunning woman, her soul steeped in malice. She had an aura of squalid unease, a dirtiness of spirit.

'He was always one for the ladybirds.' She continued: 'Prostitutes.' Adele sniggered. 'Well, not now.' She fingered the silver chain around her thick, sweaty neck: a small gold swan hung delicately from it. Both looked out of place next to the dirt-lined seams and wrinkles of her skin. 'One in particular.' Adele sniffed. 'Edith Swan-neck is what that princess of the night called herself. Bought her this as a present, he did.'

'And?'

'The little whore disappeared, God knows where. Bardolph searched but even her sisters of the night at The Oil of Gladness couldn't tell him.'

'So the necklace?' Anselm asked.

'Bardolph claimed he found it in the cemetery at Saint

Michael's, lying in the grass. Oh, that was some time ago. Anyway, after that he'd say strange things . . .'

'Mistress?' Anselm drew a coin from his belt purse and put it on top of an upturned barrel.

'He said he would have his revenge against Parson Smollat.'

'Revenge?'

'I don't know why. Bardolph also boasted how he would be rich one day – then I would see him in a different light. I have, haven't I?' she sneered. 'Corpse light!' Again, she sniffed. 'I can tell you no more. He left this morning as usual, told me to look after the alehouse. God alone knows what happened.' Adele's fingers edged towards the coin on the barrel but Anselm picked it up and slipped it back into his purse.

'If you have anything more, Mistress, but not until then.'

They left the alehouse and walked through the gloaming towards the torches flickering on the main thoroughfare. These had been lit by the wardsmen who had also fired the rubbish heaps to create more light and some warmth for the destitute slinking out of their corners and recesses. Some of these brought scraps of raw meat to grill and cook over the flames. The smell of rancid fat swirled everywhere. Stephen kept close to Anselm for this was the haunt of the night-walkers, the brothers and sisters of the dark, the fraternity of the bone: carrion-hunters, snakes-men, moonrakers, slop-collectors and all the rest who waited for the cover of night to do their work. The two Carmelites were swiftly inspected and ignored. A group of mounted archers appeared and the bobbing shadows and weasel-faces, all cowled and hooded, quickly disappeared. Anselm took advantage of this, stopping by a fire, watching the archers clatter by.

'Magister, Bardolph?'

'What do you think, Stephen?' Anselm replied. 'What do I think? Are we thinking what we are supposed to be thinking?'

'Magister, you are talking in riddles.'

'So I am – my apologies. Was Bardolph's death the result of the haunting? Did he become possessed? Was he forced up to the top of that tower and made to jump? Or was he fleeing from some horror which crawled out of the walls?'

'I don't think so,' Stephen replied, looking to his right as the people of the dark began to gather again. 'I reflected on what happened while Adele was chattering. I saw Bardolph's corpse, all pure in its white shroud, except for that sin-eater.'

'Paganism,' Anselm intervened, 'but continue, Stephen.'

'In life Bardolph was a man cloaked in dirt and mud. We found traces of that on the tower near the place where he fell.'

'And?'

'I watched you, Magister, as we went down that tower. You found no trace of mud or dirt on the steps or stairwell. Is that right?'

'Yes, correct. You are the most observant of novices. What else?'

'Bardolph didn't like heights. True, he could have been possessed but why should demons take someone they already have? A man immersed in the lusts of the flesh.'

Anselm softly clapped his hands. 'The most subtle of novices. And?'

'I believe Bardolph was carried to the top of that tower and thrown down. He was probably taken up wrapped in a sheet or a piece of canvas which would account for no trace of mud being left on the stairs or steps.'

'Stephen, I believe the same. Yet, when Bardolph fell, was not everybody clustered around that table in Sir William's house?'

'Except for the Midnight Man and his coven?'

'I agree. Bardolph's assassins, whoever they may be, want us to regard Bardolph as the victim of secret, dark forces. He was, but those powers were of this world rather than the next.'

'Magister, what do you think is happening?'

'It is very simple.' Anselm stretched his hands out to the flame. 'Now you are cold, you draw close to this fire. What came first? Why, the idea, of course. If you were warm would you even give this bonfire a second glance? Now, Stephen, think of something unpleasant.'

'My father!'

Anselm laughed softly. 'If you must. However, do you feel your body react at the thought of this man who believes you are madcap and fey-witted, so much so that he wanted to lock you away in some convent home? He dismissed what you saw, heard and felt, as the result of upset humours. He cast you out. Now, Stephen, what do you feel? A beating of the heart? A tumult in the stomach and bowels? So, change your thoughts and think of something pleasant. Alice Palmer, the maid who kissed you?' He nudged Stephen. 'That will not be difficult. Think of her lovely lips, the gentle cusp of her cheek, her pretty eyes. Oh, God be thanked,' Anselm murmured, 'for the vision of women. You feel happy, contented, flattered?' Anselm grasped a piece of stick and prodded the flames making the sparks flutter and rise. 'The business of Saint Michael's and the abbey is very similar. Powerful emotions are expressing themselves in the phenomena we see. The cause is not human weakness but something much darker: ice-cold malice.'

'Such as?'

'Murder, Stephen – horrid, cruel, calculating murder allied to a malicious interference from the spirit world.'

'Murder?'

'Oh, yes, Stephen – the slaughter of innocents. Some hideous crime which shrieks for justice – not Bardolph's, but whose, as yet, we do not know. Now,' he sighed, 'your august but severe father asked me to educate you and so I shall.' Anselm swiftly glanced over his shoulder. 'Oh, by the way,' he whispered, 'I think we are being followed. Anyway, Stephen, have you ever been to a brothel? No, I don't think you have. Well, it's The Oil of Gladness in Gutter Lane for us.'

Anselm asked directions from a surprised beadle supervising the feeding of the different bonfires now burning merrily along the runnel. The Carmelites strode off, pushing through the now gathering throng as the Worms of London, the poor and all their associates, swarmed out of their rat-like dens to search for what the city had left them. The streets were busy as the different fraternities from the guilds dispensed their charity: the Brotherhood of the Heavenly Manna, the Society of the Crumb, the Sisterhood of Martha, the Brethren of Lazarus – men and women garbed in penitential robes pulling hand-carts and barrows full of food, meat, bread and fruit rejected by the markets. Torches glowed. Flames juddered against the whipping breeze. Smells and cries carried. Beadles, bailiffs and wardsmen wandered armed with cudgels, swords, pikes and ropes, searching for those sanctuary men who thought they could leave the safety of their havens at St Paul's and St Martin's to wander the streets hunting for food, plunder and further mischief. London's underworld had opened up. Anselm, clutching his satchel, walked fast. He kept to the centre of the street though he was careful of the filth-crammed sewer.

They reached The Oil of Gladness in Gutter Lane. From the outside it looked like a small, prosperous tavern with smartly-painted red woodwork and mullioned glass windows in all three stories. The door was guarded by two well-known water-pads: thieves who stole from barges on the river. Anselm greeted both like old friends. 'This is my companion, a novice,' Anselm declared.

The two monsters stepped fully into the pool of light created by the torches flaring either side of the doorway. 'Stephen, this is Stubface. You can see why. He had the pox which pitted his face while the other,' Anselm gestured at the smaller of the two, 'is Wintersday, called so because, allegedly, he is short and very nasty. Well, my beloveds?'

The two oafs muffled in their cloaks shuffled even further forward, their bewhiskered, ugly faces furrowed in puzzlement. Both reeked heavily of ale. Stephen was wary of the nail-studded maces they carried. Wintersday was the first to regain whatever wits he had, his misshapen, grey features cracking into a broken-toothed smile. 'Why, God bless us all, Brother Anselm! What in heaven's name are you doing here? Surely you are not looking for a mort, a doxy?'

'No, my brother in the Lord, just words with your mistress.'

'You mean the Lady Abbess?' Stubface barked.

'You can call her that,' Anselm retorted, 'I don't.' He strode between both men and gripped their shoulders. 'Let us proceed in God's name.' Anselm turned both men by the shoulder and marched them up the steps. Wintersday lifted the iron clasp on the door, carved in the form of a penis, and clattered it against the wood. The door swung open and a young woman dressed in white like a novice nun invited them in. She looked both Carmelites from head to toe, pulled a face and muttered something about everyone being welcome. She then ushered them into a small, very comfortable antechamber, its walls decorated with frescoes which immediately intrigued Anselm but made Stephen blush. The novice nun stood in the doorway a little longer, grinning at Stephen until the two burly guards, left standing in the hall, insisted she let them out. She closed the door behind her. Stephen, in his embarrassment, continued to stare down at the soft turkey cloths which covered the floor, now and again darting glances around the comfortable chamber with its elegantly carved dressers for wine and goblets, the quilted stools and leather-backed chairs.

'Interesting,' said Anselm as he turned away from the fresco depicting the god Pan playing with two fauns. 'Stephen, don't be embarrassed. I saw worse at a house in Paris. It is just wonderful,' he sighed, 'how humans are fascinated by love in all its many aspects. It constantly intrigues me.'

'Magister,' Stephen asked, eager to change the subject, 'how do you know those two guards outside?'

'Oh, Stubface and Wintersday? Once, for my many sins, I served as chaplain to the prisons of Newgate, Fleet and Marshalsea, and those two beloveds were regular members of my parish. God knows how they've escaped hanging at the Elms at Smithfield or the Forks near Tyburn stream. Of course, they have a powerful patron, our so-called Lady Abbess, proprietor of this house. Indeed, someone I also consider a former member of my parish, Lady Rohesia Clamath, self-styled Irish princess, a famous whore and former courtesan, probably knows more about the human heart than a whole convent of Carmelites.'

The door opened and a stately woman dressed completely in a dark blue veil and gown swept into the chamber, her long, unpainted, severe face framed by a starched white wimple. A gold cord circled her slender waist while the buskins she wore were of silver satin and decorated with small roses of red damask. She glared disapprovingly at Stephen but her face broke into a brilliant smile as Anselm, who'd decided to study the fresco once more, turned and walked over to her, grasping her hands to kiss them gently.

'Anselm,' she murmured, clutching his fingers, 'you have not come . . .?'

'No.' The exorcist shook his head and ushered her to a seat. He drew up a stool, beckoning at Stephen to do likewise. 'There will be no Lady Abbess nonsense here, Rohesia Clamath. Bardolph the gravedigger?'

'Blunt as usual.' Rohesia grinned. 'Still, good to see you. I will never forget . . .'

'Please,' Anselm tapped her knee, 'leave the dead to bury their dead. The past is gone. Bardolph the gravedigger from Saint Michael's, Candlewick?'

'Bardolph was a frequent visitor, like so many of his parish.'

'Mistress?'

'Almaric the curate, Simon the sexton . . .' Rohesia was enjoying herself, using her long, delicate fingers to list more names, '. . . and Bardolph the gravedigger.' She smiled.

'Parson Smollat?'

'Never but, there again, Anselm, why should he? His woman Isolda once worked here and, by all accounts, was very popular.'

'Sir Miles Beauchamp?'

'Oh, our mysterious clerk who slinks like a shadow? No, he has never graced my house with his presence, but you never know.'

Anselm sat with his fingers to his lips.

'Don't be surprised,' Rohesia caressed his cheek softly, 'that so many of Saint Michael's parish come here. Welcome to the world of men, Brother Anselm, where fornication and swiving are as natural and common as eating and drinking. You all eventually come here,' she added, softly pausing at a laugh which echoed from deep in the house. 'I am breaking confidence, Anselm, because I trust you, I like you. I am in your debt. And,' she made a moue with her mouth, 'I have also heard about the commotion at Saint Michael's – the news, the gossip, the chatter which runs through these alleyways swifter than a colony of rats. Even more so now that Bardolph has flown from his church tower, poor man.' Rohesia bowed her head, fingers picking at a thread in her beautiful gown.

Stephen sat, fascinated. He had never met anyone like Rohesia – so serene, so confident. She talked about the world of men; what, Stephen reflected, would it be like to enter the world of women? This chamber, so delicately painted, elegantly furnished, its air sweet with the most alluring of fragrances.

Rohesia stared at Stephen, her face more gentle. 'Another

man of visions,' she murmured. 'Bardolph,' she turned back,
her tone brisker, 'often came here. He was infatuated with one
of my nuns.'

'Girls,' Anselm corrected. 'Edith Swan-neck?'

'Or so he called her,' Rohesia replied. 'Infatuated with her.
Bardolph could not do enough: presents, trinkets, ribbons,
gowns, even a furred hood.'

'And?'

'Now I will tell you, Anselm. Edith disappeared,' she drew
a deep breath, 'along with others.'

'What others?'

'Brother, I talked of the world of men where we women are
regarded as chattels no better than cattle. Young women, Anselm,
are disappearing here in Dowgate and beyond. I know,' her
voice grew forceful, 'girls disappear in London every day, but
that is not strictly true. They disappear but their corpses are
found, plucked from the reed beds along the Thames, or beneath
some filthy laystall or out in the heathland beyond Cripplegate.
This is different. Young women like Edith are disappearing
without trace, never to be found again.'

Stephen glanced to his right. He glimpsed something fluttering like a bird which swoops then disappears. This comfortable chamber had grown darker. Voices whispered then faded.
He shivered from the fear which coursed coldly around the nape
of his neck.

'Magister,' he murmured, 'remember the girl from The
Unicorn?'

'What girl?'

Stephen told Rohesia, trying to hide his blush. She smiled
sweetly.

'And the others,' Stephen added. 'Do you remember,
Magister? The same day we were returning to White Friars?
The market beadle, bawling out the description of two missing
whores? I mean,' Stephen hastily corrected himself, 'two young
women.'

'Whores, Stephen, you are correct.' Rohesia smiled bleakly.
'I and others have heard the same. Whores, prostitutes, yet still
God's children. Young women who have disappeared without
trace.'

'Edith Swan-neck was one of these?'

'Yes, Anselm, but with a difference. In Bardolph's search for Edith he scoured the streets and runnels. He bribed and cajoled. I helped him but to no effect. Then, by mere chance, Bardolph decided to search the cemetery of Saint Michael's and found a necklace he had given to Edith. He came here all glowering and solemn. He suspected Edith may have lain with someone else in the graveyard. I told him not to be so stupid.'

'Why?'

'Edith only went there to please Bardolph. In fact, the day she disappeared, she had gone out looking for him but never returned. The necklace was the only thing of hers ever found.'

'And Bardolph?'

'I heard rumours that he boasted how he would be rich. He would own great treasure.' She shrugged. 'Bardolph, our Knight of the Firey Nose, was an empty gong full of sound and fury with little substance. Now, sirs.' Rohesia made to rise.

'Rohesia! Rohesia! We are not finished yet. Sir William Higden – does he come here?'

'No,' she retorted. 'They say Sir William loves books and boys but that,' she pulled a face, 'is only rumour.'

'And Edith Swan-neck before she disappeared . . . did she say or do anything untoward?'

Rohesia chewed the corner of her lip. 'Yes, she seemed pleased about something. Well, as if laughing to herself.' She sniffed noisily. 'Brother Anselm, the hour is late – I can tell you no more.' This time Anselm let her rise. They made their farewells, went out into the hallway and back into Gutter Lane. They re-entered the tangle of alleyways, the melancholy waste-land around White Friars. 'Magister, what do you make of what Rohesia said?'

'She has a bold heart, a voice of power and a strong coun-tenance,' Anselm retorted. 'Do you know Rohesia has asked to be buried with a flagon of wine and a goblet to ready herself to drink the first toast in hell? Somehow I don't think she will be drinking there.' He gestured to Stephen to walk alongside him. 'We are all going to be very surprised about who is chosen for heaven. Anyway, Stephen, to answer your question, Rohesia has pointed us, perhaps not to the truth, but certainly to the way there. Well, now I am going to find my path to a different place.'

Anselm strode on, Stephen hurrying beside him. It was lamplight time, the hour of the Jacob thieves who, armed with ladders, climbed on to the roofs of houses and moved across the narrow gaps between them, searching for an open attic window. The brotherhood of the beggar were also marshalling together with all the other counterfeits, cheats and thieves pouring out of their shabby, underground cellars. Strange cries echoed. The gathering gloom was lit only by the occasional horn box containing a burning tallow candle suspended out of some window. The midnight thieves, however, ignored the Carmelites treading through the slops and dirt of the mean alleyways. This was the dead hour and these malefactors were more interested in fresh prey or spending the fruits of their earlier hunts in the low-ceilinged alehouses and wine shops. Anselm turned and went down a runnel which was more like a covered passageway, the houses on either side closing in over their heads. No candle or lamp gleamed but a light at the far end beckoned them on. Stephen shivered. He turned to his right and stifled a scream at a face peering through the narrow slats of a fence. A pallid, white-haired woman with black, glowing eyes was holding a lamp in both hands just beneath her chin. Stephen blinked and looked again, but the woman had gone.

They reached the end of the alleyway and entered a box-like square, its cobbled ground gleaming in the light of torches fixed to the walls. In the centre of the square stood the bowl, casing and roof of a huge well, illuminated by two roaring braziers. Along three sides of the square ranged black-and-white timbered houses, their windows filled with strengthened linen or clear horn. Lamplight glowed at some of these windows. On the far side of the square rose the dark silhouette of a church, more like a barn, built out of black stone with a ramp rather than steps leading up to the great iron-bound door. A hooded figure sat on a stool to the right of this porch, warming his fingers over a chafing dish. Above him *flambeaux* fixed in iron clasps licked the air with leaping flames.

'Magister, what is this?'

'Mandrake Place. The houses belong to the Fraternity of the Suspercol.'

'Who?'

'The Suspercol,' Anselm repeated, 'short for the Latin, *Suspenditur per collem* – hanged by the neck – and that, Stephen, is their Chapel of the Damned.'

As they crossed the square Stephen remarked how clean it was – no refuse or piled mounds of rubbish.

'That's because this place is sacred to the Brotherhood of the Twilight,' Anselm explained. 'Thieves, cozeners and counterfeits. The dung-carts come here at least four times a day and the guardians wash the cobbles with water from the well.'

They reached the foot of the ramp and walked up. The guard seated on the stool rose to greet them. Stephen was aware of others lurking deep in the shadows on either side of the church. The guard pushed back his cowl to reveal a white, gaunt, bony face like that of a skeleton, his long, scraggy neck scarred by a deep red ring like some ghastly necklace.

'Half-hanged Malkin, greetings!'

'Greetings to you and yours, Brother Anselm.' The man bowed and opened the door, ushering them into the church.

'Half-hanged?' Stephen whispered.

'At Tyburn Forks ten years ago,' Anselm murmured, 'he hung for an hour, and when they cut him down he revived. A miracle! He received the King's pardon and is one of the guardians here.' Stephen only half-listened, already startled by the church he had entered. A long nave stretched up to a vividly painted red rood screen where pride of place was given to the Good Thief. Eye-catching frescoes, crude but vigorous, decorated the walls, their scenes brought to life by the candle spigots placed along each aisle. The floor was of plain paving stones but in the centre were two broad trapdoors sealed with a clasp. Clearly seen through the rood screen stood the main altar, stark and unadorned beneath a silver pyx and glowing red sanctuary lamp. The Lady chapel to its left was equally sparse and bleak.

The atmosphere of that desolate chapel enveloped Stephen in a sombre embrace. It was a place of sadness and hidden fears. For a few heartbeats the rood screen seemed to disappear, replaced by a luxurious, sprouting oak tree from which many corpses hung in manacles. This faded. Stephen became aware of the charcoal crackling in pots and the pleasing wisps of heavy incense.

'The Chapel of the Damned,' Anselm explained. 'Off the beaten track, not visited by many. Certainly not on the eve of the feast of Saint Mark.'

'The same day Puddlicot broke into the crypt?'

'Precisely, Stephen and, according to the records, the eve of his grisly execution two years later. All this, Mandrake Place, the church, the houses and the Fraternity of the Suspercol, were once the property of an English leper knight of the Order of Saint Lazarus. He bequeathed it to serve as a place where the corpses of those hanged in London and elsewhere might be brought.' Anselm pointed to the trapdoor. 'Beneath that stretch are extensive burial pits of soil and lime. The corpses of many executed are brought here on the death-cart which they roll up that ramp into the church. They wrap each corpse in a sheet and lower it down for burial. I went down there once – a seemingly endless sea of bones and skulls.'

'And Puddlicot lies here?'

'Yes, Stephen, he does; his corpse no more than a tangle of bones.'

'Why have we come here tonight? To catch a sighting?'

'No, I do not think anything will happen here. We will, however, tarry at this, his last resting place. We shall assure his soul that we are its benefactor, not tormentor, as well as vow to arrange requiem Masses to be sung.' Anselm walked to the edge of the vault. He knelt and began to thread his rosary beads. As Stephen went to join him the main door opened and two women entered. The first was very old and grey-haired, with stooped shoulders, one hand grasping a walking cane, the other the arm of her companion. Both were dressed in the brown robes and white wimples of the Franciscan Minoresses who had their convent outside the old city wall near Aldgate. The two nuns stood watching them for a while before walking on up under the rood screen. Anselm hardly noticed them but continued reciting the Dirige psalms. Stephen crouched at the foot of a pillar. He tried to pray but his eyes grew heavy, aware of flashes of light around him and the dim murmur of voices. A commotion at the door roused him. He hurried back to find the guardian barring the way to a group of young, heavily-armed men. Former soldiers, Stephen concluded, judging by their close-cropped hair and hard, scarred faces. They were dressed in dark leather jerkins, tight hose pushed into their boots. Six in number, their leader had already drawn both sword and dagger.

'What is this?' Anselm came out on to the porch and stood on the top step.

'Brother Anselm.' The leader sheathed sword and dagger. 'The hour is late but Sir Miles Beauchamp . . .'

'What about him?'

'We are his henchmen. I am Cutwolf.'

'He mentioned your name to me once.'

'My companions, Oldtoast and Mutton-monger.' Cutwolf waved a hand.

'You have been following us?'

'Of course, Brother Anselm. Your safety is close to the heart of Sir Miles and what he wants . . .'

'What does he want?'

'Your presence at Bardolph's alehouse, The Burning Bush.' Cutwolf grinned. 'The widow, the now dead widow, was suddenly taken ill and died over an hour ago.' Cutwolf pointed to another of his companions. 'Holyinnocent here brought the news. Sir Miles awaits.'

The Burning Bush was guarded by more of Beauchamp's men as well as royal archers from the Tower. The taproom inside was cleared, and Adele's corpse lay stretched out next to her husband. A linen cloth draped the body. Sir William and Sir Miles, together with Almaric, Simon and Gascelyn, were present. One of Adele's servitors cowered in a shadowy corner. The Carmelites moved into the circle of light around the corpses, where a nervous, shabbily-dressed physician was drying his hands.

'What happened?' Anselm asked.

'We were making ready for the burial of old Bardolph,' the street physician declared. 'Adele brought a flask of wine, broached it and drank. Suddenly her head and neck were thrown back, and her throat and stomach swelled up. Her face turned as red as the crest of a cock. Her eyes, horrible to see, started out of her head, her tongue all swollen, turning a purplish-black.'

'Possessed by demons,' Almaric whispered.

'Nonsense!' Stephen exclaimed. Everyone stared at him.

'Nonsense?' Beauchamp queried.

'Poison,' Stephen replied, 'arsenic poisoning.'

'Tell us, learned physician,' Almaric taunted.

'My father was a physician. He made me accompany him on all his visits,' Stephen retorted. 'I have seen Adele's symptoms in at least three of my father's patients.'

'Mere prattling!' Sir William replied.

'Hush, now,' Anselm demanded.

'I have seen these symptoms.' Stephen felt his confidence rise. 'A very strong infusion of raw, red or white arsenic will cause such an effect. My father unmasked two poisoners. I watched them burn in the square before Winchester Cathederal.' Stephen glared around. 'My father always made me write up the symptoms he examined. Adele's death was sudden and violent – the infusion must have been very strong. Arsenic,' he continued heatedly, 'can be bought commonly enough. Some people – fools – use it either as a cure for stomach cramps or even as an aphrodisiac.'

'But why?' Sir William scoffed. 'Why her, and how did it happen?'

'Sirs.' The servitor shuffled out of the darkness carrying a small flask, its stopper pulled back. 'Sirs, this was delivered at the door. I saw the mistress bring it in. She drank from it, put it down and a short while later she was racked in agony.' Stephen took the flask; the stopper seal had been broken. The flask was almost empty but when he sniffed he detected something acrid mingling with the strong, fruity odour of claret. 'If you still don't believe me,' Stephen fought off a wave of tiredness, 'put this down for vermin to drink – they will not survive long.' Stephen grasped a pewter goblet from the top of a barrel, poured the remaining wine into it and shook the grainy sediment out into the glow of candlelight. 'There are your demons.'

Stephen pointed at the sediment. 'The wine is heavily tainted; strong enough to snatch the soul from her body many times over.'

'Somebody wanted Adele dead,' Anselm wondered out loud. 'But who, and why? Let's search this place.'

'Why?' Sir William declared.

'I'll tell you when we find it,' Anselm quipped.

They conducted their search in the squalid taproom, the dirt-encrusted scullery and buttery, the two chambers above and the dust-filled attic. The rooms were filthy and chaotic, reeking of staleness and neglect. They emptied broken caskets and coffers, moved the straw-filled mattresses and black-stained bolsters but found only tawdry items. They all gathered, yawning and stretching, in the taproom, where someone had thrown the sheet back over Adele's corpse.

'Magister,' Stephen whispered, 'the hour is very late. I am exhausted.'

'Gentlemen,' Sir William Higden stood next to both corpses, 'surely we have finished here? I will take care of the cadavers. The hour of compline is long gone. These matters must wait for the morrow.'

Beauchamp and Anselm agreed. The royal clerk led the two Carmelites out of the shabby alehouse. Cutwolf and the others were waiting outside, torches held high. 'Come,' Sir Miles smiled through the dark, 'we will see you safely to White Friars.'

They moved off deep into the dark, the glow of torch on naked steel keeping the busy shadows at bay. The clink and clatter of weapons, the tramp of booted, spurred feet, stilled all other noise. Beauchamp walked in silence then came between Stephen and Anselm. 'You do realize what was wrong with our search?' he asked.

'We didn't find anything,' Anselm murmured. 'We should have done. More curious still, Bardolph and Adele were parishioners yet never once in that shabby, mean house did I find a crucifix, a statue, a set of Ave beads or any other religious artefacts.' Anselm pulled his cowl up against the night breeze. 'In fact, I suspect that someone went through that house before us and removed certain items.'

'What?' Beauchamp asked.

'Oh, anything associated with magic and the black rites,' Anselm replied. 'I suspect Adele, perhaps even Bardolph, were members of a coven.'

'The Midnight Man's?'

'Very possible,' Anselm replied.

Stephen quickly crossed himself against a thought. Was it sinful, malevolent or the truth? Was the Midnight Man someone very close to them?

ooOOoo

Words Amongst the Pilgrims

The physician rose and walked to the canopied hearth where he warmed his hands, rubbing them slowly, staring into the jagged flames. His fellow pilgrims sat in silence for a while before busying themselves. A few hastened out to the latrines and closet chambers. Minehost of The Tabard asked for some platters of dried meat, bread and fruit 'to ward off' as he put it, 'the demons growling in their stomachs'. The food was served, the jugs refilled.

Chaucer watched the physician, who had turned slightly and was now peering over his shoulder. Chaucer followed his gaze. The physician was staring at the Wife of Bath, now recovered from her former state of quiet surprise. She raised her goblet in response to the physician's stare. Chaucer rose and walked over to the far wall as if interested in the painted cloth, describing in rough brushwork the great epic of Roland and Oliver. He waited. The physician left, walking into the garden, the Wife of Bath soon after. Chaucer, allowing curiosity to reign over courtesy, quietly followed. The buttery yard was empty. Chaucer walked across to the lattice screen over which wild roses sprouted from a thick green bush. Soft-footed as a cat, he stopped short of the flower bed: in the faint light he could see the brittle twigs which would snap under his boots.

The physician and the Wife of Bath were sitting on a turf seat on the other side of the rose-covered fence. Straining his ears, Chaucer heard snatches of their hushed conversation. 'Do souls still hover?' The Wife of Bath's question trailed clearer than the whispered reply of the physician. 'Sometimes,' Chaucer heard, 'they sweep in,' but the rest was hidden by the screech of a night bird deep in the garden. Chaucer heard the phrases 'grisly murder' and 'that hideous burning'. A sound made him turn. The summoner stood in the doorway to the tavern. Chaucer walked over. In the pool of light the summoner's face appeared leaner, more purposeful than the usual vacuous, slobbery-lipped look, nose red as a rose, skin scabby as a leper's.

'Good evening, Master Chaucer. What do you think of our physician's tale? Truth? Fable?'

'Do you know, master summoner? I suspect some of the characters of this miracle play do live and breathe and are not so far from us.'

'Really?'

'Summoner, what is your name? Do not reply, we are legion because we are so many. I suspect your demons thrive at the bottom of a deep-bowled wine goblet.'

'True, true,' the summoner glanced over Chaucer's shoulder, 'but now our physician returns.'

'Your name, friend?'

'Why, Master Chaucer, I am Bardolph, come again,' and, laughing softly to himself, the summoner went back into the taproom.

'Master Chaucer?' The physician, the Wife of Bath trailing behind him, strode through the darkness. 'Master Chaucer,' he repeated, 'you are curious whether this is fable or fact?' He grabbed Chaucer by the elbow. 'Believe me,' he whispered hoarsely, 'the dead do speak to the living, as my tale will prove.'

ooOOoo

The Physician's Tale

Part Four

'Questions.' Anselm tapped the table in Sir William Higden's chancery chamber. 'We will deal with this as we would a problem in the halls of Oxford. Put forward certain questions to be addressed. Sir William, Curate Almaric is taking notes for you. Stephen will do the same for myself and Sir Miles. Gentlemen,' Anselm pointed to Simon the sexton and Gascelyn, 'you may listen and,' he shrugged, 'and add anything we may have overlooked.'

'Is this really necessary?' Sir William looked peevish after what appeared to be a poor night's sleep. The powerful merchant knight's face was shaven and gleaming with oil, but the dark rings under his eyes betrayed the fact that he had drunk too deeply of the claret he apparently loved. While Anselm made soothing noises, Stephen glanced around the luxurious chamber. He was particularly fascinated by the brilliantly hued tapestries of blue, red, green, silver and gold depicting the legends of King Arthur, be it the Knights of the Round Table or Galahad's pursuit of the Holy Grail. Stephen recalled how his own father had taken him to the great Abbey of Glastonbury where Arthur and Guinevere were supposed to lie buried, their tomb being discovered during the reign of the present King's grandfather. Were those happy days? Stephen wondered. The past seemed so distant, so strange, as if he was recalling someone else's life. His time with Anselm had so changed him . . .

'We should begin,' Beauchamp insisted. The royal clerk, elegant as ever in a dark green cotehardie over a white cambric shirt and black hose, pointed to the green-ringed hour candle in the centre of the table. 'Soon the Angelus will ring.'

'I was only wondering,' Sir William protested, 'why a second exorcism cannot take place? I mean . . .' He wandered off into a litany of speculation. Stephen picked up a quill pen and sharpened it. He felt refreshed and eager for the day. Anselm and he had risen early, celebrated a dawn Mass then broken their fast. Afterwards Anselm, without explanation, had instructed Stephen to pack his panniers with a change of clothes and all he might need for a long stay away from White Friars. The exorcist had refused to elaborate but had promised the novice he would like the surprise.

'Questions.' Anselm's voice cracked like a whip, making everyone sit up and concentrate. 'First question: Saint Michael's Church is undoubtedly haunted as well as plagued by malevolent spirits, yes? Second question.' Stephen was now busy writing, using the cipher Anselm had taught him, very similar to that employed in the royal chancery. 'Second question,' Anselm repeated. 'Who are they and why are they acting like this?'

'Puddlicot?' Beauchamp broke in.

'Third question.' Anselm nodded at the royal clerk in a moment of realization. 'Why is Saint Michael's haunted by the ghost of Richard Puddlicot? True, this was his parish church. He took sanctuary here but, despite this, was dragged out. He now protests at the outrage while he also haunts the crypt of Westminster Abbey. The poor soul is lost in his own tormented past. Fourth question,' Anselm tapped the table, 'we now tread on firmer ground. At the last All Souls the Midnight Man and his coven celebrated their black rites here at Saint Michael's. Perhaps they did the same at Westminster? At first we considered the choice of Saint Michael's to be random – now we are not so sure. This brings us to our fifth question: was the purpose of the Midnight Man's satanic celebration to search for Puddlicot's buried treasure? If so, how did they know about it? Sixth question: did they find some of the treasure? Undoubtedly so! The Cross of Neath and Queen Eleanor's dagger but how, where and when? Question seven.' Anselm paused to take a sip of water. 'Was Rishanger a member of the Midnight Man's coven? How did he seize such treasure? Who killed him and his Mistress Beatrice? Question eight, Bardolph's death: was he driven to the top of that tower – was he possessed, forced to commit suicide? Question nine: Adele, Bardolph's wife, a member of this parish – yes, Parson Smollat?'

The priest, pale-faced with anxiety, nodded in agreement.

'Why was she murdered in her shabby alehouse which possesses not one religious artefact? Oh, by the way, Parson Smollat, did you bring your book of the dead as I asked?'

The parson lifted a sack from where he had placed it, close to his feet, and drew out the leather-bound ledger. 'What do you want with it?' Smollat's voice quavered.

'In a while,' Anselm replied. 'Sir Miles, your men are ready?'

'Of course!'

'What is this, Anselm?' Sir William asserted himself. 'You ask questions but surely you are here to provide the answer to why Saint Michael's is haunted.'

'As yet I cannot do that properly. I do not know what lies at the root of all this. I have one more question, or perhaps two. So, question ten: Bardolph the gravedigger. He desperately searched for his lady love, Edith Swan-neck. He found a necklace he had given her lying in Saint Michael's cemetery. What happened to Edith, and what are these rumours about other young women disappearing?'

The chamber fell silent. Stephen stopped writing. Abruptly he raised his head. He was sure, certain, that he heard faint chanting.

'So what do you suggest, exorcist?' Sir Miles sat, hands clasped, half-concealing his face. 'I must also give answers to those in authority.'

Anselm snapped his fingers at Parson Smollat. 'My friend, I want you to give us the names of the last four people buried before the thirty-first of October last year and, when we are ready, take us into the cemetery where, I hope, with the help of your men, Sir Miles, to open their graves.'

'Why?' Smollat stuttered, 'For God's sake, that is sacrilege!'

'Not if we are searching for the truth.'

'Anselm!' Sir William's face tensed with anger. 'Why this, why now?'

'Because, Sir William, I am trying to answer my own questions. Listen now.'

'I beg your pardon,' Almaric interrupted, 'you said you might have two other questions. Do you have a second?'

'Yes, you did,' Gascelyn confirmed.

'Oh, that,' Anselm smiled icily, 'is linked to my final propo-sition. Bardolph, unlike us, God forgive him, discovered some-thing. I am sure it was to his great profit but, more than that, I cannot say.'

'So what now?' Sir Miles asked. 'Anselm, don't you have any firm conclusions?'

'Oh, I have propositions, hypotheses. Let me explain. I believe the Midnight Man, whoever he is, discovered the secret of Puddlicot's treasure. How and when I don't know.' Anselm breathed in. 'I believe he and his coven discovered two items from that lost hoard. How, when and why? Again, I do not know. I believe Rishanger was a member of his coven. He stole those items and tried to flee – he and his mistress were both killed. Rishanger fled because he realized that the Midnight Man had not only failed to establish the whereabouts of the rest of the treasure through the practice of the black arts but had summoned up much more malignant forces. In doing so, the Midnight Man had attracted the attention of both Court and Church. I also suggest that perhaps Bardolph – certainly his wife, Adele – was part of the Midnight Man's coven.' Anselm shook his head at the cries of protest from Parson Smollat and Almaric.

'I confess, I am not too sure about Bardolph but I would suggest Adele definitely was. She was silenced because of what Bardolph may have discovered or may have told her.'

'Which is what?' Parson Smollat queried.

'In truth, I don't know, parson. Do you? Didn't Bardolph go to you to be shrived? Did he confess? Can you tell us anything outside the seal of confession?'

'Nothing.' Parson Smollat sighed, licking his lips. 'Bardolph talked of his love for Edith Swan-neck. He asked if I knew of any other young maidens who had disappeared.' Smollat's voice faltered. Stephen stared at him. He had met the parson a number of times over the past few days and the priest was certainly changing, becoming more nervous and agitated. A troubled spirit, Stephen concluded, but was he wicked, malicious? Parson Smollat certainly seemed to be losing his confidence by the day, his anxiety clearly expressed in his unshaven face, unkempt robes and dirty fingernails, which constantly scrabbled over the table top.

'What do you want?' Smollat bleated. 'Brother, what do we do now?'

'Sir Miles.' Anselm gestured at the royal clerk. 'I want your men to open the graves of the last four people buried in Saint Michael's Cemetery before the Feast of All Souls last.' Anselm rose to his feet. 'Parson Smollat, Sir William, I suggest you supervise this. Sir Miles, once your henchmen have reached the coffins or shroud cloths of the dead, they are to seek us out at The Unicorn in Eel-Pie Lane or elsewhere.'

Stephen hid his confusion and surprise as Anselm prepared to leave. Sir Miles summoned Cutwolf and the others into the chamber, giving them strict orders on what to do. Parson Smollat was now feverishly consulting the book of the dead, Simon the sexton peering over his shoulder, watched by a very taciturn Sir William. Gascelyn and Almaric had already adjourned to one of the spacious window embrasures, quietly discussing what the exorcist had suggested.

Once they had made their farewells and walked out into the street, Anselm and Beauchamp strode ahead, deep in conversation, with Stephen hurrying behind. The lane was busy, thronged with crowds, so Stephen was pleased to be by himself. He could also reflect on why they were going to The Unicorn and desperately hoped to catch a glimpse of the fair Alice. He only exchanged a few pleasantries with one of Beauchamp's henchmen, Holyinnocent, who had been chosen to escort them to the tavern. The day was certainly busy. The constant chatter, tramping of feet and crashing wheels of the high-sided carts were a constant din. Hucksters, peddlers, apprentice boys and tinkers screamed and shouted for business, desperate to catch the eye or grasp a cloak to sell some trinket, pot, pan, knife or piece of cloth. Strange sights appeared and merged into the moving crowd. A babbling half-wit rolled a barrel into the street then upended it to stand on; once ready he proclaimed to the puffed up, ribbon-bedecked gallants who gathered around to poke fun at him that he was the Prophet Jonah come again. Beadles and market marshals strode pompously with their wands, ready to wrap the back and legs of those trading without licence. Funeral processions merged with guild solemnities in a bobbing confusion of lighted candles, swinging thurifers as well as different chants and prayers. Anselm and Beauchamp strode on through this noisy bustle. Now and again Holyinnocent would recognize a friend and exchange good-natured banter. Occasionally they had to stand aside for malefactors, all dirty and bedraggled, being marched down to the pillories, stocks and thews. A bawd and her pimp followed tied to the tail of a cart while a fat, sweaty-faced beadle lashed their naked backs and bottoms with a rod, splashing himself and passers-by with specks of blood.

Stephen was aware of the world closing in around him, a stark contrast to the simplicity and serenity of the cloister. Cartwheels squeaked, bawds shrieked, porters grumbled. 'The Children of this World', as Anselm called them, swarmed either side in filthy rags or sumptuously embroidered silver brocaded clothes, shuffling and shouldering each other, jostling and jeering, haggling and hustling. They reached The Unicorn, a pleasant-fronted tavern standing in its own courtyard, which stretched up to the main door. Stables and outhouses flanked two sides. The tavern itself was a lofty, three-storey mansion of black timbers and pink plaster on a stone base. Stephen was surprised they did not enter. Instead, Holyinnocent was told to take the baggage in and rejoin them. As soon as he did, Anselm winked at Stephen and declared they had other places to visit. 'Minehost has your baggage,' Holyinnocent whispered to Stephen as he rejoined them. 'And we are off to Newgate.'

They took the broad alleyway leading up to the formidable prison built into the ruins of the old city wall. A grim, slimy-walled lane with every second house a tavern under its creaking, battered sign. The Sanctuary of Dead Man's Place: this was the haunt of thieves who stared out through chinks and gaps in doors and shutters. They recognized Beauchamp's insignia and let them pass through. A hunting horn wailed a warning while a hoarse whisper, 'King's Man', ran before them up the long, dark tunnel. The message kept the bullies with their swords and staves, as well as their harridans armed with spits and broomsticks, from sallying forth. They left the alleyway and entered the great, fleshing market, which flourished in the shadow of the huge sombre towers of Newgate, a place swimming in blood. The carcasses of poultry and livestock were being swiftly slaughtered, hacked and then hung from hooks above the stalls. A shambles of blood, stinking guts, entrails and boiling salt. Red-spattered butchers and their boys roared for business while beggars, dogs, cats and kites fought for the juicy scraps.

Beauchamp, escorted by Holyinnocent, elbowed and thrust his way forward. They gained entrance through a narrow iron door into the prison proper, a true vision of hell: a warren of evil-smelling passageways where the reek and stench poisoned the nostrils and stifled the throat. They passed open chambers where key-clanking janitors guarded what they scornfully called 'human vermin' – prisoners with long filthy beards and straggling wild hair, all swathed in dirty rags. The keeper who led them into the stygian darkness screamed at everyone to step aside, only to be answered by raucous shouts and curses. They went down some steps lit by flaring torches. The smell grew more rank and unbearable. The walls glistened with snail slime. Spiders big as bumble bees spun their webs to span niches and corners. They reached a circular cavern called Limbo. In the centre rose a huge stone called Black Dog with a squat tallow candle burning on top. Holyinnocent pointed to the heavy doors which faced them, whispering how these were the condemned cells. While the keeper unlocked one of the cell doors, Holyinnocent explained how many a condemned felon had dashed his brains out against Black Dog rather than take the ride in the death-cart.

Stephen, holding a sponge soaked in vinegar against his nose, went and sat on one of the battered benches. This was a truly evil place. The atmosphere oppressed him. Cries, despairing and pleading, pestered his ears. A feathery shadow crept across the floor, spilling over him, creating a wave of deep fear and panic. A haggard face came shooting out of the murk, its bone-white features twisted in an angry snarl, bloodshot eyes full of some nameless fury.

'Stephen, Stephen?'

The novice shook his head. Anselm stood, beckoning him. The cell door was now flung back. The turnkey had dragged out a shambling figure loaded with iron fetters, barefooted and dressed in the long black gown of the condemned. He was virtually unrecognizable, his head and face being hidden by a mass of tangled hair, moustache and beard. The turnkey pushed the prisoner down a passageway. Beauchamp told Holyinnocent to stay while he and the two Carmelites followed the turnkey along the slime-covered passageway, up a short flight of steps into a surprisingly clean, neat chamber. The walls were painted a brilliant white and a crucifix hung beneath the barred windows high in the wall. There was a sturdy table with benches on all four sides. The turnkey lit the fat tallow candle in the centre of the table and left. Beauchamp made sure the entrance was free of eavesdropping, slammed the door shut and, going across, pushed the prisoner down on a stool.

'This is the chaplain's room,' Anselm explained. 'I insisted it be fashioned like this. I used to come here to shrive the condemned. Are you condemned?' Anselm sat down close to the prisoner. All Stephen could glimpse were the man's bright, smiling eyes.

'This is another kind of shriving,' Beauchamp murmured. 'Everything will be in a whisper. Brothers, may I introduce Roger Bolingbrok, former Dominican friar, also known as William Chattle, Peter Waltham and so on and so on. One of my most redoubtable spies or Judas men. Isn't that right, Roger?'

The prisoner smiled in a flash of white teeth, lifting his manacled hands to clear the hair from his face.

'I cannot show you any mercy.' Beauchamp's voice was barely above a whisper. 'At least not now.'

'Will he hang?' Stephen asked.

The prisoner grinned and winked at the novice.

'Oh, no,' Beauchamp replied. 'Tomorrow a writ will arrive which confirms Master Bolingbrok's claim to be a cleric. He will be handed over to the Church, tried before an ecclesiastical tribunal at Lambeth and exiled to some monastery in the wilds of Northumberland. He will be shaved, bathed and given fresh clothes for the journey. He will travel no further north than Saint Albans, where Master Bolingbrok will escape to reappear in London under another guise. Now,' Beauchamp became brisk. 'Brother Anselm, Brother Stephen, I have made reference to the Midnight Man's exploits in the cemetery of Saint Michael's. How his black Mass and dark rites went so wrong he had to flee.'

'Were you there?' Anselm asked the prisoner.

'No, but Rishanger was.'

'How do you know?'

'As I told Sir Miles when I was first taken up,' Bolingbrok explained, voice all cultured, 'I was condemned and thrown into the common hold before being moved,' Bolingbrok grinned, 'to a more comfortable chamber. People regard a condemned man as already dead so they chatter as if you are. The villains of Newgate know all about Rishanger. He was a thief, a receiver of stolen property. He also had a nasty reputation as a warlock. He tried to buy safe passage abroad without a licence. He told a Gascon sailor what had happened at Saint Michael's – how he had been a spectator of something which had gone horribly wrong.'

'What?'

'He didn't say, except that a notorious warlock had tried to raise the spirit of a dead man but instead summoned up all the powers of hell.'

'Why should Rishanger tell that to a Gascon sailor?' Stephen queried.

'Oh, that is easy enough, isn't it, Sir Miles?' Anselm replied. 'To leave England without proper licence, especially for a goldsmith, is very dangerous and just as much for the captain of any ship.'

'Rishanger daren't lie.' Bolingbrok moved in a clatter of chains, his rags exuding an odious smell. 'He couldn't point to some petty misdemeanour to explain his flight so he told the truth, as far as he could. Not that he was a member of a coven – merely an observer.'

'Which is why,' Anselm broke in, 'when Rishanger was attacked at Queenhithe, the captain of the cog refused to help any further.'

'True,' Bolingbrok agreed. 'Safe, quiet, illegal passage is one thing, sword and dagger play on one of London's wharfs is another. Rishanger paid heavily for that passage in more ways than one.'

'And since then,' Beauchamp asked, 'what else have you discovered mingling amongst the dead men?'

'The assassins who attacked Rishanger, who may have killed his mistress, though Rishanger himself could have done that, must be members of the Midnight Man's coven. No one knows anything.' Bolingbrok licked dry, cracked lips. 'You will be out of here soon enough,' Beauchamp soothed, 'eating and drinking merrily.'

'Rishanger,' Bolingbrok explained, 'was attacked at Queenhithe. He fled along the river to be murdered in the King's own abbey. Rumours abound of a great treasure being found with him. Such news runs like flame amongst the stubble. Usually people know those responsible for such an attack but, on this occasion, nothing! No one, and I mean no one, knows anything about what happened in the abbey.' The prisoner shook his chains. Stephen became aware of the appalling cries from above.

'The crying, screeching, swearing, roaring, bawling and shaking of chains,' Bolingbrok whispered to him, 'are the plain chant of Newgate, but they hide the true business of London's Hades, the real chatter. Who does what to whom, where, when, how and why? But not on this business.' He pushed back his matted hair.

'Sir Miles, I assure you, I am done here.'

'Tell me,' Stephen spoke up, 'is there chatter amongst all this chaffing, swearing and shaking of chains about young women disappearing?'

Bolingbrok looked at Beauchamp, who nodded. 'Why is a young Carmelite interested in that?'

'Because I am,' Anselm retorted. 'Is there?'

'There is,' Bolingbrok whispered. 'Some of the pimps are full of it. Young women disappear, but they also reappear in one form or another. This doesn't happen here. Whispers crackle. They say a blood-drinker is on the loose.'

'Blood-drinker?' Stephen asked.

'Brother Anselm, Sir Miles.' Bolingbrok rubbed his brow on the back of his hand. 'You, like me, have served in the King's armies in France. You, Sir Miles, also read the reports of sheriffs and justices from every shire. You know who the blood-drinkers are.'

'Blood-drinkers,' Beauchamp's face was sombre, 'are usually men who have served in the array – lunatics, dangerous ones. They like to take a woman and kill her. Oh, yes, Stephen, for them that is the only way their seed can burst out. They lie with a woman whom they terrify; this excites them, even more so because they know this woman is going to die. Abroad in enemy towns and villages, these men hide behind the mask of a soldier. They can do what they wish. They return home but they cannot stop hunting. They regard women as quarry as hunters would a deer.'

'Any names?' Anselm asked.

'No one knows,' Bolingbrok replied, 'but they say there may be more than one.'

'And the Midnight Man?'

'Why, Brother Anselm? Rumour abounds – they say he could be a priest.' Bolingbrok grinned. 'Even a Carmelite.' Bolingbrok's smile faded. 'Or someone powerful.' Bolingbrok sounded not so confident. 'Someone who likes whores but not in the way I do. This blood-drinker likes hunting and killing them. Sir Miles, I can tell you no more.'

'We should go.' Anselm rose and sketched a blessing over the prisoner. He walked to the door and turned. 'You were once a friar, Bolingbrok?'

'Will you always be one, Brother?' the prisoner retorted. Anselm smiled, shrugged and opened the door. Once free of the prison, Beauchamp and Anselm stood in one of the shadowy recesses of the gatehouse, heads together, murmuring. 'Stephen,' Anselm called out, 'we will visit Rishanger's house.'

'Cutwolf!' Sir Miles stepped from the enclave and whispered into the ear of his henchman. Cutwolf nodded, winked at Stephen and sauntered off. Stephen wished he could question his master but Anselm seemed in a hurry. They crossed the blood-soaked cobbles of the Shambles. The exorcist grasped Stephen's shoulder and whispered how time was passing, the graves at St Michael's were about to be opened and they had to be there when it happened. Anselm moved on to walk with Beauchamp. Stephen felt a deep, cloying fear, an agitation of the heart. He stared around, not interested in the slaughter stalls, the hacked flesh or the bizarre characters who thronged the noisy crowds.

The reek from the tanner sheds and tallow shops faded, as did the strident noise. Stephen felt as if something was going to happen; he had experienced this before. His father called it a form of the falling sickness, a deep foreboding which seizes all the senses.

As soon as they reached the entrance to Hagbut Lane the warnings swept in. Rishanger's house, narrow and tall, stood forlornly on the corner of an alleyway. The place reeked of evil. Beauchamp tore at the seals along the rim of the door and kicked it open, leading both the Carmelites into a long, ill-lit passageway. Stephen entered cautiously. This was no longer a house but a gloomy valley. On one side savage fires roared while on the other a storm of white hail and sleet pelted down. At the far end a pit glared with hell's dark fires. A figure was walking towards Stephen. It reminded the novice of a painting he had glimpsed of the hideous, legendary Medea, who stalked lonely crossroads leading a legion of suicides, their very passing making the fiercest dog howl and shiver.

'Stephen, Stephen!' He opened his eyes. There was no valley, only that stinking, dark passageway. Anselm was peering at him. Beauchamp stood further along, cloaked in darkness.

They entered what must have been Rishanger's chancery chamber; the room was stripped of everything. Beauchamp, protesting at the dank air and gloom, unlocked and threw back the shutters. Columns of light pierced the oiled linen panes. Stephen started as a mouse, jet black, shot across the floor. Anselm, also alerted to the gathering evil, had drawn his Ave beads and wrapped these around his fingers. They moved from chamber to chamber. Stephen was sure that Beauchamp, although blind and deaf to the visions he and Anselm were experiencing, was still sensitive to the oppressive evil which followed them around this soulless house. The longer they stayed, the closer the sheer wickedness perpetrated here wrapped itself around them, a heavy pall of unnamed terrors. A quickening of the breath. A lurching of the heart. A pitching of the stomach as their skin crawled. There was nothing tangible to explain this. The King's surveyors had stripped the house. The place was relatively clean, yet a cold darkness hung like an arras around them, so much so that Stephen wildly wondered if he would ever be allowed to leave.

'Magister, what are we searching for?'

'Anything.' Beauchamp drew his sword and drove its point into the plastered wall of the clean, swept buttery they had entered. 'A secret compartment, a hidden casket.' The clerk walked over to the staircase built into the corner of the entrance hall. They climbed the steps. Stephen blinked at the flashes of light, the leaping sparks which swam before him. Small bursts of red fire, each containing a face which came and swiftly went. Voices cried, including that of a child. Screams and yells echoed. A voice, low and sombre, quoted that dreadful verse from the Apocalypse: 'I saw a pale rider and his name was Death and all hell followed in his wake.' Another voice answered, 'Hell-born souls drift like columns of blackness. This is the night of the weighing of souls. Doom-laden they are, born of hell, fit for hell. Eternal punishment will be theirs.'

'Ignore them, Stephen,' Anselm hissed. 'Dismiss them as shadow dreams, nothing more.'

'Chilling!' Beauchamp declared as he led the way into the upper gallery. 'Even I can feel it.' He grinned at the two Carmelites. 'I never did last time I was here. You must attract the spirits.'

'Our enemies,' Anselm retorted.

They entered the bedchamber: the outer wall was wet, the liquid gleaming like some evil sweat. The broad, linen-filled window provided some light but the shadow of brooding evil hung even heavier here. The sense of doom thickened. Voices echoed through Stephen's mind. '*Miserere, miserere* – have mercy, have mercy.'

'Oh, be quiet!' a voice growled.

Stephen started as a door downstairs opened and banged shut. Heavy footsteps on the stairs sent Beauchamp hurrying from the room sword out, his left hand clawing for the dagger in its scabbard on the back of his belt. Shapes, faint wisps of mist, trailed across the room. A harsh, barking cough made Stephen whirl around but there was nothing. Cold fingers caressed the side of his face. Anselm was shivering, moving away, flicking his hand to drive off whatever confronted him.

'Priest!' The coughing bark was like that of a dog. 'You shit-ridden priest! How dare you come here?'

'In Christ's name,' Anselm bellowed back. 'Begone, begone . . . !'

'Oh, don't be a killjoy!' The voice changed to that of a wheedling, pampered child. Anselm held up his Ave beads to bless the air. The door to the bedchamber opened and shut with a crash. Silence descended.

Beauchamp kicked the door open and walked in, mouthing curses. 'Don't,' Anselm warned. 'No curse, no foul language. Evil feeds on evil, like a dog on its vomit.' Again he blessed the air, breathing out noisily, dramatically, as if using his own life force to drive away the malignancy. The tension disappeared; the chamber just looked forlorn, gaunt and empty.

'This,' Anselm declared, 'was certainly the abode of a malevolent, stagnant soul, immersed deeply in wickedness against the innocent. Yet the source is not here, Beauchamp. We must find it.'

'The royal surveyors,' Beauchamp replied, 'were most thorough.'

'Not thorough enough!' Anselm led them out, clattering down the stairs and along the hollow stone passageway. Anselm opened the door and went out into the overgrown garden, nothing more than rambling bramble and briar, grass and sprouting weeds which had burst out of the soil, covering the herb borders, paths, small carp pond and bird house. The garden was enclosed by a high wall on all three sides with no wicket gate or garden door. The small orchard at the far end, a deep cluster of greenery, was completely unpruned and untended. Stephen followed Anselm. Beauchamp, rather reluctantly, hung back.

'There is nothing here,' the royal clerk called out. Anselm ignored him. He found a rusty scythe under a clump of bramble and began to hack away. Stephen stood on the rim of the broken fountain. Anselm was searching for something. Stephen stared around. The garden was overgrown but the paving stones just beneath him were covered in branches and other decaying refuse which had been cut. He climbed down and kicked away this thick, matted cluster to reveal a paving stone with an iron ring carefully inserted into a niche.

'Magister!' Anselm and Beauchamp hurried over. They lifted

the stone, which came up as easily as an oiled trapdoor. They slid it to one side and stared at the neatly cut steps leading down into the darkness. Stephen went first. He put his hand out and felt the walls. Finding a fully primed-sconced torch, he used Anselm's tinder to light this. He continued down, lighting some more, Anselm and Beauchamp close on his heels. The chamber at the bottom of the steps was circular. Oil lamps and lantern horns stood in carefully carved wall niches. Stephen lit these. He fought back the horrors clinging with icy fingers to his back. The hair on the nape of his neck curled; his stomach twisted. He found it difficult to breathe. He turned, resting his back against the wall. Anselm and Beauchamp, torches lifted high, were inspecting the chamber, especially the grille in the ceiling, cleverly constructed and concealed by the undergrowth above, yet sufficient enough to allow in some light and air.

Stephen sensed the change in the air around him. He braced himself against what was to come. Two shapes raced out of the murk – square-faced gnomes garbed in leather jackets and blood-spattered butcher aprons. Stephen closed his eyes and turned away. When he looked again there was nothing. Anselm and Beauchamp crouched in the centre of the chamber, examining a canvas mattress above which hung a chain fixed to the ceiling. Beside the mattress lay a great black iron dish containing tongs, pincers and fleshing hooks with points as sharp as dragon's teeth. Stephen crossed to join them. The mattress was soaked in blood. A deep dread seized Stephen, chilling him to the very marrow. Anselm was right: horrid murder had been committed here.

'Who?' Beauchamp spoke for them all. 'Why?'

'Some devilish practice,' Anselm replied, rubbing his arms. 'It's cold,' he breathed. 'This place reeks of evil. We should not stay here long.'

Stephen heard a sound and turned. Shapes, swift and darting, furry shadows like those of a nimble monkey or scurrying squirrel, crossed the wall just below the ceiling.

'Let us leave here!' Stephen hissed. He hurried up the steps, gulping the fresh air, turning his face to the sun. Anselm and Beauchamp followed. The exorcist sat on the rim of the broken fountain. 'You say this was once Puddlicot's house?' Anselm asked.

'Yes, our crypt robber set up household here with his leman Joanne Picard.' Beauchamp, rubbing his hands, sat down next to the Carmelite, his face pale and drawn.

'This is what I think,' Anselm declared. He gestured round the garden. 'The corpse of Rishanger's mistress was found here?'

'In the orchard,' Beauchamp agreed.

'I suspect Rishanger purchased this house,' Anselm continued, 'so that he could discover whether or not Puddlicot buried his treasure here.'

'And did he?'

'No, I don't think so, though I do wonder about those two items. Anyway, Puddlicot's treasure is only a part of this bloody tapestry of murder and abomination. Rishanger was a blood-drinker. A man who liked to entice young women, imprison them in that hideous cavern and subject them to all forms of abuse for his own pleasure. He sated his lusts; such bloody acts loosened his seed.'

Beauchamp, alerted by shouting from beyond the walls, got to his feet. 'One of my henchmen,' he murmured as he unsheathed his sword.

'I haven't yet finished,' Anselm remarked as he rose. 'Forget the overgrown herbers, vegetable garden, flower plots – all of this is a disguise. Trust me, Beauchamp. So, alert the ward. Raise the hue and cry. Shout, "Harrow harrow!" Have this entire garden dug up. You will find a carefully concealed burial pit containing the pathetic remains of young women – Rishanger's victims.'

'Did he practice his black rites here?'

'No,' Anselm replied, 'they need consecrated ground for that. This house stands alone, the garden protected by a very high wall. Inquisitive neighbours can't peer in. It's the perfect place to entice a young street-walker to be taken down to that ungodly crypt to become Rishanger's plaything.'

'But Edith Swan-neck's necklace was found in Saint Michael's cemetery. Do you think her corpse is buried here?' Stephen asked.

'I do not know, Stephen. I cannot answer that.' The exorcist paused as Holyinnocent came into the garden, shouting that the graves at St Michael's had been opened and now awaited their inspection.

By the time they reached St Michael's a crowd had gathered outside the lychgate. The ward was now alerted. The throng of angry people were resentful at what was happening, openly grumbling at this disturbance of the dead following so soon after the macabre death of Bardolph the gravedigger. The afternoon was greying over, the clouds gathering low and threatening. The sunlight had faded, heightening the feeling of sombre menace which Stephen always experienced when entering the cemetery. Cutwolf and his men, who had drunk deeply at a nearby tavern to fortify themselves, had exchanged harsh words with the angry parishioners. The henchmen now sprawled with their backs against tombstones and crosses but scrambled to their feet as Sir William Higden, followed by Almaric, Gascelyn and Parson Smollat, strode out of the church to greet the royal clerk and the two Carmelites.

'I hope this is necessary,' Sir William snapped. 'The graves are open.'

'I now doubt if we will find anything here,' Anselm crossed himself, 'just as we didn't discover anything at Rishanger's house. Sir William, you are a royal justice in this ward, yes?'

Sir William, his face now concerned, nodded.

Anselm gestured at Beauchamp, who described in sharp, curt sentences what they had found and what they intended to do. 'Cutwolf!' The royal clerk waved at Sir William to hold his questions. 'Cutwolf, go to Rishanger's house, take your men and impress every layabout between here and that dead demon's abode. You have my authority and that of the local justice. Dig up the entire garden until you find what is undoubtedly buried there. Now, Parson Smollat, the first grave?'

They moved across to the deep pit Cutwolf and his men had cleared. At the bottom lay a mouldy coffin, nothing better than a cheap arrow chest. Gascelyn, Smollat and the sexton, helped by the others, seized the ropes Cutwolf had lashed around the coffin and slowly began to raise it.

The chest swayed, hitting the sides of the pit. Shards of wood and lumps of soil broke free. A chilling, difficult task, as if the corpse inside was resisting this violent interruption to its eternal sleep. At last the coffin broke free of the earth, and as they settled it on the side of the grave, the top part of the chest broke away to reveal a yellowing, twisted skull, jaws gaping in a ghastly grin. 'Master Ralph Fluberval,' Parson Smollat announced. 'Once a tanner, certainly a sinner.' The parson laughed at his grim joke. 'A widower, miserly he was, went to God after suffering a violent bout of the flux. Bardolph dug the grave.' Anselm knelt down, making the sign of the cross over the skeleton's head. Ignoring the protests of the others, he ripped off the rest of the coffin lid, examined its grisly contents and went to stand over the grave. Gascelyn, without being asked, clambered into the yawning hole and dropped down. Sir William handed him a spade which he dug into the packed soil. 'Brother Anselm,' he called up, 'there is nothing here but dirt.'

'Of course there isn't,' Anselm replied, 'let us examine the others.' They moved away. Stephen crouched on the grass. He felt hungry, tired and wished they could return to The Unicorn. He watched them walk away. A door banged. He glanced over his shoulder at the church. The corpse door, shifted by the breeze, opened and shut again. Stephen rose, stumbling across the mounds, kicking aside the trailing briar branches and ankle-catching weeds. He reached the corpse door and stepped inside. The church was dark. Light still poured through some of the leaded lattice windows. Strokes of sunlight scarred the paving stones beneath. Candles flamed yet they seemed from afar like the fire of a forge deep in dark woods.

'More horned than a unicorn,' a throaty voice mocked. 'For all your chastity, novice, you have a nose for smelling out a dainty bit, haven't you, Stephen? Eager to get to her, are you?' Stephen stood, his back against the rusty, creaking corpse door. He peered through the gloom; his throat turned dry. A shadow against one of the drum-like pillars separated itself and moved towards him like a hunter speeds soft-shoed across the grass. 'Like a heron pokes a walnut shell, isn't it, Stephen? Thinking of getting between her thighs, are you?' Darts of fire flickered and died. The hand of the shifting shadow came out, grasping Stephen's wrist in an eagle's grip. Just then he heard a knocking on the door behind him. Breathless, sweating, he turned, eager to escape from the nightmare. He opened the door. An old woman holding a lamp stood waiting. She was almost bent double, clothed in rags, hair covering her shrivelled face. Around her head was a dirty dishcloth, while her face, neck and hands were a mass of wrinkles; toothless, her lips receded over blood-red gums. All around her purple lips sprouted tufts of soft, white hair which gave her the look of a whiskered, demure cat, apart from her eyes – small black holes dancing with malice. 'Come with me.' The old head bobbed like that of a sparrow. Her movements were jerky, her eyes glittered and her lips twisted in a grin. She gestured with her hand. 'Come with me.' The voice curled in a viper-like hiss. Stephen looked beyond her. There was no graveyard now, just a long, dirty room. The plaster on the walls was crumbling, the blackened beams dotted with cruel hooks. Cobwebs hung thick and heavy as tapestries. A cat lay sprawled on an ash heap; when it lifted its head its face was human like that of the harridan. The cat opened its mouth and spoke. 'Ah, Stephen,' it purred, 'man's flesh is viler than the skin of a sheep. When sheep are dead their skin still has some use, for it is pulled clear and written upon. But, with men, flesh and blood profit nothing.'

Stephen hastily stepped forward, only to find himself falling.

'Stephen, Stephen!'

The novice shook his head and opened his eyes. Anselm crouched beside him, gently tapping his face. Close by stood Beauchamp, a dark shape, just like that black shadow which had confronted him in the church. 'I saw you go into Saint Michael's,' the clerk drawled, 'but then you never came out so . . .' his voice trailed off.

'Does he suffer from the falling sickness?' Parson Smollat bustled up. Stephen gazed past him at where the rest stood, heads together.

'Stephen, you're just hungry, aren't you, lad?' Anselm asked. The novice clambered up. The day was drawing on. Dusk was creeping in. Somewhere a lych bird, the ever chattering nightjar, made its chilling call.

'There is nothing here,' Anselm declared, 'nothing but old bones, shroud shards and crumbling wood. Let us go.'

The Carmelites made their farewells and, accompanied by Beauchamp and his retainers, re-entered the narrow lanes of Dowgate.

'Who will re-inter the dead?' Stephen asked.

'Let Parson Smollat take care of that,' Anselm replied. 'I must say our parson does seem a much preoccupied man.'

They continued up the lanes. Trading was drawing to an end and citizens were making their way home along the messy thoroughfares. Apprentices still shouted. Beggars shook their clacking dishes. But, as Anselm murmured, the day was done and they were all for the dark. A cold, stiff breeze forced them to keep their cowls up across their heads. Garish signs displaying all kinds of heraldry, mythical beasts and guild insignia, creaked on rusty chains. Lanterns, lamps and tapers flared at windows or glimmered through the chinks of shutters. They reached The Unicorn, where the stable yard was busy with a line of sumpter ponies and two huge carts delivering purveyance. Coals glowed from the small forge in its narrow shed where the smith still pounded the anvil. The air was a fog of different smells: burning hair, smoking charcoal, the rich tang of manure and the various cooking smells from the kitchen and buttery. Two pie men, who had used the tavern bakery, came out with their trays slung about their necks, eager to entice passers-by with cries of 'Warm patties, really hot! Warm patties, scorching hot!' Stephen and his companions shoved through these. Beauchamp's men went ahead into the tavern. Stephen followed and closed his eyes momentarily in pleasure at its cloying warmth and savoury smells. Alice appeared along a passageway, looking rather dishevelled. Flour dusted her blue veil and gown as well as her hands and face. Nevertheless, she still gave Stephen the sweetest smile and swiftly called for her father, a tall, balding Minehost with a fine face and deep, welcoming voice. The apron he wore was clean, as were the napkins over his left arm. He bowed at Sir Miles and the two Carmelites before ushering them into the taproom; this was very spacious though rather low, with an arched ceiling resting on a huge pillar painted green and gold. Common tables ranged either side of the room with private spacious booths in the large bay windows partitioned from the rest by vividly painted screens.

Minehost, who introduced himself as 'Master Robert, formerly of Bristol,' guided them to one of these window-tables. Three places had been laid. The taverner, his voice betraying his West Country burr, assured Beauchamp that Cutwolf, whom he knew very well, and all his companions would be well looked after. Alice stood just behind him, wiping her brow on the back of her wrist, those lovely, smiling eyes still dancing at Stephen. Suddenly her smile faded. 'They say,' she called out, 'you are looking for corpses at Saint Michael's and Rishanger's house. News flies faster than swallows in Dowgate.'

'Hush now, girl.' Her father made to remonstrate but Sir Miles, who'd doffed his cloak and sword belt, busy making himself comfortable, held up a hand, smiling so appreciatively at Alice that Stephen felt a stab of jealousy.

'Mistress, you are correct – we are looking for corpses.'

'Margotta Sumerhull?' Alice's voice trembled; her father put his arm around her shoulder and gently led her away. Servitors came to take their orders. Sir Miles declared he would pay and for the best ale and wine, which were brought. Cormanye, pork fillets in wine and black pepper, aloes of beef steeped in thyme and sage with a pot of lumbard mustard, white, soft bread cuts and dishes of buttered vegetables were ordered. Anselm recited the Benedicite and blessed the table. They washed their hands in stoups of rose water and settled back to enjoy the delicious smells coming from the kitchen. Stephen hoped Alice would reappear but her father thought otherwise, serving them himself. They ate in silence until Beauchamp put down his horn spoon. He stretched across the table, grabbed Stephen's wrist and squeezed it. 'What really happened to you at Saint Michael's? Is it the falling sickness?'

'I don't think so,' Anselm intervened.

'It has happened before,' Stephen added.

'And the cause?'

'Magister, you explained it once.' Stephen forced a grin. 'You remember, the Irish?'

'I soldiered in the Holy Isle,' Anselm confessed. 'I served Dermot, Prince of Leinster. He defeated a rival clan. After the battle about two hundred heads of his enemies were laid at Dermot's feet. Dermot turned each head over. When he recognized a face he did a dance of joy like some mummer at midsummer: he was mad with delight. I was in the retinue of an English lord sent from Dublin to help the King's ally. It was autumn. There were fruit trees nearby, damsons full and ripe. After the battle we plucked these. I was tortured by thirst. I remember eating them as Dermot did his macabre dance. Anyway,' Anselm sighed, 'that prince, as lunatic as any moon man, lifted to his mouth the decapitated head of an enemy he particularly loathed and, grasping it by the ears, gnawed at the nose. A cruel and most evil act. I was revolted and sickened. I vomited what I had eaten.' Anselm paused, taking a gulp of water. 'I still tremble at the sheer wickedness. Even after all these years, God bless me, the smell of damson juice is enough to take me back to that day of slaughter and outrage and my belly turns nauseous.' He pointed at Stephen. 'My friend, you are no different. Scenes, memories come rushing back when the bell in your soul peals out what it has learnt, even if your mind has forgotten it.' Anselm tapped the table. 'In your case, Stephen, other forces swoop in, eager to exploit such forgotten, hidden memories. So, let it be. Let us not grieve about yesterday.' He raised his water cup in toast. 'To us three.' Beauchamp and Stephen responded. The novice felt relaxed. He gazed around the taproom. Hungry for a glimpse of Alice, Stephen still rejoiced in the ordinariness, the latent merriment of his surroundings. So different from those cold churches, sombre burial pits and haunted houses.

'You will stay here,' Anselm declared. 'It is good for you, Stephen. Don your old clothes, help Minehost.' He smiled. 'Get to know Alice better.'

'Why?' Stephen exclaimed. 'Why, Magister?'

'Are you intended for our order, Stephen? Are you really? You, not I, must answer that question.' Anselm waved his horn spoon around. 'A good place for a good life. A man of peace dwells here. I sense that as do you.'

'Master Cutwolf and his coven,' Sir Miles added, 'will protect you. Become our eyes and ears, Stephen. Immerse yourself in the life of the tavern, the street, the ward. Watch and listen.' Stephen fought to hide his excitement. He wanted to leap up, to sing and dance a jig like some moonstruck madcap.

'You will be given a small chamber under the eaves,' Anselm explained. 'You will help Minehost in a myriad of tasks. Ordinary things along with the Eucharist, prayer, fasting and good works are the best defence against what the sinister Lords of the Dark can hurl against us.'

The next such assault occurred the following morning. Just after the bells for Prime boomed across the ward, Stephen was awakened by Anselm, who'd slept on the floor of the garret the novice had been given, a small but very comfortable chamber with a bed, table, stool and lavarium. The walls were white-washed a gleaming cream and boasted a large painted cloth depicting a maiden feeding a unicorn, and a thick turkey carpet covered the polished wooden floorboards. 'Stephen, Stephen!' Anselm urged.

He woke and sat up.

'Stephen,' Anselm insisted, 'it is dawn. Sir Miles is here. We must return to Rishanger's house.'

'Dark of soul, hideous in appearance!' growled a voice. Stephen caught his breath. 'Night of the cutting knives, the splashing of blood.' Faces, young and fearful, swam before his gaze. 'Trapped in darkness and unable to move on!' The cry was piercing.

Stephen grasped Anselm's wrist. 'I feel . . .'

'I know,' Anselm urged, 'but come, Sir Miles awaits us. We must go. Ignore what you see, hear and feel.' Stephen hurriedly dressed in his clean attire: jerkin, hose, boots and cloak. Anselm packed what he called in a merrier mood 'his holy pannier'. They tumbled down the stairs. Beauchamp was waiting for them at the entrance. The royal clerk looked dishevelled, unshaven and heavy-eyed. He gathered his cloak about him as if to hide what lay beneath and, Stephen noticed, tried to unravel the rosary beads wrapped tightly around his right hand. 'They are waiting,' he announced.

The royal clerk led them into the street where Cutwolf and the others were gathered, torches gleaming against the greying light. Shapes and shadows moved. A dog howled; a cat shrieked in defiance. An early river mist had drifted in, distracting the eye and muffling sound. They left the tavern, moving in a pool of light with swords drawn through the morning murk. Bells clanged.

Shouts and cries echoed. Carts rumbled, creaking and crashing. But, for Stephen, all that existed was this cortège moving through the morning mist to confront the host of wickedness. He tried to ignore the hasty voices, the pleas for help, the strident cries clamouring his ears. He wanted to concentrate on what he was doing but this did not help. Shadowed faces moved before him and vanished. He glanced at a cat squatting on a pile of refuse. The cat assumed human features, a devilish grin. Ghostly fingers caressed Stephen's face. A hand clutched his belly and squeezed hard. He exclaimed loudly at the pain. Anselm turned and whispered the Jesus prayer; the sensation faded.

The morning was dull and the river mist had yet to dissipate. The creatures of the night, not ready to return to their rat holes to sleep, ate, lurked and waited again for twilight. The streets were filthy with slops of every kind. They passed the pillories and stocks, the malefactors still cruelly fastened there by neck, wrist or feet. During the night the ward watch had surprised a group of housebreakers and carried out summary justice, hanging them from iron brackets fastened to the walls, their corpses dangled by the neck, purple faces twisted into hideous grimaces. Cats slunk beneath the swaying corpses. A yellow-ribbed mongrel sniffed the puffy hand of one of the hanged. Warning shouts carried. Figures hurried down the alleyways into the mildewed cellars where the night-walkers gathered. Stephen felt the weight of depression descend on him, then his hand was touched. He turned. Alice, heavy-eyed with sleep, a cloak wrapped about her, hair a gorgeous tumble about her smiling face, was walking next to him. She pressed a small linen parcel into his hands, kissed him swiftly on the lips and then she was gone, racing back up the street towards The Unicorn.

'Lucky fellow.' Cutwolf, striding beside him, winked at Stephen.

'Love,' Anselm murmured. 'How truly boring life would be without it.' Stephen felt elated. The darkness no longer clung to him. He grasped the linen parcel like a trophy, his lips still burning from the kiss. The sun would rise. The mist would thin and fade. All hell might be invoked against him but Alice was wonderful. She was thinking of him. He felt like dancing, singing alleluia. Stephen opened the parcel and stared at the manchet loaf cut, buttered and laced with thin slices of ham. He broke this, distributing it to his companions.

'Manna from heaven,' Anselm whispered. 'Have you ever tasted anything so delicious, Stephen?'

The novice blushed, hastily swallowing his portion as they moved across an alleyway, stopping before Rishanger's house. Beauchamp had been busy. Tower archers boasting the royal livery ringed the abandoned mansion. Inside the King's serjeants in their blue, red and gold tabards guarded the various chambers. Beauchamp swept past these into the gloomy garden, now lit by flaming cressets lashed to poles driven into the ground. These revealed what Anselm could only whisper as the 'abomination of desolation'. At least six burial pits had been uncovered, each containing a white tangle of bones and skulls.

'So many,' Beauchamp breathed.

'My Lord,' Cutwolf retorted. 'They were buried with their possessions.' He pointed to a pile of tawdry shoes, slippers, bracelets and other dirt-encrusted jewellery. 'They were all young women.'

'But killed some time ago,' Anselm declared, moving to the edge of one of the burial pits. 'They have been in the ground some time.'

Pausing at the chattering song of a nightjar, Stephen wondered if demons nestled in the branches of the clustered orchard trees. Did the malign ones stare out, gabbling their malevolence? Stephen could not look away. The sheer misery of that place was suffocating. Anselm was correct: these skeletons belonged to the long dead – at least a year. They would not find Edith Swan-neck here.

Stephen returned to the house even as Anselm, cross in hand, solemnly cursed the perpetrators of these wicked acts. 'May they be cursed by the sun, moon, stars, grasses and trees,' he declared. 'May their corpses be left unburied to be devoured by the dogs and birds of the air. May their souls enter the eternal darkness of hell where grief, without consolation, gnaws the heart and evil flourishes like weeds. May their souls be cursed to wander for ever.'

oooOooo

Words Amongst the Pilgrims

The physician coughed and raised his hand, rings sparkling in the light. 'I have said enough for the moment,' he declared. 'My tale runs on but, there again, we promised a late start for the morrow.' The physician moved to stand once again before the hearth. The other pilgrims also stirred, quietly discussing what they had heard. Master Chaucer, aware of their sharp and changing mood, watched intently. He did not mean to be so curious, yet he felt like a hawk on its branch, keenly surveying the field before him. The Wife of Bath was tearful. She sat crying but quickly wiped her face and rose, demanding to know where the latrines were. Other pilgrims moved. Chaucer noticed how the burly haberdasher had grown very agitated. The summoner, too, had changed, no longer the scab-faced, lecherous, hot-eyed court official, he sat on a stool tapping his fingers against the long Welsh stabbing dirk in its scabbard on his belt.

Master Chaucer felt the tension. A mystery play was being staged behind the veil of this long spring evening. Ghosts were gathering. People were doffing masks and donning others. Chaucer, dry-mouthed, watched the haberdasher holding his crotch; the man moved swiftly out of the taproom towards the latrines. Immediately the summoner followed, his hand on the hilt of his knife. Chaucer rose to his feet and pursued both men. The haberdasher was walking across the lawn to the lattice fence with the summoner on his heels. Chaucer saw the glint of shimmering steel. The dagger was drawn. Mischief was afoot. The haberdasher paused by the fence, admiring the wild tangle of roses. The summoner, soft-footed, dagger out and hanging by his side, made to follow. Chaucer coughed loudly. The summoner's dagger disappeared beneath the folds of his robe. The haberdasher turned, his burly face flushed and slackened by wine. He forced a smile and continued on around the lattice fence. The summoner strolled back to Master Chaucer. The court official did not look so bumbling but purposeful and deliberate. He paused beside Chaucer and grinned in an array of jagged, yellowing teeth.

'The dagger?' Chaucer queried.

'Nothing.' The summoner simply tapped the coiled hilt of his knife. 'Even here, Master Chaucer, in the midnight garden of a Kentish tavern, one should be very careful.' He brushed Chaucer on the shoulder, attempting to pass him by. He tensed as Chaucer grabbed his arm. The summoner's hand reached again for his dagger.

'Peace, peace,' Chaucer whispered. 'The physician tells a tale yet there are strong echoes of it here amongst some of our fellow pilgrims.'

'Some stories,' the summoner retorted, freeing his arm, 'never finish and never will, even if all the souls who throng that tale lie cold in their graves. Remember that, master poet.'

The summoner walked back into the tavern, while Chaucer waited for the haberdasher. The bulbous-eyed individual came from the latrines beyond the fence; he appeared nervous, fumbling, trying to tie the points on his hose. He walked falteringly, his swollen belly full of wine. He staggered by Chaucer and stopped, swaying on his feet. 'What are you looking at, sir?' he slurred.

'I was wondering that myself,' Chaucer quipped. 'Who are you really, sir? Do you not realize that our physician's tale has stirred memories amongst our companions?'

'Has it now, has it now?' The haberdasher put his face in his hands. 'Oh, God,' he murmured, 'the demons still pursue us.' He took his hands away. 'This hunt will never finish. I recognize the summoner now.'

'Master Chaucer?' The physician stood in the light of the taproom door. 'Come,' he beckoned. 'Come!' he repeated. 'And bring your friend.' The physician's voice was tinged with sarcasm. 'My tale is set to resume.'

ooOOoo

The Physician's Tale

Part Five

Stephen tried to forget the grisly horrors of Rishanger's macabre house. Anselm and Beauchamp busied themselves about the removal of the remains to the city cemeteries. Stephen, on the other hand, now free of the Carmelite rule, settled into his life at The Unicorn. He came to love that warm, welcoming tavern with its sweet-smelling taproom, kitchen garden, scullery, buttery and large stone kitchen. Minehost Master Robert allowed Stephen the free run of the hostelry before deciding that he was best suited to the kitchen. He was soon instructed into the mysteries of that great, stone-flagged cooking chamber with its yawning hearth, furnished with a spit, side ovens, grid irons and what the cook called his 'sizzling pans and cauldrons'. Stephen was shown the various knives, stone mortars with their wooden pestles, the vivarium for fish, the hooks for fleshing, the skillets and different bowls. He watched the cooks and spit boys prepare a wide range of dishes: fillet of cold boar glazed with honey; capon braised with sweet wine stock; sole in yellow onion sauce. He embraced the world of chopping, smoke, steam and a host of delicious thick smells which tickled his nose, watered his mouth and teased his stomach.

Master Robert also used him to fetch stock from the different markets: meat from the blood-puddled stalls under the grim hulk of Newgate; chicken and geese from the fowl sellers along Poultry as well as the produce from the various herb and vegetable markets of Cheapside. Alice went with him. She was merry – even shameless – in her flirting. She seized his hand, making Stephen run along with her through the lanes, breathlessly pulling him into some shadowy nook to kiss him full on the lips. Stephen was, in both heart and soul, much taken with her. Every day was an adventure. He would rise early in his small garret, try and recite some prayers, then visit the nearby chapel of St Frideswide, as Anselm had told him to stay well away from St Michael's, Candlewick. After he had attended Mass, recited an Ave before the Lady chapel and lit a taper for the soul of his mother, Stephen was caught up in the hurly burly of the day, which he thoroughly enjoyed. Alice, impetuous and passionate, chattered as merrily as a spring sparrow on the branch. Neat and clean, she greeted him every day with a smiling face and brushed hair, always dressed in an immaculate smock and apron. She adored her father, Master Robert, who proved to be a genial host. He was fair and honest, making the tavern scullions and servants work hard but paying and feeding them well, ensuring they had safe and comfortable lodgings.

Alice explained how her father's family had owned two such taverns on the outskirts of Bristol with a similar holding on the Old Roman Road near Bath. On the death of his wife Master Robert had sold all three, moving to Dowgate in London with Alice and her younger sister Marisa where, Robert had vowed, they would manage the best tavern in the city. Stephen was caught up in all the runnings of this, be it the purchase and import of food or Master Robert's determination to extend the tavern gardens and produce his own vegetables for the kitchen. The Unicorn was certainly popular, the favourite choice of tradesmen, tinkers, ermine-robed lawyers, scarlet-cloaked serjeants, dark-garbed clerks and sailors from nearby Queenhithe as well as the citizens of Dowgate.

Stephen worked hard from daybreak until noon. Once the Angelus bell sounded, Alice would take Stephen into what she called her 'secret bower in the greensward where they could sit like Robin and Marion in Sherwood'. In truth, that part of the tavern garden was overgrown, a mass of tangled bushes and climbing sturdy flowers. A former owner had built the bower by twisting saplings together and allowing an array of wild roses to overgrow it. Inside stood a high turf seat and a rickety old table for pots of flowers. The only fly in the ointment, as Alice observed, was her baby sister, Marisa. Alice's mother had died giving birth to her and Master Robert believed the life force of two souls was trapped in that little body. Marisa was a vivacious handful: six to seven years of age, she was a bundle of energy with a rosy face framed by yellow curls and a constant gap-toothed grin. She was, as Stephen came to realize, a sprite in all her ways. Marisa needed very little sleep – merry as a robin, she rose early to seek him out. From the start, Marisa had decided that if her sister liked Stephen, so would she and she acted accordingly. Where Stephen and Alice went, Marisa always followed, their noonday meetings being no exception.

Alice tried to ignore her younger sister, more concerned about the dire events in Dowgate. 'Margotta Sumerhull and I would often come here after the Angelus,' Alice declared as she made herself more comfortable, placing the linen napkins containing cold meats and fresh bread on the table. She took the tankards of ale from Stephen and placed them down, turning to grasp his hand firmly, her loving eyes now solemn. She would always lean forward and kiss him roundly on the mouth, then draw back. Stephen sometimes wondered if Alice was slightly fey; he had never met a young woman like her – demure but direct.

'We always met here,' Alice continued, parcelling out the food. 'We would discuss meeting our perfect gentle knight as the troubadours say we should. Well,' she pushed a piece of bread between Stephen's lips, 'I have met mine. I took to you, Master Stephen, as soon as I met you in the street with Brother Anselm.' She smiled. 'You looked so innocent, so trusting, despite all the commotion at the church. You are the young man I decided I should marry.'

Stephen gulped what he had eaten. 'But I am a novice,' he replied, 'entrusted to the Carmelite order.'

'But you have only taken simple vows, not solemn ones,' Alice declared blithely. 'I have checked that. Brother Gilbert – you know, the Benedictine who sells us his produce from the orchard at Westminster?' She didn't wait for Stephen's reply. 'Well, I have asked him. He explained the difference. He knows about you and Brother Anselm. He says you visited Westminster.' Alice cut a portion of meat, neatly diced it with a sharp, curved knife, picked up the pieces and popped them into his mouth. 'You see visions, don't you? Are you seeing them now?'

'No!' Stephen exclaimed with a fervour which surprised even himself. 'No, I am not – not since I came here.' He swallowed the diced meat and grinned. 'Perhaps you frightened them off?'

'I probably have.' Alice chewed on her bread, watching him curiously. 'I heard about what they discovered at Rishanger's house. Did you know he used to come here? A weasel-faced, hard-hearted rogue. I never liked him.' Alice put down the piece of manchet loaf. 'God knows,' her eyes filled with tears, 'one of those may have been Margotta Sumerhull. Tell me,' and she'd revert to her usual litany of questions, which he tried to answer as best he could.

Stephen came to realize that Brother Anselm had left him at The Unicorn for many reasons. The exorcist himself had disappeared, lost in his own business. Stephen began to sense that Anselm was not only trying to determine his vocation but also learn what was happening along the needle-thin runnels and alleyways of the Parish of St Michael's, Candlewick. Stephen remained vigilant. The deaths of Bardolph and his wife, the opening of the graves, the rumours about hauntings, had alarmed everyone. People were now glad that Sir William Higden had decided to keep the church under close ward. Many argued that the church should be closed completely. Sir William should pull down the entire edifice, clear the cemetery, fill the charnel house and begin a new building. The dark rites of the Midnight Man and his coven were common gossip, as well as the horrid finds at Rishanger's house. Lists of the names of young women who had disappeared were hastily drawn up in this alehouse, tavern or cook shop and passed from lip to lip. Alice, however, was only interested in one name: her bosom friend, Margotta Sumerhull. She pestered Stephen, who could only answer that all they had found was a tangle of bones. Nevertheless, he promised he would ask Anselm and Sir Miles if they could offer further help. Secretly, Stephen wondered more about Edith Swan-neck, Bardolph's mistress. Stephen, from what he had learned from his father, knew that her corpse would not have decayed completely, so where was she?

At times, although immersed in the joys of The Unicorn and Alice's loving presence, Stephen openly fretted about the apparent disappearance of both Anselm and Beauchamp. Alice, in their daily meetings in her 'secret bower', would often question Stephen about his master. Did he have secret powers? Could he see the spirits of the departed? Stephen, sworn to silence on such matters by Anselm, could only answer evasively, so Alice would move on to Beauchamp. Stephen had also heard rumours about the royal clerk. How he lived in apparent splendour in his own elegant mansion in Ferrier Lane. 'A man of great discretion' was how Alice described Sir Miles, who sometimes supped at The Unicorn. Rumour had it that he was a ladies' man, yet he was most reluctant to entertain at home and more inclined to visit this tavern or that, constantly escorted by his henchman Cutwolf. Rumour babbled about that enigmatic royal clerk's private life, though it was more of a case of much suspected but nothing proved. At times Stephen was relieved to be distracted by the young Marisa, who regarded his daily meetings with Alice in their bower as part of a delicious game. The little girl would creep through the garden, or be there hiding already, only betraying herself by a flash of colour or her irresistible giggle. Alice would rise and go searching until she caught her young sister, dragging her out of her hiding place, trying not to laugh at the gap-toothed grin before sending her packing back into the tavern. Marisa, however, also regarded Stephen as hers and, when her sister was not looking, would grasp his hand, jumping up and down, begging to be taken out to this stall or that.

Cutwolf appeared. He, too, took lodgings at The Unicorn, a narrow, low chamber near the stables. At first he kept to himself, busy with his master's affairs. Cutwolf could give Stephen little news about Anselm, who had apparently disappeared into the muniment room at the Tower while Beauchamp was absent on Crown matters, though exactly what was never discussed. During the second week of Cutwolf's stay at The Unicorn, as Minehost and his servants prepared for some May-time celebrations, Cutwolf became more sociable. He took to joining Master Robert and the tavern servants in the taproom after the usual customers had left. In the glowing light from a roaring fire and the shafts of flame from candles and tapers, Cutwolf would regale them all with stories about London's Hades, the dreadful underworld thronged by a host of dark but colourful characters: Melisaunde, the arch mistress of wicked wenches and Duke Jacob Hildebrod, a monstrously fat old man with one gleaming eye in the centre of his forehead. How Duke Jacob ruled what was commonly called 'The Shire of the Lords of the Huff', which included all the naps, foists, coneycatchers, cozeners and forgers of London. How this lord of hell could whistle up a blizzard of swords and cudgels as well as a legion of hideous hags who rode on broomsticks. The rifflers and the rufflers from the dank, pig-licked cobbles of Southwark and Smithfield were also his retainers . . .

Stephen, with Alice next to him on a bench close to the inglenook, Marisa sitting on the floor between them, would listen round-eyed as owls as Cutwolf described the evil smelling 'Hole-in-the-Wall' tavern with its spacious bailey, 'The Court of Miracles'. Here the Ringers of the Dead would summon all the thieves of London to account to their lord, Duke Jacob. Cutwolf would delight them with such tales of mystery while Minehost passed around a steaming posset in a broad-rimmed, loving cup, along with dishes of finely-sliced bread and roast meat. Stephen's admiration for Cutwolf deepened as the henchman proved that verse from the Gospel – how the children of this world are more cunning in their affairs than the children of the light. Stephen discovered that Cutwolf was in fact a royal clerk schooled at Stapleton Hall, Oxford; a mailed clerk who had fought in battle. A secret, subtle man who hid his true identity beneath the mask and guise of a street riffler. Cutwolf was not just acting the troubadour, the jongleur, the travelling minstrel, he was also Beauchamp's spy. Cutwolf was a clever spider, spinning a web to cover them all and entice others into the trap. Once he'd finished minstrelling, he would invite others to make their contribution about life along the alleyways of Dowgate and the surrounding wards. Everyone was eager to participate and, in anticipation during the day, garner as much tittle-tattle and gossip as possible.

The bloody, mysterious affairs at St Michael's and Rishanger's house were raised in disgust. The common opinion was that Bardolph had been hurled from the tower by a demon who lurked in the cemetery and stalked the tombs. Stephen held his peace because, as the days passed, he realized that Cutwolf was after greater prey – the identity of the Midnight Man! That title certainly cast its own deep shadow of evil over the ward. Warlocks and wizards, witches and moon women were common enough, but the Midnight Man and his coven were different. One evening Cutwolf opened his purse and laid six thick silver pieces on the table, bringing the candle spigot closer and allowing the precious coins to glitter like gifts from heaven. These, Cutwolf promised, would be given to anyone who brought fresh information about the Midnight Man and his company. Master Robert openly supported Cutwolf. More people thronged the taproom before the curfew bell tolled and so more remained to share the gossip after the main lantern horns were doused and the tavern door officially locked and sealed for the night. The ward patrol took no issue with this; instead its members would knock on the courtyard gates and be granted admission. Yet, if Cutwolf hoped for a revelation, he was disappointed. Legend and lie abounded about the Midnight Man. Rumour had it that Rishanger was one of the coven, even its leader, yet the identity of that notorious warlock remained stubbornly hidden.

One night Simon the sexton appeared in the taproom. He was so deep in his cups that he failed to recognize Stephen but sat slack-mouthed, listening to Cutwolf, when the henchman produced his coins and asked about the Midnight Man. Stephen, deep in the shadows around the inglenook, wondered if Simon had come of his own accord or been sent by Parson Smollat. Any doubt about that dissipated the following evening when the good parson himself, accompanied by the sexton, also attended Master Robert's joyous vespers. On that particular evening Cutwolf related a chilling ghost story about St Mary-le-Bow, the gathering place of Laurence Duket's ghost, who had taken sanctuary there decades earlier and was found hanging from a window-bracket. Afterwards the discussion returned to the hauntings at St Michael's. Everyone glanced curiously at the parson who, red-faced with drink, could only shake his head and stutter at what he slurred was, 'the sheer wickedness of the thing'.

'The Midnight Man must be a powerful person,' Alice declared, her lilting voice ringing through the taproom. 'Someone who can dominate and terrify a soul.' Everyone agreed, nodding their heads at the horror surrounding this warlock. Cutwolf realized he would learn little from the evening and, as he always

did, turned the conversation back to some other topic. Alice's
intervention, however, had forced Parson Smollat to stare in
Stephen's direction. Despite his many gulps from the loving
cup, the parson recognized Stephen and afterwards, just before
he left, pompously sauntered over. He did not question why
Stephen was there or why he was not wearing the Carmelite
robe, but clutched the novice's arm and demanded to know the
whereabouts of Anselm. Why had he disappeared, and what
could be done about the strange doings at his church? Despite
Parson Smollat's wine-soaked arrogance, Stephen felt his real
fear. He could only fend off his questions as he helped the priest
through the door and into the cold night air. The parson called
for the sexton to wait for him before tapping the side of his
red, fleshy nose as if he and Stephen were fellow conspirators.
'Cutwolf is right,' he slurred. 'That malignant, the Midnight
Man, must be found. He is the root of all this evil nonsense.'
Parson Smollat sighed noisily. 'God knows, I am tired of all
this. I wish I was free of Saint Michael's.' Turning away, he
walked off into the darkness to join Simon. Stephen watched
them go. The lane leading to the tavern side door emptied, silent
except for the slipping and slurry of hunted and hunter across
a pile of refuse further down. Stephen was about to return to
the cheery taproom when a glow of light abruptly appeared. A
cowl, empty except for blackness, swam towards him out of
the dark.

'See what fear man's bosom rendeth,
When this from heaven the judge descendeth.
Wondrous sound the trumpet flingeth,
All before the throne it bringeth,
Nature's struck and earth is quaking . . .'

'Stephen!' Cutwolf was beside him, shaking his shoulder;
both vision and voice faded. 'Stephen!'

'Your master?' the novice asked, still staring into the darkness. 'Where is your master, Beauchamp, Cutwolf? Why doesn't
he entertain visitors at his house?'

'Because my master is not what he appears to be.' And,
saying no more, Cutwolf turned away.

Anselm appeared a few mornings later. Stephen was in the
kitchen being initiated into the mysteries of preparing stewed

collops of venison basted in spiced wine. He was carefully mixing the ingredients into a large pan: meat stock, peppercorns, a stick of cinnamon, six cloves, and was about to add the ginger, vinegar and salt when he looked up. Anselm stood like a prophet of old in the doorway, beckoning at him. 'Stephen,' he called, as if they had been parted for a short while instead of weeks. 'Stephen, you must come.'

Stephen smiled his apologies at the cook who had been instructing him, grabbed his cloak from a peg and joined Anselm, who was already striding across the cobbled stable yard.

'Magister, how are you? I have missed you over the last few weeks.'

'No, you haven't.' Anselm paused at the gates and stared down at him. The exorcist's lean face looked more austere than ever, though his eyes were friendly. 'I missed you, Stephen, I really did.' He paused and coughed, wiping his mouth with a linen cloth. Stephen's heart lurched when he glimpsed the bloody flecks. Anselm followed his gaze and pushed the cloth up the volum-inous sleeve of his gown. 'It's nothing,' he rasped. Stephen caught the laboured wheeze in Anselm's chest.

'Magister.' Stephen slipped his hand into Anselm's. 'Magister, you are coughing blood. I know . . .'

'And so does the prior of Saint Bartholomew's. I have been there, Stephen, and elsewhere. Anyway, he tapped my chest and listened to my breathing. He has given me a strange concoction: dried moss mixed with soured milk. It seems to help. I have also been to the Tower and elsewhere while you have been with Mistress Alice, lost in her eyes no doubt!' He strode out into the lane, not waiting for an answer. Stephen, swinging his cloak about him, followed on. Only then did he glimpse the two women dressed in the dark brown robes of the Friar Minoressess. Stephen immediately wondered why they were so far from their house near the Tower. He stared hard. Both women were old, one of them most venerable. Stephen recalled chatter from the tavern, and how these two had been glimpsed before. In fact, the more he stared, the more convinced Stephen became that they were the same two nuns he had glimpsed at the Chapel of the Damned. The women stared back and turned away, the older one leaning heavily on her companion's arm. Anselm passed them without a glance. Stephen hurriedly followed.

'It's Saint Michael's,' Anselm declared. 'Well,' he stopped to allow a legless beggar crawling on wooden stumps to cross the runnel, 'it would be, wouldn't it?' They hurried on.

'Sir Miles and I were to meet Sir William Higden,' Anselm explained, 'about a possible second exorcism. Our good merchant, however, wants the entire building torn down. I cannot truly fault him on that. We were to adjourn to the church. Simon the sexton was instructed to meet us there with the keys but we cannot find him or gain entrance.'

'Why did you come for me?' Stephen asked, fearful that today he would not meet Alice in their secret bower.

'I am sorry.' Anselm paused to cough. Stephen caught the bloody flurry on the rag in his master's hand. Anselm swiftly pushed it back. 'Enough of that!' He smiled at Stephen, grasping him by the arm. 'Here we are!'

They reached the lychgate guarded by Cutwolf and his coven. 'No joy yet!' the henchman declared sombrely.

The two Carmelites entered the cemetery. The morning air was cool and crisp, and fleecy clouds streaked the blue sky with white wisps. The sun was strong, yet the light and warmth failed to bring any life to that dismal place. The sprouting weeds and the long, wild grass had grown even higher, masking the tombstones and other monuments of the dead. Before them loomed the sombre, craggy mass of the church with its dark tower and slated roof. Figures moved between the steps leading up to the main entrance and the corpse door to the side of the church. Abruptly a crow called, sharp and strident. Stephen glanced up and the vision descended. A hideous scream shrilled, while the deepest shadows raced swiftly through the long grass of the cemetery. These abruptly stopped. Eyes, red as blood, peered out between black weed stalks. The shapes shifted, fast and fleeting like some night swallow. These wraiths skimmed the bramble tops, turned and vanished.

'See the night of the deep ploughing!' a wheedling voice mocked.

'Close fast like a trap!' another answered. Stephen stumbled. He glanced down in horror at the white, claw-like hands creeping out from the undergrowth, fingernails long as talons and caked with dirt. 'Give mercy!' a soft voice whispered. 'Give mercy. Have pity on the surprised, unprepared dead.'

'*Jesu Miserere*,' Stephen replied. 'Jesus, have mercy.'

'You are well?'

Stephen glanced up. For some strange reason he had crouched down as if to clean soil from his boots. He stared up at a smiling but haggard-looking Beauchamp.

'I am well.' Stephen rose to his feet. Anselm had gone ahead, climbing the steps and pulling at the great iron ring on the main door of the church.

'We cannot get in.' Sir William Higden, followed by Smollat, Almaric and Gascelyn, came around the corner. He nodded briefly at Stephen. 'The corpse door is locked. We are tired of hammering. Is Simon asleep, drunk? We need him – we need his key.' The merchant knight's face was flushed and petulant, eyes glittering, lips pursed. A hard man, Stephen reflected, insistent on having his own way. Almaric the curate looked sleepy-eyed, rather vacuous. Gascelyn, as unkempt as ever, kept playing with his dagger hilt, staring back over the cemetery as if searching for a glimpse of that eerie death house. Parson Smollat looked and acted as if he was deep in his cups, unshaven, red-eyed, not too steady on his feet.

'Let's force the door!' Gascelyn exclaimed.

'The corpse door is heavy,' Almaric retorted. 'The sacristy door would be easier.' A brief discussion ensued and the decision was made. A moss-encrusted log was hauled from beneath one of the ancient yew trees, the branches of which hung down like the bars of a cage. They moved to the narrow sacristy door. Stephen stood back and watched. Cutwolf and the others hurried to help. Sir Miles Beauchamp, wiping his hands, once more tried to force the door.

'It is locked and bolted,' Almaric confirmed. 'Brother Anselm, you have tried the corpse door and the main entrance? Simon must have locked himself in.'

'Begin!' Sir William shouted, drawing his sword as if besieging an enemy castle. The group of men grasping the log drove its blunt end into the door, aiming for the lock. The door shuddered but held. Again they tried, stopped, rubbed their hands with spittle, grasped the log and returned to the assault, moving their aim from the lock to the thick leather hinges embedded deep in the lintel. At last the ancient wood began to buckle, splinter and crack. The top hinge yielded first, snapping back, followed by the second. The door was pushed open.

'Wits sharp, pray fervently,' Anselm whispered to Stephen as they followed Beauchamp into the gloomy sacristy. 'Check the door!' Anselm hissed. Stephen did so. The bolts were badly buckled, while the key hung twisted in the lock. The sacristy was musty; cobwebs stretched across the corners. They hurried through into the sanctuary. A cold breeze swept Stephen's face, bringing the bloody stench of the Shambles.

'Welcome.' The muffled voice seemed to come from his left. 'Welcome to the banquet of Cain, the fruit of his loins.'

'Master Simon,' Parson Smollat called from the top of the sanctuary steps. 'Master Simon, where are you?'

They went down the steps and began their search. 'Here!' Gascelyn called from a darkened transept, and they hurried over. The sexton lay in a wide, congealing puddle of his own blood, turned on his back, eyes staring up, the savage cut across his throat gaping like a second mouth. His sprawled arms were outstretched, his own dagger grasped in his right hand. Stephen stifled his cries as the others exclaimed at the horror lying there. Anselm demanded some sacking be brought from the church tower. He placed this around the corpse and immediately administered the last rites, whispering hoarsely the words of deliverance followed by the prayers for the dead. Parson Smollat was shaking so much Gascelyn had to take him to sit on the sanctuary steps.

Beauchamp, aided by Sir William and Almaric, immediately searched the church, going into every nook and cranny, but Stephen knew it was futile. This place was a barren wasteland peopled by restless ghosts now clustering hungrily around them. Something crept across Stephen's booted feet. He glanced down at the moving shadow trailing like black smoke. Tendrils of wet hair swept the side of his face. Cold fingers pressed against his brow. Anselm was still intoning the prayers for the dead. The sacking he knelt on squelched blood which began to bubble. Stephen, mouth dry, had to step away. He flinched at the disfigured, twisted faces drifting out of the gloomy transept: pale and thin, eyes glaring madly, jowls twisted in anger. He glanced over his shoulder. Gascelyn had struck a tinder; he was lighting the torches as well as different candles. Parson Smollat was blubbering like a child, shoulders shaking. Anselm's voice rose. 'I command you, Michael Archangel and all the heavenly hosts, to go and meet him.'

'Ours in life, ours in death!' a voice snarled in reply.

'I command you,' Anselm retorted. 'Begone to your proper place and stay there. Stephen,' Anselm insisted, 'kneel, pray!' The novice did so, yet all he could think about was Alice, of sitting beside her in that rose-garlanded bower with young Marisa spying on them from the brambles. He prayed but he could only think about them as the cold breeze returned with its offensive stench.

'Remove the corpse,' Anselm ordered, getting to his feet. 'Let us leave here swiftly. This is no longer a place for God or man.' Anselm swept by Stephen, tapping him on the shoulder as a sign to follow. The exorcist hurried up the sanctuary steps, pausing to deal with a coughing fit which bent him double. Stephen again glimpsed the red specks on the linen cloth but Anselm waved a hand and, taking a deep breath, straightened up. He walked across the sanctuary, took a stool, stood on it and unhooked the silver pyx. He removed the round white host and reverently ate it. He stood for a while, hands clasped, murmuring the Eucharistic prayer, 'May the body of Christ be to my salvation, not to my damnation', followed by the 'Anima Christi' poem.

Stephen stood with him and, by the time they had returned, Beauchamp had organized Cutwolf and others to use more sacking as a makeshift stretcher. The corpse was removed from the church. They left by the sacristy door. Parson Smollat, now partially recovered, murmured about the corpse door remaining bolted and locked and how its key was still missing. Stephen was just relieved to leave that abode of shadows. He turned, revelling in the sunlight and the pleasing breeze. He watched as Cutwolf hurriedly searched the corpse, now stretched out on the sacking. The sexton, however, only carried a few paltry possessions: coins, rosary beads, a small cross and a few nails but nothing else. No key to the corpse door could be found.

'Take his corpse back to the priest's house,' Beauchamp ordered. 'Brother Anselm, you accompany it, see that all is well. Sir William,' Beauchamp turned to the merchant knight, 'we shall meet in your chamber within the hour, yes?'

Anselm whispered to Stephen to follow him. The exorcist went to walk on but paused, crouching to examine dark stains on the paved path which went round the church. He picked at the congealed specks, plucked a piece up and sniffed at it, rubbing it between his fingers. He scrutinized similar droppings then rose to his feet. 'Strange,' he murmured, 'but let us go on.' They walked through the cemetery towards a small wicket gate which led into the enclosure before the priest's house, a fine pink-plastered, black-timbered dwelling built on a grey stone base with a blue-slated sloping roof. Parson Smollat explained how the sexton had two chambers, which could be approached by an outside staircase. The exorcist intoned the *De Profundis* as they approached the steps.

Stephen, however, remained distracted. He felt as if they were being followed: the sound of dry leaves whirled and rasped behind them, yet when he looked back there was nothing but the swaying wilderness of wild grass. He glanced back at the church. A shape like a gargoyle or babewyn was crouched on the sloping slate roof, black and hideous like some wild ape. He glanced again but it was gone. Stephen's eye was caught by movement at the top of the tower – shifting shapes as if bowmen, hooded and cloaked, clustered there. 'Stephen, Stephen!' a woman's voice called. He glanced across the bending grass which parted to reveal a black tombstone – from this a wicked white face, hair all a-tangle, glared furiously at him. Stephen stumbled and swiftly crossed himself.

They reached the wicket gate and went through on to the cobbled courtyard before the pretty-fronted priest's house. Isolda, wimple all awry, hands outstretched, came out. She began to chant a hymn of mourning until Parson Smollat gathered her in his arms and led her away. They took Simon's corpse up the outside staircase. The door to his two chambers hung unlocked, and they entered. Stephen was immediately struck by their ordinariness. Two white-washed cells with crucifixes and painted cloths on the walls, a few sticks of furniture, coffers and caskets. They placed the corpse on the narrow bed but, even as they arranged the dead man's limbs into some form of dignity, both Anselm and Beauchamp were busy about the chamber. They examined the tattered, grimy sheets of parish records piled on the chancery table in the second chamber. Coffers and caskets were opened. Stephen was surprised at how swiftly both Beauchamp, looking rather tired and absorbed, and Anselm sifted through the dead man's possessions. Parson Smollat, accompanied by a now comforted Isolda, came up the outside stairs. Beauchamp asked the woman to look after the corpse, adding that he would leave Cutwolf and his companions to assist her in cleaning and washing the body. 'We must go,' the royal clerk declared. 'Parson Smollat, we shall wait for you below.'

Beauchamp, Anselm and a slightly nervous Stephen left the chamber and went down to wait in the courtyard. 'Magister,' Stephen pleaded, 'where have you been, what have you been doing?' He glanced swiftly at the royal clerk. 'You are coughing blood. You should not be involved in this.'

'Brother Anselm.' Beauchamp grabbed the exorcist's arm. 'What is this spitting blood? Have you been poisoned?'

'No, no.' The exorcist smiled, exerting all his charm and beckoning them away from the door of the priest's house. 'I have been studying here and there and my cough is as old as I am. Now, Stephen, do not fret or worry.' He rubbed the side of the novice's face. 'Be at peace,' he urged. 'Think of God's goodness and,' he teased, 'Alice's smile. You have enjoyed yourself. No,' Anselm wagged a finger, 'I will not talk about myself. Let us talk more about poor Simon.'

'We discovered nothing,' Beauchamp declared. 'Nothing at all.'

'Except this.' Anselm twisted a piece of parchment, small and greasy with age between his fingers. 'A mere scrap.' He handed this to Beauchamp, who simply pulled a face and passed it to Stephen. The novice read the scrawl repeated time and again in dog Latin, Norman French and English. The message was simple and stark: 'Now Lucifer was the friend of Saint Michael.' As the Angelus bell abruptly tolled, Stephen thought about the arbour and sitting next to Alice.

'Stephen?'

'Er, nothing, Magister.' He handed the strip of parchment back to Anselm. 'I don't know what that means. Look, the others will be waiting.'

They all, Parson Smollat included, eventually gathered in Sir William's elegant chancery chamber. The perfume of the quilted leather chairs and stools mingled with the fragrance from the flower pots, chafing dishes and braziers. Stephen wondered how such exquisite beauty could exist alongside the horrors they had just witnessed. 'Well,' Sir William asked, lacing his podgy fingers together, 'we really must close the church now. Yes, Parson Smollat?'

The priest gulped noisily but nodded in agreement.

'What happened?' Anselm demanded.

'From the little we know,' Sir William replied, 'Simon went into the church. He entered by the corpse door. Once inside he pulled across the bolts and locked the door. He must have taken the key with him.'

'And this has not been found?' Anselm intervened.

'Yes,' Sir William agreed. 'Apparently it wasn't on his corpse.'

'I searched the church with Almaric when you took poor Simon's corpse back to his chambers.' Gascelyn spoke up. 'Brother Anselm, that key has disappeared.'

'So,' the exorcist demanded, 'how did the sexton die?'

'We've discussed that,' Sir William replied. 'Brother Anselm, it is a mystery except for one conclusion.'

'Which is?'

'The sacristy door was locked and bolted – you saw that. So it would seem that Simon entered by the corpse door, drew those bolts, locked it and threw away the key or hid it somewhere. He then went into that darkened transept, pulled his dagger and cut his own throat.'

'Impossible.'

'What other solution is there?' Almaric sniffed. 'Go back, examine the corpse door. The bolts were drawn. If you draw them back, the door remains locked because the key is missing. Simon must have killed himself, or was forced to, or some secret assassin entered that church. But how? There are no tunnels or secret passageways. Some demon, surely, Brother?'

Almaric grew more loquacious and Stephen suspected that the curate had drunk deeply from the goblet of claret in front of him. 'Surely,' he repeated, 'a man can be so terrified by demons, by the horrors which lurk behind the veil as to take his own life?'

'I would agree,' the exorcist conceded, 'and you all think that?' He stared around the polished walnut table, slightly dusty from the great bowl of lilies in the centre, their yellow seeds now peppering the polished top. Everyone nodded in agreement. Beauchamp looked rather askance, even sullen as he mulled over his own dark thoughts. The royal clerk caught Stephen's glance and stared coolly back. The novice wondered if Cutwolf had told him everything, including Stephen's own suspicions about this mysterious and enigmatic clerk.

'In which case,' Anselm tapped the table top, 'Saint Michael should be placed under interdict until it is cleansed and purified.'

'Or pulled down?' Sir William declared. 'I have petitioned both the Crown and the Archbishop. The entire church should be razed to the ground.'

'In the meantime,' Parson Smollat asked, 'what do I do?' The priest looked agitated, his balding brow laced with sweat.

'It is not the end of the world, parson,' Sir William said kindly. 'You can look forward to a new church.'

'If the King and the Archbishop should agree.' Beauchamp asserted himself, resting his arms on the table. 'But for the moment,' he emphasized his points on his fingers, 'we do not know who the Midnight Man is or his coven. We do not know how he learned about the lost treasure or the robber Puddlicot, yet he has. He has used, to little or no effect, the black arts to learn more. He performed those rites at Westminster and at Saint Michael's, Candlewick. We know he failed but not how or why this ended in failure, causing such a fierce stir amongst the living dead. Hence the hauntings, the demon infestation of Saint Michael's and the abbey. Somehow or other,' Beauchamp paused, 'I believe the Midnight Man discovered two items of the lost treasure. Rishanger seized these, attempted to flee and was murdered.' The royal clerk carefully rubbed his hands together. Stephen sensed something false, as if Beauchamp was not revealing his true thoughts. 'Now, Rishanger was undoubtedly a member of the warlocks coven,' the royal clerk continued. 'He may even be the Midnight Man himself, for that sinister figure has fallen remarkably silent. Rishanger was certainly a blood-drinker. He abducted and murdered young women, then buried them in that dire garden of his. Beatrice, Rishanger's leman, was also murdered, her corpse abused by Rishanger or others – we do not know the truth. Finally, were Rishanger's other victims the object of his murderous lust or were they used in his diabolic rites?' Beauchamp shrugged. 'Again, we do not know.'

'Then there are the other mysterious deaths,' Anselm declared. 'How did Bardolph fall from the top of that church tower? And Simon, his throat cut, locked in a church? Adele, poisoned by a mysterious visitor? Who this was or why they should murder her is, again, a mystery.'

'Why can't you free us from all of this?' Parson Smollat almost shouted. 'You are the exorcist. Anselm. You failed and then you disappeared.'

'Yes, I failed. I did so because I have failed to dig out the root of all this, a malignant human wickedness. Yes, I did disappear but I have been very, very busy. I have searched the records. I have also travelled to the great Abbey of Glastonbury in Somerset.' His words created an immediate silence.

'Now it comes!' a voice hissed into Stephen's ear. 'Now the wheel spins yet again.' Stephen glanced over to the corner where a figure sat, a blood-red translucent veil covering its head, face and body. Stephen's heart skipped a beat. He watched those red-mittened hands: the ends of the fingers were like long white worms, the nails painted a deep blue. Stephen murmured a prayer. The hands were moving. Stephen panicked. They must, he prayed, not pull up that veil and reveal the sinister face beneath – a witch's face! Stephen abruptly pushed back his stool.

'Glastonbury,' Sir William spluttered. 'Why there?'

Stephen rocked backwards and forwards on the stool. He glanced over again: the corner was empty but a drum, deep in the house, began to beat, followed by the faint trails of a trumpet blast. '*A l'outrance!*' a voice cackled. '*Usque ad mortem* – to the death, so the tournament begins.' Stephen felt a blast of heat, as if an oven door had been thrown open and he had been thrust before it.

'Stephen,' Beauchamp gestured at the wine dresser, 'do you want something to drink?'

'No.' The novice rubbed his clammy hands along his jerkin. 'No, I am sorry, I was daydreaming.'

'As was I,' Anselm added quickly. He had noticed his novice's discomfort and was eager to distract attention. 'Sir William, you asked about Glastonbury? Well, I also searched the records in the Tower, studying every item of treasure stolen from the crypt. Now, as you know, during the reign of Edward I, the present King's grandfather, the monks of Glastonbury allegedly opened Arthur's tomb in their abbey. Arthur's body, a veritable giant, was discovered along with his flaxen-haired Guinevere. However, according to the abbey chronicle and local legend, they also found Merlin's Stone and other magical items belonging to that great magus.'

'What,' Beauchamp asked abruptly, 'is Merlin's Stone?'

'The philosopher's stone,' Anselm replied. 'The means to perform alchemy, to transmute base metals into gold.'

'Rishanger believed in that nonsense,' Sir William barked. 'I told you the murderer came here, begging me for money to achieve that, do you remember?'

'I certainly do,' Anselm agreed. 'Anyway, I travelled down to Glastonbury; the almoner of that great abbey is a friend of mine. He showed me Arthur's grave and in the library chronicle, a most fascinating account of the discovery.'

'I have never been there,' Sir William intervened. 'I would love to.'

'Yes, yes, you must go. Anyway, Edward the King took the stone and the other magical items and kept them amongst his trophies.'

'Was Puddlicot a warlock?' Parson Smollat asked.

'No evidence exists for that.'

'This business . . .' Beauchamp was eager to bring attention back to the matters in hand.

'Ah, yes, this business.' Anselm paused. 'I thought, prayed, reflected and speculated.' The exorcist rubbed his hands together slowly. 'Undoubtedly the Midnight Man and his coven were blood-drinkers. Rishanger certainly was. They used that desolate house and that infernal pit in its dismal, isolated garden to entice young women and subject them to every kind of abuse. No wonder the place was haunted. However, the cemetery at Saint Michael's, Candlewick is different.'

'Yet undoubtedly haunted?' Parson Smollat interjected.

'Of course, but why?' Anselm added hastily. 'Rishanger could carry out his gruesome rites in his own dark temple. However, would young women willingly go into a cemetery? Even if they weren't enticed but abducted, they could resist, protest – eventually such a crime would be noticed. I mean, God knows who used to wander that place – beggars, lovers, the curious?'

'I agree,' Parson Smollat slurred, 'and yet it is haunted.'

'When I first thought some innocents had been taken there and murdered, I did wonder if they had been killed and buried in graves already dug.'

'But that means, Brother Anselm,' Sir William declared, 'you suspected Bardolph, even Parson Smollat?'

'No, no,' Anselm retorted. 'Remember, I asked about burials there. A grave is invariably dug the day before the requiem Mass, yes?'

'Correct,' Parson Smollat agreed.

'Accordingly, I wondered if the assassin would use such occasions to kill and, under the cloak of darkness, bury his victim in a grave already dug, then cover her with soil. The funeral takes place. The coffin or shroud cloth is lowered. The grave is filled in and no one is any the wiser!' Anselm straightened up. 'I was mistaken. However, I still believe that corpses, horribly murdered, lie somewhere else.' Anselm gathered together his writing satchel. 'As for poor Simon's death – and I rightly call him poor Simon – believe me, my friends, a fiend did that, though not from hell but from Dowgate.' Smiling grimly at his companions, Anselm rose, made his farewells, then left with Stephen.

Once outside the house the exorcist made his way back towards St Michael's. The day was quiet. A Franciscan stood on a plinth, begging alms for a group of lepers clustered a short distance away, their faces and hands swathed in bandages. Only their eyes, frenetic and desperate, peered out at a world that had forsaken them. Stephen ran up and told the friar to take his little flock to The Unicorn, where Master Robert would undoubtedly see them well. The Franciscan hopped down as nimble as a cricket, kissed Stephen on the cheeks and shouted at his charges to follow. He led them off singing the '*Salve Regina*' while the lepers followed at a distance, shaking their rattles and bells. Children, playing with an inflated pig's bladder, scattered at their approach. Women shouted from the windows of houses, begging their little ones to be careful. A false trader came racing up the lane, breathless and sweaty, as he dodged and twisted in a desperate attempt to escape pursuing market beadles. No sooner were they gone than a relic seller stepped out from an apothecary's shop, a tray slung around his neck, offering miniature portions of soap. Each was wrapped in a linen cloth which, he proclaimed, Joseph of Arimathea had used for the Lord's body on the first Good Friday. Stephen stood and watched these sights, aware of the different smells from the various shops and stalls. He glimpsed a necklace of gleaming copper being hawked by a tinker and immediately wondered if Alice would like it. He was about to walk across the lane when a cold breeze wafted against his face. A voice whispered something about the devil's wolf, hungry for the hunt. Stephen whirled around. A sense of pressing danger agitated him. Were those two beggars at the mouth of the runnel watching him? Or the man, heavily cloaked, who now stood just beneath the sign of the apothecary shop? Was he masked? Was his hand resting on a dagger hilt? The people milling around did not seem so welcoming now. Glittering eyes peered from deep hoods. A bulbous-eyed servitor, apron stained with blood, hastened by then paused to stare slyly at Stephen. Above him a window casement flew open and a man leaned out. Stephen thought he was holding a crossbow, yet when he looked again the casement slammed shut. A fierce whispering broke around him, like the humming of a noisome cloud of flies. Stephen felt the terrors seize him. He was not safe here. He broke free of his panic and hurried after Anselm, finding the exorcist standing at the lychgate to St Michael's. Stephen paused and took a deep breath.

Anselm turned. 'Believe me, my friend,' the exorcist leaned against the heavy wooden gate, 'this truly is the Kingdom of Cain. Murder was committed here but how, Stephen? Why and when?'

'Magister, what shall we do?'

'I'll stay here.'

'Stay here?'

'Yes.' Anselm left the gate and crouched down with his back to the cemetery wall. 'I just want to watch and see what happens.' He shaded his eyes, squinting up at Stephen. 'You have some money?'

'Yes.' Stephen grinned. 'Why? Are we to beg?'

'No, to eat,' the exorcist replied. 'Stephen, I am famished. A pastry full of minced beef with peppers and a dash of mustard? Master Robert sells the best!' Stephen, his terrors forgotten, needed no second bidding. Swift as a lurcher he ran to the tavern, bursting breathless into the kitchen, surprising the cook who gently mocked his eagerness, saying that two pastries and a pie were easy to serve. However, the lovely Alice had accompanied her father to St Paul's to meet a merchant beneath the Great Cross.

Stephen blushed, then grinned at the teasing. Once the linen parcels were ready, stowed in an old leather sack, he left the tavern, turning back into the street. A shout echoed through his mind. A woman's voice whispered, 'Ave, ave.' Stephen whirled around as four figures, hooded and garbed in black leather jerkins and hose, soft boots on their feet, merged out of the shadows. These were no phantasms. They breathed noisily behind their masks while their wicked knives winked in the light. 'Good morrow, little friar. You must come with us.'

'I must not.'

One of the nightmare figures stretched out his blade. 'What are you, little friar, you God-mumbler, you prattler of prayers? You stand there like some rabbit, jerking and trembling at the rustle of life.'

Stephen felt the anger well within him. He stepped back, determined to resist.

'God save you all! God save the King! God save Holy Mother Church!' Cutwolf, as if appearing from nowhere, sauntered down the alleyway. Behind him was his companion, face and head all oiled and shaved – Stephen knew this must be Bolingbrok, just by the way he swaggered. Beyond them, at the mouth of the alleyway, others thronged. Stephen heard a sound. He glanced back. His sinister assailants had disappeared into the spindle-thin runnel which stretched through the old houses in this quarter. Breathing in deeply, Stephen tried to ignore the clamouring voices. Cutwolf and Bolingbrok approached, sauntering along without a care in the world, confident in their own strength, the weapons strapped to their war belts. Bolingbrok stopped before him and bowed. 'The Lord hath delivered thee,' he intoned, 'as he did Israel from Og King of Bashan and Sihon King of the Amorites.'

'Blueberry.' Cutwolf laughed. 'That is what he is calling himself now. But we shall always know him as Bolingbrok. Anyway, young Stephen, we have kept you under close scrutiny. You really should be more careful.'

'Who were they?'

'Oh, undoubtedly the Midnight Man's messengers, but come,' Cutwolf beckoned, 'Brother Anselm is starving.'

'What did they want with me?'

'To see what you know, because the trap is closing, Stephen. But don't you worry. Where you go, your shadows will also follow.'

'Why didn't you try to arrest them?'

'For what? No, my friend,' Cutwolf grinned, 'too dangerous and, I suspect, they are merely hired bully boys who know very little.'

They returned to St Michael's. Anselm still sat sunning himself against the wall, watching the people drift by. Stephen joined him, handing over the linen parcel, making no mention of what had happened. Cutwolf and his companions drifted into the cemetery, squatting down in the long grass, shouting and laughing with each other. Stephen bit into the still-warm pastry and watched, as Anselm did, the shifting scenes. A group of pilgrims, armed with iron-tipped staves and preceded by a priest swinging a smoking thurible, hurried down to Queenhithe, chanting the litany of St James of Compostella, whose shrine at Santiago they hoped to visit. Tumblers and tinkers, moon men and mountebanks, jongleurs and the tellers of tall tales swarmed by. Cutwolf and Bolingbrok joined the two Carmelites, sitting like young boys with their backs to the walls, faces to the sun, commenting on all who passed: the court fops in their prigging fineries, the beadles and bailiffs, the staggering drunks and sober-clad officials.

As the daylight began to fade, the more colourful of Dowgate citizens, those who lived in the Mansions of Darkness, emerged fresh for a night's mischief. Cutwolf knew many of them by name and reputation. 'Hedge-Popper' and 'Hob the Knob' were two pickpockets; 'Peck Face' a professional beggar and 'Rattle Ears' a well-known cheat. Anselm seemed to enjoy himself and yet the more Stephen watched, he realized his master was mostly interested in the young drabs, whores and doxies who passed by. 'I have learned something,' Anselm breathed, 'the Holy Spirit be thanked. I confess my arrogance. I can now begin to learn.'

He finished the pastry and was about to get up when the two Franciscan Minoresses suddenly appeared in the mouth of the alleyway opposite and hobbled across. 'Light immortal, light divine,' a voice whispered, only to be answered by the snarl of a fierce dog – a chilling, resounding sound which sent Stephen scrambling to his feet. He wiped the sweat on his jerkin as the two women approached. The first was very elderly and venerable with a seamed, wizened face, eyes like small black currants in a flour-white skin. The other was also old but still vigorous, sharp of eye and firm of mouth, with the natural authority of a Mother Superior. They paused and bowed at Anselm, who returned the courtesy. 'You are Anselm, the Carmelite, the exorcist?'

'Yes!'

'We have much in common, Brother Anselm.'

'Such as?'

'Richard Puddlicot.'

Anselm just gasped.

'Puddlicot!' Stephen stared at the older woman, thinning hair peeping from beneath her wimple, eyes milky blue, mouth chomping on pinkish-red gums.

'Who are you?'

'Joanne Picard,' the old woman whispered. 'God have mercy

on me, and on him. I was Puddlicot's mistress. Now I am his relict.'

She leaned on her companion and smiled. Despite her age, Joanne Picard was resolute in both speech and manner.

'You must be . . .?'

'Close to my eighty-eighth winter.' The old woman laughed softly. 'I was barely sixteen when I lost the love of my life.' The bony, black-spotted, vein-streaked hand clutching her companion squeezed hard. 'And this is Eleanor, our daughter.' Anselm stood surprised and shocked.

'Magister?'

'Not here, Stephen, sisters.' Anselm grasped both of them by the hand. 'Stephen, run ahead and tell Master Robert at The Unicorn that he has guests.'

'But not the royal clerk,' Eleanor Picard declared firmly. 'Not him!'

'Why not?'

'I trust you, exorcist, we trust you, novice, but not him.'

Anselm glanced at Cutwolf, gently shaking his head. The henchman just lifted his hand in reply, then he and Bolingbrok sauntered back into the cemetery to join their companions. Stephen hurried off. Master Robert and Alice had returned to The Unicorn. Busy in the taproom, hair a little dishevelled, her pretty face tickled with sweat and her eyes rounded in mock grief, Alice confessed, flicking flour from her sleeves, how she'd had to distract herself while her beloved had disappeared without a word.

Stephen recited a list of apologies, which only put Alice into a fit of giggles. She kissed him merrily on the mouth and demanded to know why he was in such haste. When he told her, Alice immediately called her father and, dragging Stephen in to help, they prepared the most private of the window-seats. Anselm eventually arrived with the two ladies and Stephen joined them behind the screen. Now he could tease Alice, shaking his head in mock solemnity at her enquiries. Both women refused to eat, saying they would do so later in the day at their convent, although they gratefully accepted a jug of Rhenish and a dish of marzipan which Joanne merrily declared to be her favourite. Anselm did not need to question them.

Eleanor Picard, once she had taken a deep mouthful of the sweet white wine, moved the decorated horn box with its bright tallow candle to the centre of the table. She talked swiftly and pointedly. She declared how her mother had been Puddlicot's mistress after he had returned to London from Flanders. A carpenter by trade from a reputable Oxford family, Puddlicot had dabbled in the export of wool, which had been severely disrupted by Edward I's sharp disagreement with the Flemings. Puddlicot arrived in London full of anger at the King and determined to make a fortune at the Crown's expense by robbing the crypt. Eleanor described how Puddlicot had suborned the leading monks of Westminster and others, enticing them into his outrageous scheme. Finally she explained how both Puddlicot and his gang had been broken by a royal clerk, John Drokensford, later Bishop of Bath and Wells.

'My father, as you know,' Eleanor fought back tears, 'fled for sanctuary at Saint Michael's, Candlewick.' She took a deep breath. 'He sheltered there. The parson at the time, Henry Spigurnel, gave him sanctuary.'

'Was he part of your father's coven?' Anselm asked.

'I think so. I suspect he helped my father hide most of the looted treasure.'

'Where?'

'Richard never told me,' Joanne Picard whispered. Despite her age, Stephen realized that her wits were sharp, even wary of eavesdroppers in the tavern.

'What did he tell you?'

'How the treasure lay under the protection of God's guardian!'

'Saint Michael the Archangel?'

'I suppose so.' Joanne laughed quietly. 'I visited him when he was in sanctuary. Puddlicot was a true roaring boy. He didn't give a fig about life or death. He told me how he'd buried two pieces of treasure, the Cross of Neath and Queen Eleanor's dagger, in the garden of our house in Hagbut Lane.'

'The same one occupied by Rishanger?'

'The same,' Joanne agreed. 'Richard told me that and how he had left me a message with those two items about how he'd put the rest of the treasure under the protection of God's guardian. He said he would give me further details but later that day he was taken by force. During the attack Parson Henry Spigurnel was injured and died shortly afterwards.'

'Spigurnel resisted?'

'Yes, yes, he did. He received a blow to the back of his head which staved his crown in. He never regained either his sense or wits but died in his sleep. I never saw my beloved again.' The old woman wiped her tear-streaked face. 'They took Richard to the Tower. They confined him close. Once they had finished – and I know they did not break him – they bound him in a wheelbarrow and paraded him through the city before hanging him on the gallows outside the main gate of the abbey. The King let his corpse dangle for a day then ordered Richard's body to be flayed and the skin fixed to a door close to the abbey crypt.' The old woman swallowed hard. 'They hired a skinner from the Shambles to do it. He peeled Richard's skin as you would an apple, hanging it like a costume next to Richard's blood-red corpse.' She paused, crossing herself. 'They later cut his corpse down and carted it like a hunk of meat to the Chapel of the Damned. I believe you saw us there.'

'And so it ended.' Eleanor spoke up. 'My mother was pregnant with me. She searched the garden of her house but could find nothing.'

'I had to be careful,' the ancient one intervened. 'The King's surveyors were watching. I had no choice but to return to my family in Somerset. My father was kindly; he supported me. Eleanor was born. I eventually received my inheritance and moved back to London to work at what I am gifted – a seamstress. The old King was dead; his son then ruled. I lived comfortably enough.' She paused. 'I truly loved Puddlicot.' Only then did her voice break. 'I truly did. I visited our old haunts. Of course, all those involved in his great escapade were either dead or witless. I heard his skin had been left to rot on the abbey door.'

Joanne caught her breath and greedily slurped from the goblet. 'I also heard the stories. How both the monks' cemetery as well as that at Saint Michael's, Candlewick were haunted. By then my lover's name had entered legend and folklore. According to the common tongue Puddlicot's ghost could not, would not, rest.' She paused, head down, her thin, bony shoulders shaking.

'The harrowing of hell has begun,' a voice lisped close to Stephen, 'sharper than the eagle's talon is the vengeance which ploughs the infernal meadows. The trumpet sounds, a clarion call. Stephen, the dead gather. The fires burn!'

The novice glanced in the direction of the window and saw faces pressed there, eyes beseeching, lips curled in supplication.

'I tried to make peace,' Eleanor's voice rasped, drawing Stephen from his reverie. 'I wanted to live a normal life. I became betrothed but that was not to be. As I grew older I became more and more aware of my father, his spirit, the evil he had done. I visited the Franciscans at their house in Greyfriars and confessed all. The good brothers gave me wise counsel. I decided on a life of reparation. I sold all my possessions. I joined the Minoresses and entered their house at Aldgate on one condition: that my mother was given a corrody there, a pension. The good sisters agreed.' She paused. Stephen ignored the tapping on the window, like that of a sharp-beaked bird or the fingers of someone desperate to get in.

'We settled down. We loved the horarium of the house. Brother Anselm, we found peace until the present troubles began. We heard of Rishanger, his murder in the abbey, the two treasures found and the stories about the hauntings at Saint Michael's.'

Stephen tried to shake off the keen cold; he peered around the screen in the hope of catching a glimpse of Alice. Cutwolf stood there, deep in conversation with Master Robert. The henchman glanced up. Stephen withdrew behind the screen.

'We watched you,' Eleanor continued, 'we heard of you, Brother Anselm. We needed to trust you.'

'But not Sir Miles Beauchamp?'

'Oh no, not the royal clerk. Drokensford was a royal clerk. He dragged Puddlicot from the sanctuary, loaded him with chains and sent him to the Tower. After he had been condemned, Drokensford put him in a wheelbarrow – an object of derision – and had him carted through the streets to a gruesome death.' Eleanor sipped at her wine. 'Drokensford never allowed my mother to visit her beloved. Afterwards, I understand, he harassed her constantly.'

'Just for a while.' Joanne spoke up. 'He thought I had information.' The ancient one grinned, pert as a sparrow. 'I did,' she
sighed, 'but what was the use?' She blinked, staring up above
their heads as if searching for something. 'Richard organized
that robbery. He brought the treasure to our house and then
moved it to Saint Michael's. I believe Parson Spigurnel was
going to help by securing safe passage abroad for both of us,
but then Drokensford struck. So yes, I don't like royal clerks,
particularly Beauchamp with his secretive, sly ways, hiding in
that strange house which only his henchmen enter. Anyway,
Richard had to flee to Saint Michael's at the dead of night. I
only visited him once. I drew as close as I could to the sanctuary
chair. I know my daughter has told you this but it is worth
repeating: Richard whispered how he had left me a package,
wrapped in a leather casing buried in our garden, containing
the Cross of Neath and Eleanor's dagger, along with a message.
I asked him about the rest of the treasure – that's when he
repeated the message that it was under the protection of God's
guardian. I suspect he hoped that I would find the treasure and
perhaps use it to negotiate with Drokensford, but I could not
– that clerk was too sharp. He had already ransacked our house
and the garden. Remember, Anselm, I was only sixteen and
bearing a child. I was truly terrified.' She began to sob. Eleanor
put a protective arm around her shoulder.

'Tell me,' Anselm leaned across the table, 'did Puddlicot ever
talk about the Merlin Stone? I will be even blunter, mistress:
did Puddlicot ever dabble in the black arts?' The ancient one
glanced up, watery eyes creased in an impish smile. 'God bless
you, Brother Anselm, but I find that amusing. Puddlicot was a
merry fellow. He could dance a jig and tell a tale. He was a
jongleur, a bully boy, deeply in love with life. He did not pray.
He lived recklessly for the moment so he had no time for magic,
wizards, witches or warlocks. He dismissed them all as
charlatans.'

'The Merlin Stone,' Anselm insisted, 'was part of the treasure
stolen from the crypt?' The ancient one looked at Anselm then
threw her head back, cackling with laughter. 'I do remember
that, small and round as a ball, smooth and polished.' She wiped
her tired eyes on the back of her hand. 'Merlin Stone!' she

scoffed. 'Richard tossed it into the carp pond as a useless piece of rock. He claimed it was man-made, the type of stone you carve from a falling star which has burned out and fallen to earth. He said the good monks of Glastonbury must have been hard at work to smooth that out! As far as I know,' she chuckled, 'Merlin's Stone is still lying at the bottom of that carp pond!'

Even Anselm grinned, lifting his goblet of water in salute. He then told them about the Midnight Man, the disappearance of young women and the grisly murders at St Michael's. Both women sat in shocked silence. Eleanor raised her hand. 'Brother Anselm, how will this end? You say my father's ghost still hovers, that even our prayers have not helped. Will my father's spirit ever find peace?'

'How will it end, Eleanor,' Anselm replied kindly, 'is in the hands of the Lord. I shall tell you something I have not yet told others. I am beginning to understand what happened and that opens further doors. Rishanger was undoubtedly a member of the Midnight Man's coven; that nest of vipers always had an interest in Puddlicot's treasure, probably because of the Merlin Stone. Rishanger and his fellow demons searched that house but found nothing. However, they were also blood-drinkers, feasting and revelling on the bodies of young women whom they slaughtered and buried in that hellish garden. During one such foray, Rishanger stumbled on those two treasures as well as the information Puddlicot had buried with them. This provided further impetus; hence the satanic revels at Westminster and particularly at Saint Michael's. They were intrigued by the written reference to Puddlicot's plunder being guarded by God's protector.'

'The church of Saint Michael's?'

'Of course!' Anselm agreed. 'So, Mistress Eleanor, they performed their rites but these became entangled in some other wickedness and came to nothing.'

'What wickedness?'

'I shall tell you, mistress. I trust you. I will tell you something I have not yet told Sir Miles and the rest: somewhere in that church or cemetery lie other corpses.'

'Why do you say this?'

'Satanic covens need consecrated ground for their filthy blood sacrifices. More practically, I suspect, Rishanger's garden could not hide any more corpses.'

'So many were slaughtered?'

'We are talking of a coven, all blood-drinkers. Perhaps a few of them are women but mostly men.' The exorcist paused. 'I do wonder why cemeteries fascinate the human soul. Is it all the ceremony which goes into them? I have been to the Innocents in Paris, a forest of ornate, carved stone. The rich even try to make their dead flesh sweet, paying butchers to scoop out their entrails and fill their insides with fragrant spices.' Anselm laughed sharply. 'It only makes them tastier for the worms. What does it matter? I was also in Paris when the Pestilence returned. I heard her swish her scythe as she combed the streets, gathering her victims. I saw corpses piled high, the flesh turning a purplish-black, bereft of all soul and spirit. If people like the Midnight Man reflected on such an end, they would give up their filthy ways.'

'Brother Anselm,' Eleanor intervened gently, 'when will you put paid to these nightmares?' The exorcist did not reply but rose to his feet, helping her and her mother, who had now grown sleepy-eyed. The exorcist simply blessed them. Stephen helped both women out from behind the screen. The taproom was now filling up. Tradesmen and tinkers jostled each other. A wandering scholar, his pet weasel in a cage, was offering to chant a poem but no one took any notice. Two relic sellers were inspecting the contents of their sacks. They caught Stephen's eye and invited him over. He ignored them and escorted the two women to the door. The sunshine had gone and a thin drizzle peppered the cobblestones. A man strode through the gates, face hidden in a deep hood, dark cloak billowing out like the wings of a bat. Cutwolf! He did not stop but glanced, mice-eyed, at the two ladies, brushed past Stephen and into the tavern. The ancient one patted Stephen on the arm and leaned heavily against her daughter, who smiled at Stephen.

'So young! I hope what we told your master is of use?'

'I am sure it is,' Stephen reassured her. 'As he said, all these are pointers to the truth.'

'Will we ever be free of it?' Eleanor murmured. 'Years ago I heard a story about a child who found an evil-looking toad in a field. The girl was so frightened, she killed it. That dead toad pursued her night and day, giving her no rest. The girl killed it time and again but the pursuit continued even after it was torched to ashes. The hapless, persecuted girl, to be eternally free of the torment, let her loathsome enemy bite her but escaped death by cutting away the venom-filled wound. Vengeance appeased, and the toad was seen no more.'

'Mistress?'

'Sometimes evil dogs our lives – a host of bats blacking out the sunlight.' She leaned over and kissed Stephen on each cheek. 'I do believe your master will free us from the evil which seems to hound our souls. But remember, Stephen, there will be a terrible price to pay.' Then they were gone, two lonely figures shuffling into the gloaming.

Stephen returned to the taproom to find Cutwolf closeted with his master in the window-seat. 'Sir Miles wants to know what our two guests told us,' Anselm declared drily. 'I have given Brother Cutwolf the gist of it. Sir Miles believes more mischief is afoot, but we also have an invitation to dine with him. You, me, Master Robert and Mistress Alice – it will be grand.'

'My master is most appreciative of your work.' Cutwolf, despite the heavy cloak over his mailed shirt and clinking war belt, was friendly enough. 'The day after tomorrow, just before vespers, he insists that you sup with him.' Cutwolf's voice became teasing. 'Master Stephen, you did ask about my master's house . . .?'

Stephen blushed.

'And now,' Anselm rose, 'we have an appointment with a soul bound for God. Master Bolingbrok awaits us inside Saint-Olaf-all-alone.'

'A small tavern, deep in White Friars,' Cutwolf answered Stephen's puzzled look, 'as different from this as hell from heaven. Don't be disappointed,' Cutwolf added kindly, 'Mistress Alice will be here when you return and remember, the evening after tomorrow, we have our festivities to celebrate.'

Stephen hid his disappointment. He gathered his cloak and sword belt with its long stabbing dirk and sought out Alice. He feverishly kissed her then joined Anselm and Cutwolf, already

striding across the tavern yard. They went up through the
constant drizzle towards St Michael's, a dark mass against the
cloudy sky. They paused for a while by the dripping gates of
that evil-festering cemetery with its heap of tumbled stones and
crosses. Anselm stood staring out over the desolation. Stephen,
busy with his cloak and belt, his mind still full of regret at
leaving Alice, felt the crowding ghosts close in. He gazed down
the empty lane. Figures moved. A shadow rose out of a puddle;
others followed. Restless shapes, as if a mob of demons and
spirits, were mustering. Faint traces of song and conversation
teased Stephen's ear. A waft of heavy perfume came and went.
A raucous voice shouted, 'Harrow! Harrow!' The air turned
abruptly cold. Cutwolf clapped gloved hands on the hilt of both
sword and dagger. Stephen caught his breath. He glanced
towards St Michael's. The cemetery was no longer just a stretch
of moving grass. Tall trees now grew there bristling with thorns,
their leaves like blades of red-hot iron. Near the lychgate a
cauldron, seething with oil, pitch and resin, belched flames of
black, smoky plumes. A huge snake, coiled round the cauldron,
reared its ugly head and breathed out fiery sparks which assumed
a life of their own. Somewhere in the darkness a filthy, grunting
herd of swine rooted and snouted for food, their stench hanging
like a heavy veil. The drizzle seemed to be raining down fresh
horrors.

'Stephen, Stephen!' Anselm was shaking him. The novice
broke from his nightmare, trying to ignore the stabbing pain in
his own head. 'Stephen,' Anselm whispered, 'I can feel the
same. This night is as restless as an evil conscience in a tumbled
bed. Something is about to happen. Pray God we keep safe!'
They walked on. Cutwolf drew sword and dagger as they left
the thoroughfares of Dowgate. They entered the little, crooked,
dog-legged alleys of White Friars, which ran under houses so
dingy they'd turned black, and were so ancient and corrupt they
had to be supported by wooden crutches. Now and again little
knots of figures would break from wallowing in the dirt and
dart like bats into the doorways or alley-mouths. Here human
wolves alongside crime, filth and disease lurked in the shadows
or behind dark doors leading down to even darker vaults and
cellars. Underfoot the path was nothing more than slimy mud

and stinking water. The dungeon-like doors and prison-like windows remained shut. Nevertheless, voices called and trailed. An occasional light flared and dimmed. Cutwolf was recognized, the two Carmelites noted as they made their way through the squalid, hellish maze of the needle-thin paths, their ill-dug sewers crammed with disgusting refuse.

Stephen had to cover his mouth against the constant, pressing, infected smell. He felt frightened. A hideous presence hovered close, hurrying breathless to his right then to the left, only to slip behind him like some threatening assassin. The sweat started on his body. Stephen fought the mounting panic until suddenly, without being bidden, Cutwolf broke into song, his harsh voice intoning St Patrick's Breastplate, a powerful invocation for God's help.

'*Christ be with me,*
Christ behind me,
Christ before me,
Christ beneath me.'

Anselm joined in. Stephen grew calm, and also took up the refrain:

'*Christ in danger,*
Christ in the mind of friend and stranger . . .'

The darkness thinned. The terrors receded as they swung into a narrow street and stopped before the ill-lit St-Olaf-all-alone, the creaking sign with its rough depiction of the northern saint almost hidden by dirt and grime. They pushed open the door into the drinking chamber, a gloomy place lit by the occasional taper glow. The taverner, standing by the board, recognized Cutwolf and snapped at the two oafs guarding the makeshift staircase built into the corner to stand aside. These gallowbirds, who rejoiced in the names of 'Vole' and 'Fang', stepped back into the darkness. Cutwolf led the Carmelites up into the stygian, stinking blackness along a narrow gallery lit by a lantern horn perched on a stool, and into a shabby chamber. Bolingbrok crouched by a pile of sacking which served as a bed. On this sprawled a narrow-faced man; in the mean light of the tallow candle his pallid, unshaven skin shimmered with sweat and blood bubbled between chapped lips as he clutched his belly wound, a soggy, gruesome mess.

'This is Basilisk,' Bolingbrok murmured. 'Thief, assassin, God knows what else. Stabbed over a cogged dice and now bound for judgement.' He leaned down. 'Aren't you, my bully boy?'

Basilisk could only gasp. '*Miserere!*'

'Yes, yes,' Bolingbrok replied. 'I keep my eyes and ears open for the likes of Basilisk. He needs a priest. He couldn't care now about this or that. He has told me one thing, even though he recognized me as a cast-off priest, a defrocked one. We have chattered, Basilisk and I, and he has confessed.'

'To what?'

'To being a retainer of the Midnight Man's coven.'

'As God be my witness,' Basilisk still had his senses, 'I was recruited over a year ago.'

'And how do you meet?' Anselm pushed his way forward to kneel by the bed. Bolingbrok gently withdrew, allowing the exorcist to lean over the dying man. 'The day after every full moon,' Basilisk gasped, 'the summons is posted in terms only we understand. On the great post near the Si Quis door at Saint Paul's. The date, the time and the place.'

'But anyone curious could note these?'

'No, no,' Basilisk whispered, 'the place is numbered – fourteen, for example. We then look for a second bill, written out simply, the number reversed so it is forty-one, which stands for Saint Michael's. The places are well known to us, usually along the mud flats or beyond the city walls.'

'And the Midnight Man?'

'He appears hooded and masked, well-guarded.'

'And the ceremonies?'

'No.' Basilisk glanced at Anselm beseechingly. 'I was only a guard, a retainer – not a member of their coven. I was not present at their filthy rites at Rishanger's house or elsewhere.'

'So what did you do exactly?'

'He was an assassin,' Bolingbrok hissed. 'He was summoned whenever there was killing to be done.'

'Who?' Anselm placed a hand gently on the dying man's chest. 'Who?' he repeated. 'You are to go before God's dread judgement, Basilisk. Hell awaits you, that blind world, mute of all light, dark, deep and cloud-filled. Hell is a horrible valley

where the devils rain down the souls of murderers to melt like
lard in a frying pan and seep through the iron-grilled floor as
molten wax does through a straining cloth. Do you wish to
escape such a place? Then repent, confess, be absolved!'

'I and others,' Basilisk whispered, 'imposed order on the
coven.'

'You mean those who strayed or disobeyed?'

'In *morte veritas*,' Basilisk whispered, 'in death truth.'

'You are schooled? You are a clerk?'

'As God be my witness, a clerk, schooled in the hornbook.
A scholar of Oxford. I served in the King's array and returned
steeped in blood.'

'You were given the names of those the Midnight Man marked
down?'

'Yes, it always meant sentence of death. A grocer in Poultry,
a tanner in Walbrook. We were given both the name and the
house – we never failed. Most of the deaths were judged as an
accident: a fall from a chamber, crushed by a cart or a boating
mishap near London Bridge.'

'And Rishanger?'

'We were ordered to follow him and, if he tried to flee, kill
him. We attacked him at Queenhithe but he fought like a man
possessed.'

Basilisk paused, breathing out noisily, gargling on the blood
filling the back of his throat. He abruptly braced himself against
a shaft of pain.

'I gave him an opiate mixed in heavy wine,' Bolingbrok
whispered. 'He cannot last much longer.' Basilisk began to
ramble, chattering in Norman French, the words 'Mother' and
'Edith' being repeated time and again. Stephen, who had stood
with his back against the shabby door, wiped the sweat from
his face. The chamber was growing unbearably hot; the only
window was a mere arrow slit. Stephen's gaze was drawn to it.
He tensed at the bony, taloned fingers which grasped the rim
of the narrow opening as if some repulsive creature clung to
the rotting masonry outside, desperate to pull it out and force
an entry. 'The hour of greatest darkness!' a voice murmured.
'See the fluttering banners of Hell's Host. The Lords of the
Night gather. The Knights of the Pit prepare for *chavauchée*.

The Dragon's archers string their bows. Judas time! Darkness falls! The Armies of Hell have received their dread writ of array.' Stephen forced himself to look away, to concentrate on Anselm, who was gently stroking the dying man's face. The exorcist paused in a fit of coughing, shoulders shaking at the violent retching. Stephen's heart missed a beat. When this was over, he promised himself, Anselm must visit the best physicians. He wondered if he should write to his own father.

'Rishanger?' The exorcist recovered from his coughing fit.

'We pursued him. Killed him in the abbey but we were unable to find the treasure he had hidden.'

'And?'

'The Midnight Man was furious. We were summoned to a meeting in the ruins of Portsoken but did not go. Since then all has been quiet. There are rumours of a great stirring but . . .'

'A great stirring?'

'The Midnight Man is whistling up his coven – that is all I know.'

'And the other two who were with you at Rishanger's death?'

'Dead,' the man gasped. 'Strange, isn't it? We failed so we, too, were marked for death.'

'And the Midnight Man?'

'I know nothing of him or his coven. Father, please absolve me.'

'Stay outside.' Anselm spoke over his shoulder.

Bolingbrok, Cutwolf and Stephen stepped into the ill-lit narrow gallery. Beauchamp's henchmen stood silently, shadows against the shadows. Stephen glanced through the narrow window – nothing was there, yet he could hear a distant chanting. Stephen closed his eyes and prayed. The gathering was imminent. He recalled Eleanor's words. She was certainly right: this would end in blood. They stayed for a while. The door opened. Anselm stepped out. 'He could tell me no more.'

'He still lives?' Bolingbrok asked.

'Just.'

Bolingbrok stepped around Anselm and, opening the door, entered the chamber. The bolts were drawn; a short while later they were pulled back. Bolingbrok, dagger in hand, stepped out. 'He is gone,' he murmured. 'A mercy cut. No physician could save him. When the opiate faded he would have known hideous pain. He is past all caring and gone to God. We must leave.'

Anselm put his fingers to his lips and, abruptly, without warning, burst into tears. Cutwolf seized his arm but the exorcist shook him off. 'I weep,' he explained, 'at the sheer, soul-harrowing sadness of it all.' The exorcist took a deep breath and crossed himself. 'Let us go.'

They left St Olaf-all-alone and walked briskly back through the streets. Even before they reached Dowgate the smell of burning curled heavy in the air, while a bright orange glow suffused the night sky. Bells began to toll. Lantern horns appeared. Doors opened and shut as they turned through the maze of lanes leading to Saint Michael's. 'The church is on fire!' Anselm exclaimed. They hastened on; the closer they drew, the deeper their alarm. Stephen followed his master who, he noticed, had to stop to relieve his hacking cough. Tendrils of smoke brushed their faces; the smell of burning grew thicker. They rounded a corner and stared in horror. A fire raged through St Michael's; its vivid glow illuminated the church set on top of a slight rise. The windows of the nave were bright with an unholy light. Tongues of flame shot up through the roof. The ward had been alerted. Sir Miles, swathed in a cloak, stood under the rain-drenched lychgate. Beside him, Sir William Higden, Almaric and Gascelyn. A figure lurched out of the dark-ness, slipping and slithering on the grass. Holyinnocent stepped into the pool of torch light. 'The very fires of hell!' he exclaimed. 'Sir Miles, you must come. It is safe. You must see this.'

Beauchamp turned to the two Carmelites, 'Good evening,' he whispered, '*pax et bonum*. You met Master Bolingbrok?'

'We did.'

Sir Miles nodded and indicated that they all accompany Holyinnocent across the cemetery. Stephen followed, staring fearfully at the furious inferno ravaging the black shell of the nave. Window glass had disappeared and all wooden structures must have burst into flame.

'How?' Anselm called out.

'We do not know,' Sir William replied. 'I was a-bed when the tocsin sounded and the alarm was raised. I thought your man Holyinnocent was guarding the lychgate?'

'He was,' Beauchamp snapped tersely, 'while your squire was in the death house.'

'I heard nothing,' Gascelyn declared. 'I woke to the roaring flames. It was so sudden.' Any further conversation was cut off as Holyinnocent led them under the great, canopied yew tree where they'd found the log to breach the sacristy door. At first Stephen thought it was a vision: two shapes hung above the ground, moving soundlessly from side to side. Only when Holyinnocent walked across, joined by Cutwolf, who had fired another sconce, was the full horror revealed. Necks twisted, faces a ghastly blueish-white, eyes popping, mouths gaping, Parson Smollat and his woman Isolda hung from the end of ropes, the nooses tied so tightly around their necks that their flesh was ploughed a rough, bloody furrow. Smollat was dressed in his robes; one boot had slipped off, lying next to the bench both must have stood on then kicked over. Isolda was garbed in a simple robe, soft buskins on her swinging feet, her hands, like those of Smollat, hanging listlessly by her side. Both just dangled, slightly twisting, the yew tree's branches now creaking in protest.

'Their hands?' Holyinnocent muttered.

Anselm inspected them, lifting them up. Even in the poor light, Stephen, standing beside the exorcist, could see that they were blackened. Anselm sniffed at Parson Smollat's and let them drop. 'Oil,' he declared, 'possibly saltpetre. Did they start the fire then come here and hang themselves?'

'So it would seem,' Beauchamp answered. 'Let us inspect them more closely. Bolingbrok, cut them down.'

Sir Miles walked off towards the blazing inferno now consuming St Michael's; even as he did, part of the roof cracked and collapsed in a furious surge of fire and spark. Standing behind him, Stephen stared back across the cemetery.

At the gate Beauchamp and Sir William's retainers were holding back the gathering crowd, assuring them there was nothing to be done. The fire would be left to burn. Sir William had already proclaimed that as there were no buildings standing nearby, the danger was slight. So, apart from the usual warnings about every household being wary of sparks and to have ladders, hooks and buckets of water at the ready, there was nothing to be done for the church.

'A cleansing fire, eh, Stephen?' Anselm, who had finished his inspection, came up to stand beside him.

'What truly happened here, Magister?'

'God knows, but Saint Michael's church is finished.'

Anselm turned away as Beauchamp, along with Cutwolf, strode off towards the priest's house. The henchman's flaring cresset streaked the darkness, the flames flickering in the direction of the church as if they were eager to join that violent conflagration. Stephen continued to watch the fire. Molten lead streaked down the walls, a grey, moving sludge, and the fire had now spread to the tower; an ominous red glow already lit the high open windows. The more Stephen stared at that maelstrom of flame, the deeper his anxiety grew – a chilling apprehension that this fire would do little to cure the evil which hung over this place just as heavy and as real as the thick clouds of smoke now pouring into the night. Stephen caught his breath. He glimpsed movement against the hellish red nimbus around the windows. Figures and shapes moved swiftly, as if the gargoyles and babewyns had come to life and were leaping about the fire.

'*Sanctus, Sanctus, Sanctus,*' the voices sang. '*Dominus Deus Sabaoth* – Holy, Holy, Holy, Lord God of Hosts.'

The choir of voices shrilled across the cemetery. Stephen looked over his shoulder; Bolingbrok and the rest were cutting down the corpses. Gascelyn had managed to provide canvas sheets. They worked unaware of anything apart from the burning church and those two ghastly bodies. The singing, however, low and carrying, came from the other side of the cemetery. Stephen walked across and stared into the night. He swallowed hard, clenching his mouth tight against the apparitions. No longer tendrils of mist or vapour but figures, stark and clear, now gathered threateningly amongst the tombstones and crosses. He could not make out individual faces but they stood unmoving, staring across at either him or the burning church. Gathering his courage, Stephen walked slowly towards them. The cowled figures shifted gently in the gloom. 'Light and peace,' a voice whispered. Stephen started as something raced through the gorse in front of him, rustling the grass: a dark, darting shadow of an animal, snorting and snarling like some fierce dog. Stephen blinked at the abrupt flashes of light. He felt himself shoved in the chest. A face, horrible in every aspect, gasped and mouthed before him. Crouching down, Stephen tried hard to control his panic. The vision disappeared; nothing but the bleak night lit by that conflagration.

Stephen rejoined the rest. Bolingbrok had finished sheeting the corpses. They followed the torch-bearers through the cemetery, across the enclosure and into the priest's house. Stephen was immediately struck by its ordinariness: the kitchen was clean, well-swept and tidy, the great carving table scrubbed a dull white, clear except for a bunch of keys lying on top of a piece of greasy parchment. The rushes on the floor were green and wax-like, the pink-painted walls shiny in the candlelight. The fire in the grate had burnt low, the small ovens either side still warm, the copper and brass pans, pots and cutlery hung orderly on their hooks. The corpses were laid out on the floor. Stephen stared at the ghoul-like faces, twisted and frozen in their final death agonies. Beauchamp and Cutwolf, who had conducted a swift search of the other chambers, strode into the kitchen. 'Nothing!' Beauchamp declared. 'Nothing at all.' Everyone remained silent while Anselm administered the last rites. Once completed and the corpses covered, Cutwolf and the rest guarded the door. The two Carmelites, Beauchamp, Sir William, Gascelyn and Almaric gathered around the great kitchen table.

'The fire broke out suddenly, without warning,' Sir William began. 'It would seem Parson Smollat, God save him, together with his woman Isolda, started it. They moved oil, kindling and other combustibles into the church.' He pointed at the keys. 'Parson Smollat apparently had these all the time. Brother Anselm, you found them and that scrap of parchment on his corpse. Both his hands and those of Isolda were stained with oil and pitch, saltpetre and even grains of cannon powder.'

'I would agree,' Anselm declared.

'Did they commit suicide?' Stephen asked abruptly.

'So it would seem.' Anselm sighed. 'There is no trace of force or imprisonment on their corpses; I was most vigorous in my inspection. My only conclusion is that Parson Smollat and Isolda, for God knows what reason, started that fire then hanged themselves in the shade of that yew tree.' He gestured around. 'Look at this house. Sir Miles, you have searched as carefully as any royal surveyor – nothing is out of place! Both the parson and Isolda appear to have lived a normal life. They apparently finished their evening meal in the kitchen then decided on their own deaths and the destruction of the church they served. Parson Smollat must have quietly purchased oil and other materials.' Anselm paused to clear his throat. 'Parson Smollat even wrote what might be a confession. We shall come to that. However, did he and Isolda act in their right minds? I don't know. The parson also held the keys, which raises the strong possibility that he may have had a hand in Simon the sexton's mysterious death. Was all this deliberate? Or did the infernal powers which haunt this site possess both him and his woman?' Anselm shook his head. 'Sir William, I would be grateful if you would make a careful search of what Parson Smollat bought over the last few days.'

'I can answer that.' Almaric spoke up. 'Parson Smollat was very busy. A cart-load of purveyance was delivered just before Nones today. I thought they were the usual supplies but he must have bought oil and the other kindling.'

'Perhaps,' Sir William spoke up, 'the poor be-knighted fool thought he could cleanse this place.' The merchant knight scratched his unshaven, sweaty cheek. 'Perhaps he and Isolda then regretted it and decided to take their own lives. I shall miss them,' he added sadly. 'Smollat was a good man, though easily frightened. Perhaps he viewed all that had happened as a judgement on himself. Yet in a way he was correct about the purification.'

'What do you mean?' Beauchamp asked sharply.

'Sir Miles, our church is burning. There is nothing we can do about that – let it burn. The ward has been alerted – let the flames spend themselves. Once it is done, we will cleanse this site. I promise,' Sir William became more invigorated, 'a new and splendid church will rise like a phoenix from the ashes.'

'The corpses?' asked Anselm gently. 'If they are suicides, can they have Christian burials? When the news spreads, Sir William, not everyone will be as charitable as you. They will demand that both cadavers be taken to a crossroads outside the city, a stake driven through their hearts and their remains buried beneath some gallows post. Deranged, possessed?' Anselm stretched across the table. 'I cannot say. Parson Smollat certainly scrawled this note. He had it with the keys.' Anselm picked it up. 'It is Parson Smollat's writing?'

'Undoubtedly,' Sir William replied. 'Both myself and Almaric have compared it to other documents found here. Yet it is strange, Brother Anselm. Read it again.'

'"*Habeo igne gladioque destruxi ecclesiam nostram*" – I have, with fire and sword, destroyed our church.' Anselm shrugged. 'Is that a confession? Is he admitting to the fire?'

Beauchamp leaned across and took the parchment script. He read it and handed it back, a fleeting smile crossing his lean, saturnine face. Anselm, too, stared at the parchment and gave it to Stephen, who studied the large bold letters, '*Habeo igne gladioque destruxi ecclesiam nostram*'.

As the novice stared down at the text he felt a shift, a tug at his very soul. 'Now!' a voice whispered. 'All will be revealed. For the fowler's snare will spring, as it shall on every living soul.'

'We should leave.' Beauchamp rose, gathering his cloak and staring at Anselm. 'Let the fire burn itself out. Keep the wardsmen vigilant against sparks. Sir William, I will have my henchmen remove both corpses to the Chapel of Saint Peter Ad Vincula in the Tower. The chaplains will bury them there. No one need know. I have searched this house – there is nothing to prove Smollat or Isolda were members of any coven. Once the corpses are removed, my men will lock and seal the house . . .' He stopped short at the sound of a hideous crash which echoed across the cemetery. Beauchamp picked up his cloak and hurried out, the others following.

'It's the roof,' Cutwolf explained. They entered the cemetery and stared across, the flames leaping through where the roof had been. 'So intense,' Stephen whispered.

'Remember,' Anselm murmured, 'the benches, the chantry chapels, the pulpit, all the furnishings, the drapes, the carvings, those heavy rafter beams. Parson Smollat must have soaked the place in oil.' Anselm's voice trailed off. 'Sir Miles is certainly correct – there is nothing more to be done, and all,' he added in a whisper, 'for a piece of useless rock which is probably lying at the bottom of a slime-filled pond.'

'And the rest of the treasure,' Stephen added.

'That, too,' Anselm declared. 'So many deaths, Stephen – for what? Does it really profit a man if he gains the whole world's treasure but suffers the loss of his immortal soul?'

ooOOoo

Words Amongst the Pilgrims

The physician paused in his tale and filled his water cup. This time no one stirred; his fellow pilgrims realized he was approaching the climax of his story and waited restlessly. Chaucer glanced swiftly around. The haberdasher was drinking so heavily, Chaucer wondered if the man would be fit to ride the next morning. The Wife of Bath's plump red cheeks were wet with tears. The summoner just sat with a sombre look on his face.

'I remember this.' The knight spoke up. 'I, too, was on secret business for the Crown. There were whispers about blood-drinkers roaming the streets and alleyways close to the river, though they weren't the monsters I hunt. And the fire? I was in London at the time. In the end a fine new church was built. Sir William must have . . .'

'Hush now, Sir Godfrey,' the physician called out. 'Softly, let me finish.' The knight nodded in agreement, going back to cradling his tankard.

'Yet this tale is certainly true.' The usually taciturn shipman spoke up. 'Master physician, I have kept a still tongue in my head but I was on board the cog which Rishanger tried to reach. I served my apprenticeship with its captain,' he grinned sourly, 'from whom I learned so much. I watched Rishanger's clash with those assassins on the quayside, his flight up river.'

'Oh, yes,' the physician assured him. 'This is all true.'

'Cloaked in secrecy, it was,' the franklin rose, fingering his snow-white beard.

'What was?' the friar demanded.

'The business at Saint Michael's,' the franklin replied, pointing at the physician. 'A hideous tragedy, yes?'

'Gentle pilgrims all,' the physician stretched out his hands, 'please let me finish my tale.'

ooOOoo

The Physician's Tale

Part Six

The fire at St Michael's had burnt itself out by late the following morning. A heavy pall of smoke hung over the blackened remains of the church. The roof and east wall had collapsed, as had the top sections of the tower. At Beauchamp's order the mysterious deaths of Parson Smollat and Isolda were kept secret; for the rest Sir William Higden came into his own. He hired bully boys under Gascelyn to guard both the cemetery and the church. Of course the gossip and tittle-tattle swept through Dowgate swifter than the wind. Anselm absented himself, returning to White Friars, promising to meet Stephen the following evening at The Unicorn before going on to Beauchamp's house to enjoy a great and splendid supper. Stephen felt a deep disquiet about his master. Anselm was more secretive than ever and the novice sensed that something had happened between the exorcist and the royal clerk.

Alice, however, was full of curiosity about what had occurred. Bright of eye and pert of tongue, she would sidle up to Stephen and ask if this or that were true. Was that rumour genuine? Where was Parson Smollat? What would Sir William do? And did Sir Miles have any news about Margotta Sumerhull? Alice danced around him as merry as a robin in spring. Stephen loved every second of it, although he found it impossible to throw

off the growing sense of disquiet, a menacing threat as if some
malignancy was gathering beyond the veil.

On the night after the fire, Minehost Robert insisted that
everyone retire early as he was sure that the magnificent feast
at Sir Miles' the following evening would go on into the early
hours, long after the monks had finished their chants at Matins
and Prime. Alice, eyes all teasing, said she had to bathe and
lay out her gown and kirtle which, she proclaimed, would
outshine that of Lady Moon, Mistress Alice Perrers, the
resplendent mistress of the old King. Stephen pretended to be
shocked that Alice could even know of such things. Alice then
delved into her wallet and produced a beautiful, oval-shaped
medal of St Joseph, a thin wafer of silver on its own chain. She
slipped this around Stephen's neck, nuzzling his cheek with her
hair as she breathlessly whispered how she must fix the clasp
properly. Stephen felt her warm, full breasts against his chest
and tried to kiss her but, laughing softly, she stepped back out
of reach. Stephen glanced down at the medal. 'You told me
about your father,' she murmured, 'so I brought you a medal
of Saint Joseph. I mean, if he guarded the Lord God, he will
certainly guard you. Now,' she grinned cheekily, 'I must be
gone.' And away she whirled, but not before dragging Marisa
from a shadowy corner where 'the little imp', as she called her
younger sister, was hiding and spying once again.

As they both scurried away, Stephen looked down at the
medal with its slightly embossed figure of Joseph holding the
Divine Child. He recalled the ancient wooden statue of the same
saint on its plinth in the small chantry chapel at St Michael's.
The fire would have reduced all that to ash. A thought occurred
to him about the riddle Puddlicot, also a carpenter, had left. He
dismissed this. Stephen wanted to forget all that, at least for a
while. He bade Minehost Robert good night and climbed the
stairs. Stephen reached his own small garret and, feeling
suddenly tired, lay down on the bed. When he awoke, night
had fallen, black against the small casement window. An
ominous humming made him sit up. He stared in horror at the
figure seated on the corner stool. The old woman's face, subtle
and cruel as a hunting cat, could be seen through the red net
mesh, lit clearly by the candle pot held between her hands. She

just sat, a figure of heart-rending terror – not moving, just staring wickedly at him. Panic seethed within him. Stephen shivered at the pressing cold, repelled by the reek as if from the foulest latrine. 'In God's name!' he exclaimed. He felt his cheek brushed, turned and screamed as the old woman's face now pressed close to his, those milky green eyes, the purple lips curled back to reveal blood-red, toothless gums, her skin black-spotted with age. He threw himself off the bed, feverishly clutching the medal Alice had given him, and pulled open the door. Stepping into the stairwell Stephen felt a savage jab to his back which would have sent him crashing down the steep stairs but, catching the guide rope attached to the wall, he was able to stop and turn. The stairwell was empty. Nursing a bruised arm, Stephen cautiously re-entered the bed chamber, quietly mouthing a prayer for protection. He heard a siren's voice call his name and walked over to the casement window, pushed it open and stared down. The cobbled yard below was full of young women with straggling hair. They were staring up at him beseechingly, dark-ringed eyes in deathly white faces, hands raised in supplication. The window swung back; he caught it and looked again. The courtyard was empty.

Stephen returned to a fitful sleep. He awoke, heavy-headed, and found even Alice's glee at the prospect of Sir Miles' supper difficult to bear. Anselm appeared, coughing into his rag. He asked Stephen to accompany him up to St Michael's, where Higden's bully boys allowed them through into the godforsaken cemetery. Stephen was aware of presences, of whispering voices on the misty morning air as they walked up the winding path and through the corpse door, which had simply crumbled into blackened shards.

'Parson Smollat bought oil by the barrel – skins of it, along with saltpetre. He even obtained some precious cannon powder. Drenched the place, he did.' Anselm's voice echoed hollowly through the burnt shell of the nave.

Faint sparks still rose and trails of smoke continued to circle and twist. The church had been truly devastated. The sanctuary, altar, pulpit, rood screen, reredos and chantry chapels no longer existed. The fire had licked the plastered walls and stripped them clean. Only a pure stone statue of St John the Baptist, its face now unrecognizable, remained. Stephen walked over to the chantry chapel of St Michael's and stared at the devastation.

'The entire site will be levelled,' Anselm intoned. 'Not one stone left upon another.'

'As the lightning strikes from the east,' a voice called, 'and appears in the west, so sudden will it be.'

'The gloom gathers,' another voice shrilled, 'the darkness deepens. Where the corpses lie, the vultures will gather.'

Stephen glanced around. Were those dancing sparks, the trails of black and grey smoke, the remains of the fire or something else? And were those motes milling through the air only an outward sign of inward things? 'I feel apprehensive, Magister.'

Fingering the medal Alice had given him, Stephen wandered over to where the small chantry chapel of St Joseph had stood: everything, including the beautiful wall paintings, had been destroyed. Anselm came over and Stephen showed him the medal. Anselm simply stared then, quietly whispering to himself, walked away. Stephen stood rooted to the spot. He glanced up at the church. A pall of smoke hung over the sanctuary. Stephen started as a figure, veiled in red, moved swiftly through the murk and was gone. A voice shouted. Anselm walked over and stood staring down at the floor.

'Magister?'

'Saint Bernadine of Siena,' the exorcist declared distractedly. 'He was a Franciscan. He and his order promoted devotion to Saint Joseph. Ah, well.' They left the church and cemetery. Stephen was glad to be away. Anselm absent-mindedly remarked how they would meet at The Unicorn then he strode off, lost in his own thoughts.

For the rest of the day Stephen tried hard to distract himself as he worked in the tavern kitchen, assisting the cooks, learning the mysteries of minced chicken relish or spiced capon in a nutted wine sauce. He breathed in the fragrances of poached plaice with mustard or the sweetness of veal and custard pie. Now and again that deep sense of foreboding would close in around him; a choir of ghostly voices chanted their verses. 'Why must we stand and face the ice storm of hell's spears? The sword blizzards threaten. The she-wolf presses her paw on the swollen, fatted corpse. Hail stones fall. Cloud pebbles clash against the shield wall.' Eventually the voices faded and a face with snake-sharp eyes and angry mouth appeared, only to merge into a blaze of burning blue embers. Stephen whispered his prayers and kept to the task in hand.

At last the day finished. Master Robert handed over his tavern to the care of his steward and principal cook. The hour of Vespers was approaching; they had to make ready. Alice appeared in a beautiful gold-spotted gown of Lincoln green with a high-encrusted collar of silver lace, a girdle of gold around her slim waist. She wore blood-red ankle boots with silver buckles on her feet. She had prepared her hair and covered it with the lightest of white lawn veils, adding a little paint to her face. Stephen had never seen such beauty. He called her 'his fairy princess from the bright grassed lands of the west'. She laughed merrily then clapped her hands as her father appeared resplendent in a russet cotehardie with a matching cloak. Anselm arrived, angular, ascetic and distracted. They made their farewells to the leaping Marisa and walked the short distance to Beauchamp's fine house, standing in its own high walled courtyard. Cutwolf, all sardonic, welcomed them into the plain but sweet-smelling entrance hall and led them through the house, down the paved passageway, past rooms closed and locked and into the courtyard, which overlooked a splendid garden bounded on all three sides by a high, red brick wall.

Sir Miles, garbed in a gorgeous tabard, greeted them and led them into a specially erected garden pavilion embellished with a blue and gold awning with tassels of delicate silver. The sheets on either side had been pulled back and fastened to poles so the fine walnut table, elaborately decorated, was plain to see. Sir William Higden and Gascelyn were already there; the merchant knight, shaven and oiled, was dressed magnificently in cloth of gold robes. Sir Miles clapped his hands, ushering everyone to their seats. Brother Anselm was on his left, Sir William to his right and then Stephen. Alice was beside him and Gascelyn was on the other side, next to Cutwolf. Musicians with citoles, flutes, clarions and fiddles played gentle music in a small covered pavilion further down the garden. Matilda Makejoy, a well-known saltatrix, delighted them with somersaults and handsprings to the heart-plucking sound of an Irish harp. Servitors brought iced wine and drinks of crushed juice. Once Matilda had finished, the soup was served, ground capon thickened with almond milk and spiced with slices of pomegranate and red comfits.

Alice was beside herself with joy, clutching Stephen's hand, while Master Robert basked in the favour being shown them. Stephen glanced quickly at Beauchamp and Anselm; they sat, heads close together. Both men, despite the festivities, looked grim. They drew apart as the cook, specially hired by Beauchamp, came to announce the main dish or *entremet*: crayfish set in jelly, loach and young rabbits. The cook withdrew and reappeared with the food to a flourish from the musicians. Evening set in. The coloured lanterns, lashed to poles driven into the green lawn, were lit. Stephen turned to speak to Alice and, as he did, the nightmare swept in. For a few heartbeats, joy and splendour all shattered as the crossbow bolts struck. A musician, hit full in the mouth, half-rose, hands flailing in terror. Silence descended, and then a fresh volley. Servitors and musicians reeled away as the barbed quarrels split their flesh. Stephen rose. Black-garbed figures were scaling the high red brick wall and leaping down into the garden. The music and laughter abruptly died. Cutwolf was on his feet, sword out; Beauchamp, too, screaming over his shoulder, pushing Anselm away. Stephen grabbed Alice, who was sitting round-eyed in shock; only then did he notice the black quarrel embedded deep in her chest. He picked her up, even as the blood bubbled between her lips, aware of Master Robert and Cutwolf thronging beside him. He turned and, carrying Alice, ran back towards the house.

Beauchamp was screaming at Cutwolf and Bolingbrok that Stephen and his companions be protected. The clerk then staggered back, dropping his sword as a bolt took him deep in the shoulder. Anselm went to help but Cutwolf and Bolingbrok pushed him away, driving Stephen and Master Robert back along the stone-vaulted passageway towards the main door. Alice now hung limp in Stephen's arms. They burst through the entrance, out into the street. More figures garbed in black leather were waiting. Cutwolf and Bolingbrok fought like men possessed, swords and daggers flickering out, sharp and sudden like the fangs of a viper. At last they were clear, running along the dark-filled lanes, throwing themselves into The Unicorn where, sweat-soaked, they collapsed to the floor of the taproom. Stephen laid Alice gently down. She was past all help, eyes staring dully in her corpse-white face. Stephen crouched down beside her, bringing his knees up. He screamed all the pain and anguish which held him tight. Anselm squatted beside him for a while. Cutwolf and Bolingbrok arrived and gently prised loose Stephen's tight hand clasp on the dead girl. They lifted the corpse up and took it away. Stephen heard the soul-chilling cry of both Alice's father and the inconsolable Marisa. He laid down on the taproom floor and sobbed.

The following morning Anselm shook him awake and forced a bitter, tangy drink between his lips. Stephen fell asleep and, when he woke, he was in his chamber, lying sweat-soaked on the bed. Anselm sat cross-legged, his back to the chamber door. 'She is dead, Stephen,' the exorcist said gently. 'Alice is dead. Master Robert is in shock. Marisa cries unendingly. Stephen, we must go.'

'Where, master?' Stephen retorted, pulling himself up. 'Shall we pray in church? Gibber some litanies?'

'Hush now.' Anselm left and returned with a bowl of broth. He forced Stephen to eat this then put on his boots, collected his cloak and war belt and followed him down to the deserted taproom. The tavern was closed. Cypress branches wrapped in purple and black cloths draped windows and doors. Master Robert was nursing his own grief with Marisa. Cutwolf and Bolingbrok sat on a bench near the courtyard door. Stephen was surprised. Both men were closely shaved, their hair shorn and dressed smartly in the dark green and brown of royal clerks. Both wore chancery rings on their fingers, war belts carrying sword and dagger circled their waists beneath the sleeveless blue, red and gold tabard of the King's household. The two men were grim and resolute. They offered no sympathy, no condolences, no grieving. Stephen found this strangely welcoming. They just stood, donned their cloaks, adjusted their war belts and led them out into the mid-morning street. Others waited: royal archers from the Tower wearing the livery of the secret chancery, hard-eyed veterans who

circled them under Cutwolf's direction and led them back to
Beauchamp's house.

Stephen felt as if he was going back through a dream: the
passageway, the garden with its beautiful awning, the table, the
candles and lanterns. All signs of the attack had been cleared
away except for the occasional shard or broken platter resting
against the leg of a table. Only dark blotches staining the chairs
and paving stones or flecks of dried blood against the grass and
pavilion poles showed how some outrage had occurred. The
garden still stretched, sweet-smelling and orderly, under a
strengthening sun. Stephen caught the full echoes of the heinous
affray which had shattered his life. 'The war ghost is aroused,'
a voice murmured, 'red and slashed is the ground.' Faint shapes
swirled before Stephen's eyes. 'Welcome!' the voice repeated,
'to the dark-hued war hawks' blood bath. Beware of the grey
eagle's grasping beak.'

Stephen felt he had to break free of all this. 'Sir Miles?' he
asked.

'Stephen, prepare yourself.' They left the ornate finery of the
garden and re-entered the house. Cutwolf, at Anselm's behest,
took them from chamber to chamber. Stephen could only gape.
Every single room they entered was bleak, devoid of all furnishings except for a stark black crucifix nailed to the walls. The
kitchen had nothing but a fleshing table and stools with different
pots, skillets and kitchenware hanging from their hooks. The
buttery cupboard was devoid of anything but a loaf, a pot of
butter, a jug of milk and a flagon of wine. Upstairs was no
different: empty and bleak, free of all ostentation. Only one
chamber was in use, the huge aumbry and the deep chest beside
it crammed with quilted jerkins, hose, shirts, boots and belts.
They entered the bed chamber, as austere as the rest. Again,
nothing but the essentials of a lowly chancery clerk. A table
with all the necessaries stood beneath the window, beside it a
writing stool and an armoured chest. Beauchamp's corpse,
garbed in the flour-white robes of a Carthusian, lay stretched
out on the narrow cot bed, the cowl pulled full over his head
to frame a face so serene it looked as if he was asleep.

Stephen stumbled, hitting the chest with his knee. 'I cannot
understand,' he gasped, rubbing his leg.

'Neither can I, Stephen.' Anselm led the novice over and pulled down the Carthusian robe to reveal the sharp hair shirt beneath.

Stephen gazed at the now peaceful face, the long fingers embroidered with a set of glass Ave beads. 'What is this?' Stephen glanced at Cutwolf and Bolingbrok.

'You once wondered, Master Stephen.' Cutwolf, standing on the other side of the bed, replaced the sheet of gauze linen over his master's face. 'You did,' he forced a smile, 'wonder about my master? Why he invited no one here? Now you know, as does Brother Anselm!'

'Sir Miles.' Anselm slumped down exhausted on a stool, a linen rag to his mouth. 'Sir Miles,' he repeated, 'was certainly not what he appeared to be. He dressed and acted like a wealthy, powerful royal clerk, yet in many ways he was an ascetic. I have found only three books in this house: the Bible, Boethius' *Consolations* and Augustine's *Confessions*. I understand from Cutwolf that Beauchamp often fasted, gave most of his revenue, very discreetly, to the poor and took the Sacrament each day.' Anselm rubbed his face. 'When he wanted to, Beauchamp could act the part. Outside he would dine and entertain, even act the cynic but, like his dress, that was only for show. The hair shirt and the fast were more real to him than the silken doublet and the deep bowled cup of claret. He truly followed Christ's advice about not letting the left hand know what the right was doing.'

'My master swore us to secrecy,' Cutwolf declared. 'He told me once that, if he survived, he would leave this world for a Carthusian cell.'

'If he survived?' Stephen asked.

'Our master,' Bolingbrok declared, '"dealt with" *Res Tenebrarum*, the Things of the Dark: warlocks, wizards, sorcerers, witches, all the lords and ladies of the night. The Midnight Man was his special quarry. Sir Miles was like a hunting lurcher. He would not give up. He realized that this was a duel to the death in that implacable silence which seems to shroud such wickedness. In a word, Sir Miles recognized that he, as well as other innocents like your beautiful maid, would be caught up in the bloody maelstrom of this horrendous spiritual battle.' Bolingbrok sighed noisily. 'He always said he would make a mistake and he did. He never thought the Midnight Man would be so audacious and yes,' he held up a hand, 'we are sure that he and his coven were responsible for this.'

'Did you examine their dead?' Anselm asked.

'We had little time,' Cutwolf declared. 'Sir Miles was struck mortally in the shoulder. Holyinnocent held him as he died.' Cutwolf fought back his tears. 'Sir Miles believed the attackers came for you. He whispered that you, Anselm, would bring justice. Will you?'

'Their dead?' Anselm insisted.

'Musicians and servitors were killed. Sir William received a flesh wound but he and Gascelyn fought their way into a chamber and barred the door. Mad with fury, Sir William has returned to his own mansion. He has dismissed all his servants, fortified his house and despatched urgent letters to the King.'

'Their dead?' Anselm persisted, cold and hard as if quoting a refrain.

'Brother, we killed some of them both in the garden and in the street beyond, but they took their dead and wounded with them.'

Stephen stared at the corpse of a man he now realized he truly liked and admired. Beauchamp was all he wanted to be: courteous, learned, skilful, a powerful presence and now, he had learned shamefacedly, a man of deep spirituality. 'The wolf's mane ruffles,' a voice murmured, 'the shield wall closes against Satan, a raging boar all tuskered and fiery eyed. The blades, all crimsoned, flicker out, hungry for flesh. The war bands gather.' Stephen could only listen – he felt useless, weak.

'My master,' Cutwolf's voice was as sharp as the finest blade, 'Brother Anselm, believed you are close to the truth.'

'I am,' the exorcist replied wearily, 'much closer than I ever thought.'

'Sir Miles believed that they came for you, to capture or kill you both. You know they will come again?'

'I know,' Anselm murmured. He rose to his feet, sketched a blessing above the corpse then grasped Stephen's hand. 'Cutwolf, we shall meet later but here in this house. Worlds have died. When, why and how does not concern me so much as the evil which spawned it.'

The two Carmelites left. Stephen felt cold, as if a stone was wedged in his chest. Anselm no longer mattered. The grief and shock of Alice's swift and brutal death were only feeding the embers of an ever greater fire: hatred for those responsible, revenge for the mortal wrong these demons had inflicted. Stephen felt as if he was walking through a white-hot desert: no colour, no life, no touch, no smell, just a blazing, white rocky path which stretched into a blinding, searing light. He did not know what to do except plod on. Somewhere, surely, he thought, he would find peace and rest.

'The sunlight's died,' a voice whispered, 'stony inner parts where the flesh throbs and the blood pounds. No eyes, nothing but blinding darkness from empty, staring sockets.' A face, faithful to such a grisly description, swam in front of the novice.

'Stephen?' Anselm gently squeezed his hand. They had arrived at The Unicorn. The exorcist kissed him gently on the brow, pushed him through the half-open door and left. Stephen entered. The taproom, still sweet-smelling, was deserted. Only the chief cook sat in a darkened corner, cradling a tankard of ale. He beckoned Stephen over. 'Master Robert,' he whispered, 'will leave tomorrow. He is taking his daughter's corpse back to the West Country for burial. He,' the cook wiped the tears from his cheeks, 'does not want to look on your face again. He wants you gone.'

Stephen, eyes brimming, thundered up the stairs. He tried to enter Alice's chamber. The ostlers on guard gently but firmly drove him away. He could not stand the grief, the anger seething within him. He hurtled back down the stairs, across the taproom and out into the yard. He stopped abruptly. Anselm stood waiting by the gateway. 'I thought that might happen,' the exorcist called softly. 'Come, Stephen, let us return to our house and grieve quietly. Pray and prepare.'

They returned to White Friars. Stephen felt as if he was still imprisoned in that hot, arid wasteland, just wandering, struggling along some scorched path past bushes and brambles twisted black by a sun which pounded down like a hammer on an anvil. He attended Mass and divine office but all he could think of was staggering through the streets with Alice's body, all bedecked in beauty, dying in his arms. On the third day after his return, once the colloquium was finished and the sunlight beginning to fade, Anselm came into his cell. The exorcist's face was sharp, sallow and sweat-soaked. 'I have prayed, Stephen, I truly have. I must conduct one final exorcism at Saint Michael's, but first I must drink. You will come with me.'

They left the convent and made their way through the bustling streets. Hawkers, traders and apprentices bawled for business. Beadles lashed the buttocks of a whore pinioned to the tail of a cart. A beggar, crushed by a runaway horse, lay dying in a doorway ministered to by a Friar of the Sack; three court fops stood close by laying wagers on how soon the man would die. Windows opened and pisspots were emptied. A young moon girl offered posies of flowers for good luck. A jongleur sang about a blood-drinker who had walked the far side of the moon. Further along a trader, standing on a barrel, declared he had imported a new type of leather from Spain. Jumbled, tangled scenes. Stephen felt as if he was being hurried through hot, dusty passageways. He shook his head to be free of such fancies, back to trudging through narrow, noisy streets, where life in all its richness ebbed and flowed.

Anselm abruptly paused outside a small tavern, The Glory of Hebron. He pushed Stephen inside the dark, close taproom. Taking a table near the window, the exorcist demanded a jug of the best claret, two cups and a plate of bread, dried meats and fruit. Once the servitor had laid the table, Anselm leaned over. 'Listen, Stephen, grief is in your very marrow – it freezes your heart and numbs your soul.' Anselm paused, beckoning at him to share out the wine. 'This is the first I have drunk for years.' The exorcist supped deeply and smacked his lips. 'As Saint Paul says, "take a little wine for the stomach's sake" and the Psalmist is correct, "wine truly gladdens the heart of man". Well, Stephen.' He waited until the novice had swallowed a generous gulp. 'The confrontation is imminent; we must be vigilant. We will return to White Friars and, as the Psalmist again says, "pray to the Lord who readies our arms for battle and prepares our hands for war". I brought you here to stir your wits,' he grinned, 'and I believe they are stirred – wine is good for that.' Anselm lifted his goblet. 'You are with me, Stephen, *usque ad mortem* – to the death? I must be sure of this.'

The novice raised his own cup. 'Magister, as always, *a l'outrance de siècle à siècle* – to the death and beyond!'

They finished their meal and returned to White Friars. Stephen continued, despite his best efforts, to remain and brood in that bleak landscape of his soul. Anselm became very busy, paying the occasional visit to reassure the novice. Although Stephen tried to act courteously, still all he could think about was Alice. He returned to The Unicorn only to find it locked and barred. The watchman on guard brusquely declared how Master Robert had taken his daughter's corpse back to the West Country. Only then did the fiery flickers of anger return, a thirst for revenge, an implacable urge to confront and challenge the dark forces which had caused the death of his beloved.

A few days after returning to White Friars, early in the evening, Anselm came looking for him. Stephen was sitting cross-legged in the Lady chapel, staring hard at the carved, beautiful face of the Virgin. Anselm, cloaked and booted, carried 'his holy bag', the pannier containing sacred water, oils, crucifix and an asperges rod, all the necessary items for an exorcism.

'Stephen,' Anselm snapped his fingers briskly, 'we must go. I believe we have found the treasure.' The exorcist would say no more. The novice hurried back to his own cell, putting on a stout pair of sandals and swinging his cloak about him in readiness.

'The battle lords of hell muster,' a voice growled from behind him. 'The strong, grasping warriors of Hades swing sharp swords from their fiery scabbards. The greedy carrion birds' claws will soon redden. The hawk lords gather.' Stephen whirled around. A man, hair and face chalky white, garbed in clothes of the same hue, stood staring at him. 'The dark caves lie open. The serpents' field awaits.' The voice came soft as a breath. Stephen dropped his cloak. He bent down and picked it up; when he glanced again both vision and the voice had gone, only Anselm rapping on the door telling him to hurry.

They left and reached St Michael's. The guards at the cemetery had been withdrawn – only a surly-faced Gascelyn stood vigil under the lychgate. Stephen could feel the tension rise as they made their way up into the cracked, blackened remains of the nave. Anselm wasted no time shouting at Gascelyn, who was trailing behind them, to bring the iron bars and picks he had asked for. Once that sombre custodian of the dead had done so, Anselm, directing Stephen, began to prise loose one of the paving stones which had formed the floor of the small chantry chapel to St Joseph. 'You know why,' Anselm whispered hoarsely. 'Stephen, we could wait to be taken, or we could set our own trap. Go and look at Saint Michael's.'

The novice put down the iron bar he had been trying to wedge into a small gap between the paving stones and walked over. The floor of the chantry chapel of St Michael's was now nothing more than a pit, the paving stones from it packed against the wall. Someone had already searched there. He walked back. The church lay threateningly silent except for Anselm trying to prise loose that same paving stone. No visions, no voices – nothing but this empty clanging. Stephen went to assist the exorcist.

'Good,' Anselm breathed, 'it is time!' Stephen turned. Higden, Almaric and Gascelyn, all heavily cloaked, stood on the top sanctuary step. All three walked slowly down, footsteps echoing through the nave. 'Good evening, Brother Anselm. I received your message and here I am. What are you doing?' Higden demanded. His two companions, cloaks billowing about them, sat down on the plinth along which the wooden screen to the chantry chapel had once stood.

'I am searching for Puddlicot's treasure. He claimed,' Anselm broke from his labours, 'it was guarded by God's protector. Everyone thought this was Saint Michael Archangel, this church, the cemetery or even the chantry chapel. Sir William, I have read the writings of the Franciscan Bernadine of Siena who fostered the cult to Saint Joseph. He called him God's protector, which he was, the Guardian of the Divine Child. Puddlicot, like you, Curate Almaric, was once a carpenter, hence my deduction. The treasure must be buried here in this chapel?'

'But Cutwolf, Bolingbrok?' Sir William asked.

'They are busy on other matters. They are spent; I don't trust them.' Anselm shook his head. 'Not since the death of Sir Miles. By the way, your wound?'

'Only superficial, a cut to the arm,' Higden replied, slowly getting to his feet. He shrugged off his cloak, and his companions did the same. Stephen shivered. All three, even the curate, wore war belts, while Gascelyn carried a wicked-looking arbalest.

'Protection,' Higden murmured, following Stephen's gaze. 'We must be on our guard.' Higden's face was now feverish. He and his two companions began to help prise loose the paving stones. Stephen privately thought Anselm was being foolish. He, too, had wondered about the phrase 'God's protector', but surely? They loosened one paving stone, pulling it loose. Stephen gaped at what lay beneath. Higden shouted with joy. Anselm crouched in a fierce fit of coughing, nodding his head and pointing at the rotting piece of wood they had now uncovered. It looked like a trapdoor. Gascelyn, as excited as his master, dug in his pick and wrenched it back to expose the pit beneath.

'I suspected that,' Anselm declared, recovering from his coughing bout. Stephen's heart lurched at the sight of the blood-soaked rag in the exorcist's hand, the red froth bubbling at either corner of Anselm's mouth.

'I suspected,' Anselm breathed heavily, 'this was once the church's secure pit, a place to hide sacred vessels and other treasures during times of trouble.'

Higden and his companions ignored this; stretching deep into the pit, they drew out heavy leather sacks coated with dust and tied tightly around the neck with rotting twine. Sack after sack was pulled up – six in all. They shook out the contents: small caskets, coffers, minute chests with leather casings, all crammed with jewels, diamonds, silver and gold ornaments. Pectoral collars, rings, bracelets, gems, pearls and coins rolled out.

'If you are looking for Merlin's Stone,' Anselm murmured, leaning his back against the wall, 'well, it's not there. It lies at the bottom of Rishanger's filthy carp pond, a useless piece of black star rock.' Higden and his henchmen sobered up, eyes narrowed in their flushed, ugly faces. They got to their feet. Anselm began to laugh, which ended in a choking cough. 'A piece of stone,' he mocked, 'lying in the slime, though I reckon that's much purer than your souls.'

Stephen felt a deep coldness wrap around him.

'Brother Anselm, we came because you asked us,' Higden snapped. 'We came in peace.'

'I invited you here, Sir William, because you are the Midnight Man and these are your two minions. I invited you before you could take me and mine as you did Sir Miles.'

'Nonsense!' Higden's voice carried a hideous threat. 'Remember, I was with Sir Miles. I . . .'

'A simple flesh wound, Sir William. Your assassins were under strict orders as to whom to kill and whom to ignore. Sir Miles had to be removed because he was our protector – he knew too much, he was hunting you. Cutwolf openly proclaimed a reward for knowledge about the Midnight Man. In the end Sir Miles suspected you, Sir William – he told me so. You sensed that. He had to die, then you would deal with us. You must have wondered if we were close to the truth about this treasure – that's why you tried to abduct Stephen. I dropped hints about how close we were and you couldn't wait.'

'Brother Anselm, we are here,' Almaric protested.

'Of course you are,' Anselm pointed at Higden, 'you two alone know his true identity. The other members of your coven only see the Midnight Man as a powerful, hideously masked figure who deals out death at his night-drenched meetings. Let me guess,' making himself more comfortable against the wall, Anselm pressed home his attack, 'we now have the treasure while the cemetery is no longer guarded. Stephen and I, if we were not having this conversation, would be allowed to leave, escorted back to White Friars by Gascelyn. On the way something would happen. Another bloody attack. Gascelyn would be wounded – not seriously – but Stephen and I would die. Two more victims of the Midnight Man, yes?'

'And this treasure?' Higden taunted, squatting down. 'I just keep it? How do I know that you and Sir Miles have not drafted some secret memorandum to the Crown detailing your suspicions about me?'

Anselm pulled a face. 'And what proof would I offer?'

Higden shrugged.

'I admit there would be very little – perhaps none at all,' Anselm conceded. 'Sir William, I used to gamble. I gambled on your greed. You planned to come here. If we had not found the treasure tonight – well, our deaths could be delayed. But we have and, as I've said, something is going to happen to us on our journey back to White Friars. You, Sir William, would take all this to profit yourself. You intend to search this treasure for what you want: Merlin's Stone and any other magical items you believe might help you in the black arts. You'd keep them hidden for your own use. You would then offer the Crown the rest of this treasure hoard. You would receive, as finder, at least a tenth of its value, a fortune indeed. You would also, by handing it over, win great favour with the Crown. The King would regard you as a close friend. More favours, more patronage, more concessions, more wealth would flow your way. Any suspicions about you would be choked and strangled off. You would emerge more powerful to continue your midnight practices, be it as a blood-drinker or as a warlock. If Sir Miles and I had left any such memorandum, it would be ignored, being flatly contradicted by your actions. You would dazzle the King with this wealth. Any suspicions about your loyalty would disappear like smoke on a summer morning.'

'So you have no proof.' Gascelyn picked up the crossbow. Stephen flinched as the henchman took a bolt from the small, stout quiver on his belt.

'Proof, Gascelyn, proof – what does it matter now? You know, Sir William knows, Almaric knows. You cannot let us walk free.'

Higden edged closer, head slightly to one side. 'You're a curious one, Anselm. I am fascinated by you. We could tell each other so much.' He grinned, eyes widening in mock surprise. 'Learn from each other.' He gestured at the heaped treasure. 'This is ours, you are ours. What can you do? What proof do you really have, eh?'

Anselm got to his feet. Sir William followed, hand going for his sword hilt. Gascelyn slipped a barb into the groove of the small arbalest.

'I have already told you that I was a gambler, Sir William,' Anselm replied curtly. 'I used to be a sinner to the bone. My offences were always before me. Drinking, lechery and above all gambling.' He smiled thinly. 'I truly gambled tonight. I gambled that you would come. I wagered that I would find the treasure. I offered odds that you would act as you have.'

'Odds?'

'I was right.' Anselm abruptly threw his head back. '*De*

profundis!' he shouted with all his strength. '*Clamavi ad te Domine. Domine exaudi vocem meam* – Out of the depths I have cried to you, oh Lord. Lord, hear my voice!'

Higden and his two henchmen, taken by surprise, could only finger their weapons. Stephen jumped to his feet as a fire arrow arched through the night sky and smashed in a flutter of heavy sparks on to the floor of the nave. Two more followed before Higden and his henchmen could recover. Dark shapes appeared in the doorways and gaps of the ruined church. Hooded archers, war bows strung, arrows notched. They slowly spread out across the nave; behind them swaggered Cutwolf, Bolingbrok and Holyinnocent, their swords drawn.

'What is this?' Higden drew himself up, 'What is this?' He pointed accusingly at Anselm. 'You said you didn't trust them.'

'I was deceiving you. I also thank you for withdrawing your own guards. Master Cutwolf, Clerk of the Secret Chancery, has been watching you; he has certainly been watching me. I welcome him to this colloquium – this discussion.'

'You have levelled serious allegations,' Almaric blurted out. 'What real proof do you have?'

'Oh, I shall show you that,' Anselm replied. 'Master Cutwolf, ask your archers to withdraw slightly but be ready to loose.' Anselm sat down, gesturing with his hand. 'All of you do likewise.'

Higden looked as if he was going to protest. He looked over his shoulder at Cutwolf then reluctantly obeyed, untying his war belt to sit more comfortably, though his sword hilt was not far from his fingers. The other two followed. Stephen watched. Higden was cunning, powerful, the weight of evidence against him seemed slight; after all, he had come to this church at Anselm's bidding. They had found the lost treasure. Higden could still hand this over and appear as the King's own hero.

'You Higden, Gascelyn and Almaric, are blood-drinkers,' Anselm began. 'You hunt and capture young women. You abuse them and kill them. You enjoy the power. You love watching a woman suffer before she dies. I met your like in France and elsewhere. War, for you, is simply an excuse for your filthy, murderous practices.'

'How dare you!' Almaric snarled.

'Shut up!' Anselm paused over a fit of coughing. 'All of you, shut up! You three, together with men like Rishanger, served abroad. You plundered the French. You raped and murdered but the great hole in your soul has a deeper, more sinister darkness. You are warlocks, wizards. You dabble in the damned arts and converse with the demon lords of the air. You may have even used your victims' blood to further this. The sacrifice of cockerels and night birds is nothing compared to that of a human heart, or a chalice full of some young woman's hot blood.'

'Proof?' Higden insisted.

'Yes, proof?' Gascelyn repeated. 'You will need proof before the King's Bench, for the Justices in Eyre. Your madcap theories are not enough.'

'You returned to England and continued your filthy practices.' Anselm's voice was almost conversational. 'Rishanger's lonely garden with its secret cellar or pit was ideal. Young women were invited there. We now know their hideous fate. You act like some blasphemous religious order, cells within cells. You, Higden, your two acolytes and possibly Rishanger, knew the truth behind the Midnight Man. All of you are deeply implicated. Meeting at Rishanger's house or some other desolate place, using your wealth to swell the number of your coven – men and women like Bardolph and Adele. You also had your bodyguard, your cohort of killers, guards in black leather, to be whistled up like a hunting pack.'

'Evidence?' Higden made to rise.

'Oh, I will come to that by and by. You, Higden, became a peritus, skilled in the black arts. A true nightmare, you would cast about in search of secret rituals and precious items to deepen your so-called powers, artefacts such as the Philosopher's Stone – the key to all alchemy.'

'I threw Rishanger out of my house over that.'

'Mere pretence, a disguise to conceal the truth, a public demonstration that you had nothing to do with such a man. You had that wax figurine of yourself deliberately placed in Rishanger's house so as to portray yourself as an inveterate enemy of such a wicked soul. I suspect you never really liked or trusted Rishanger. Time proved you right.' Anselm paused to cough and clear his throat, wiping blood-flecked lips on a piece of cloth.

Stephen glanced around. Almaric and Gascelyn sat, eyes blinking, now and again the occasional nervous gesture. Cutwolf and his companions remained impassive: faces of stone, eyes almost blank as if they had already made up their minds what to do – but what?

'Now at Glastonbury, the so-called magical stone of Merlin, a rock of allegedly great power, had been found during the reign of the present King's grandfather and placed along with other precious items in the treasury crypt at Westminster which Puddlicot later pillaged.'

'I know nothing of Glastonbury. As I said, I have never been there.'

'Correct – you have never visited the abbey. I checked. I am sure you would love to do so. However, Higden, you like to keep your hand hidden – you cleverly cover your tracks. You,' Anselm pointed at Almaric, 'are different. You were born close to Glastonbury, weren't you? You were at school there. You served as a novice and became a skilled carpenter. You were taught by the abbey artisans before you left. You took to wandering. You were later ordained as a priest, becoming a chaplain under the royal banners and serving in France, where you met your true master here.'

'What nonsense!' the curate scoffed.

'Facts,' Anselm countered. 'You knew all about the discoveries at Glastonbury and told your master here. Rich and powerful, he became absorbed with finding such items, along with the rest of the treasure Puddlicot had stolen.' Anselm paused, head down.

Stephen stared around. No voices, no visions. Nevertheless, he sensed a whole host of invisible witnesses were gathering, pressing in on every side to listen. This ruined, charred nave had become a fearsome judgement hall. Cutwolf and his companions, grim and silent, were the executioners. One way or another, this would end in blood.

'You, Higden,' Anselm continued, 'searched, as secretly as you could, everything about Puddlicot, even though you openly pretended ignorance about him. You secured the advowson to this church. You moved house to be closer. I suspect Rishanger bought Puddlicot's dwelling at your insistence.' Anselm took a deep breath. 'With me and mine, whatever we did you pretended, like mummers in a play, though I noticed you always avoided my attempts to exorcise. Yet you made one mistake very early on. How did you know Rishanger's particular house in Hagbut Lane once belonged to Puddlicot? Who told you that?' Higden refused to answer. Anselm shrugged and continued. 'Time passed. You appointed Parson Smollat to the benefice – a good but very weak priest with more than a fondness for the ladies, someone you could control.'

Higden simply smirked.

'The cemetery was searched. You used Bardolph for that, digging the earth, preparing graves, but you discovered nothing. Your blood-drinking at Rishanger's house continued. Eventually you decided that enough corpses were buried there, although I suspect you hated being dependent on Rishanger. By now you had your new death house in Saint Michael's cemetery. A well-fortified, stout and lonely building with, I suspect, a prison pit beneath. You enticed your victims into it.'

'How?' Higden gibed. 'And if I did, where are they buried?'

'I sat by the lychgate,' Anselm retorted. 'I spent an entire afternoon there. I was surprised at how many young women of various means and livings go by. Before the trouble started, I am quite sure a few would use the cemetery as a place to rest. Margotta Sumerhull, the maid from The Unicorn, went there and disappeared – so did Edith Swan-neck. Who enticed them in? You, Almaric, a priest who could be trusted, or Gascelyn, the handsome squire? An invitation to talk, to sup? Would they like to walk through, perhaps see the new building? Others were easier – whores and prostitutes hired under the cloak of dark. That death house is well-named; once there, they would be imprisoned.' The exorcist paused. 'A poor dancer died there, didn't she, Gascelyn? Eleanora? She came back to haunt you with her perfume and stamping feet. Little wonder you became so wary but Higden made you stay there?' Anselm leaned forward. 'The death house will be searched. I am sure a pit lies beneath where those poor girls were pinioned before they were brutally enjoyed and murdered.'

'There is a pit,' Gascelyn, face all flushed, protested. 'But for storing.'

'Silence!' Cutwolf held up a hand, snapping his fingers. The captain of archers hurried over, pushing back his cowl to reveal a sharp, nut-brown face. Cutwolf whispered, the man murmured his agreement and left the nave with two of his companions.

'And the corpses?' Higden's steely poise had slipped.

'Oh, very easy. Saint Michael's is the parish cemetery of the ward. Many beggars die in Dowgate. They are brought here, wrapped tightly in canvas sheets, bound with cord and placed in the laystall close to the old burial pit. I have seen them. It's an ideal place. The soil there is always loose and soft from the lime and other elements caked in the ground. Who would dream of untying and unrolling the dirty shrouds to inspect the naked cadaver of some hapless beggar? However, in some cases, those shrouds contained the corpses of murdered young women such as Margotta and Edith. Buried quietly, swiftly, their bodies soon rotted.

'The pit could be opened?' Bolingbrok declared.

'Yes, it could be,' Anselm agreed. 'That burial pit was also your unholy sanctuary, Higden, a place you could practice your midnight rites. However, let us return to Rishanger's gruesome garden. Sometime last year, while burying your victims at Rishanger's house, the Cross of Neath and Queen Eleanor's dagger were found, along with a parchment script saying how the remaining treasure was under the guardianship of God's protector. This confirmed your belief that Puddlicot had buried most of the treasure somewhere in or around Saint Michael's Church, Candlewick. You made secret searches using the likes of Bardolph. He was unsuccessful so you decided to consult the dead. You organized, I am sure, the most malignant of all such ceremonies: a black mass celebrated over that burial pit during the deep heart of the night.

'I am not a priest!'

'No, but Almaric is and, as is common with such rites, something truly hideous occurred. You called into the darkness, Sir William, and a demonic chorus sang back. You raised a fiery nest: not only the hapless ghost of Puddlicot and the souls and spirits of those you had murdered both there and, I believe, elsewhere, but the prowling demons – those powerful, malevolent spirits who hunt the arid lands of the spiritual life. So fearsome were they that you and your coven had to flee.'

'Very interesting!' Higden snapped. 'Brother Anselm, I am prepared to surrender myself to the King's clerks. I will, in a different place and at a different time, demand evidence – proof positive for your outrageous allegations.'

Stephen glanced quickly at Cutwolf and Bolingbrok and a chill seized his heart. Cutwolf, just for a brief moment, betrayed his own uncertainty.

'Rishanger,' Anselm continued, ignoring the interruption, 'became agitated. His relationship with you was not as strong as that of your two henchmen here. Perhaps he resented sharing the treasure found in his garden. More importantly, he had seen your vaunted powers brought to nothing. How the disturbances at St Michael's were now attracting the attention of both Crown and Church. Rishanger decided to flee. He may have killed his mistress Beatrice, or that might have been the work of your black-garbed assassins who then pursued and murdered Rishanger in Westminster Abbey.' Anselm chewed the corner of his lips. 'You also tried to raise the dead there, didn't you, and failed? No wonder members of your coven became nervous and uncertain. You must have been truly furious at Rishanger's treachery, his attempt to flee and the bungled work of your assassins. Now the Crown knew what was at stake: they had the Cross of Neath and Queen Eleanor's dagger. Sir Miles Beauchamp and the Secret Chancery were alerted.'

Anselm paused, fingering the wooden cross around his neck. Stephen glanced up and flinched at the evil, gaunt face glaring down at him from the pitch dark. He shifted his gaze.

'Hate-made holes slick with blood. Soul weary, the spirits gather to sing sorrowful songs,' a voice taunted. Stephen glanced up at the moving, dancing shapes which floated and darted like shards of ash. A billow of dust swept by, only to dissipate in a pool of light.

'Shrouded in sadness,' the voice whispered. 'Release must come!'

'You.' Anselm's voice cracked under the strain. 'You, Higden, became convinced that Puddlicot's treasure hoard was here. You regarded my interference and that of Sir Miles as vexatious but not serious. More importantly, you needed to close this church so that you could search it thoroughly as well as control your own followers. Bardolph was not obeying. Recalcitrant, stubborn, absorbed with Edith Swan-neck, the gravedigger was not a member of your inner cell. However, I think he began to suspect your true identity, Sir William. The night we first attempted to exorcise this haunted place, Bardolph openly grumbled at the lack of burial fees. He was secretly making a barbed sally against you. How he was burying corpses, those of your victims, which brought him no income. He probably resented Gascelyn occupying the death house, assuming duties Bardolph considered his own. Above all, unbeknown to you, Bardolph had become obsessed with the whore Edith Swan-neck from a local brothel. Edith was, I believe, invited to Saint Michael's by one of your coven who had noticed her beauty when either Gascelyn or Almaric visited the The Oil of Gladness. Was she told how she had caught the eye of no less a person than Sir William Higden? Full of herself, Edith hurried away. She was inveigled into the meadows of murder. She was abducted, killed, her corpse like the rest wrapped tightly in shroud sacking and buried by Gascelyn. Bardolph searched for her. He discovered his beloved definitely left for Saint Michael's but then disappeared. He later found her necklace in the cemetery. Bardolph became furious, fearing full well what might have happened and holding you, Sir William, responsible. Full of anger and resentment, Bardolph's twisted heart turned to the prospect of blackmail. He openly boasted about his rich prospects. He may have even mentioned something to Parson Smollat. He had to be silenced. Adele or someone else in the coven alerted the master to the danger. Bardolph was killed in this church by your minions here. His corpse, wrapped in a sheet, was carried to the top of the tower, unwrapped and pushed between the crenellations. It is,' Anselm smiled grimly, 'difficult to glimpse anything at the top of that soaring tower, especially when the sun moves into the west and the light begins to fade. More importantly, I stood there when the bells mysteriously tolled; that tower top shook like a tree in a furious gale. Bardolph's corpse, resting between the turrets, simply toppled over when

Simon the sexton began to peal the bells.' Anselm spread his hands. 'Just another mysterious death in this haunted church.'

'But the sexton claimed,' Almaric taunted, 'that he heard someone walking up the steps of the tower.'

'The spirits!' Higden jibed.

'No, no,' Anselm retorted, 'that was just poor Simon's imagination and the effects of your minions going up and down the steps; trapdoors being opened, dust stirred, doors unlatched.' Anselm paused as the captain of the archers came hurrying through the darkness. He leaned down and whispered into Cutwolf's ear. 'Well?'

Higden rose and stretched, stamping his feet. Cutwolf also got up to meet him, gesturing that Higden sit down. The merchant knight did so reluctantly. Cutwolf went off to whisper to the archers and came back. 'There is a pit,' he announced, 'cleverly concealed beneath one of the paving stones of the death house. They lifted that and went down.'

'And?' Gascelyn could hardly keep the excitement out of his voice.

'Nothing!' Cutwolf replied. 'Nothing but a barrel and some boxes.'

Stephen's heart sank; Anselm sighed noisily.

'However!' Cutwolf snapped his fingers. 'In moving the bed, Master Gascelyn, we found this.' An archer handed over a small casket. Cutwolf lifted the lid to reveal a heap of bangles, cheap rings and necklaces. Cutwolf sifted amongst these and handed over a bracelet. 'Read the inscription.' Anselm examined the tawdry item and mouthed the word *Margotta*.

'You stupid fool!' Almaric snarled, before Higden shouted a warning. Cutwolf screamed into the darkness and an arrow shaft whirled through the air, smashing into the wall behind them. 'That proves nothing,' Higden spluttered. 'Gascelyn bought . . .'

'Silence!' Cutwolf took his seat, gesturing at Anselm to continue.

'Bardolph's death was necessary for three important reasons.' Anselm leaned forward, jabbing a finger at Higden who, like his two companions, was clearly agitated. Almaric sat, arms crossed, looking down at his feet; Gascelyn, hands on his knees, stared blindly before him.

'Three important reasons,' Anselm repeated. 'The same

applies to all the other mysterious murders here. First, to clear
the board, to remove anybody who might get in your way.
Secondly, to silence gossiping mouths. Finally, and most importantly, to depict this church and its cemetery as a haunt of
demons,' Anselm chuckled. 'And that would not be difficult.'

'Why?' Cutwolf's attitude had changed slightly, as if listening
to something which would convince him about what he
should do.

'Oh, as I have said – to close this church and pull it down.
Sir William would have free rein to explore, dig, pull up
and push until he found Puddlicot's treasure. Lord, the sheer
wickedness of the logic! Publicly Sir William is the generous
benefactor, promising the world a splendid church, a gorgeous
new beginning. In truth, however, he is a Satanist, a blood-
drinker, murderer and arsonist.'

'Smollat burnt this . . .'

'No, no, Sir William, let me explain further. You murdered
Bardolph for the reasons I have given. You then silenced Adele,
leaving that flask of poisoned wine in her alehouse, a special
mourning gift for her. Adele was a greedy woman – she drank
the wine full of arsenic. She had to die just in case Bardolph
had chattered. You visited her house in the guise of the local
justice so one of your minions could search and remove anything
suspicious.' Anselm wiped his hands. 'All neat and tidy.' He
gestured at Cutwolf. 'Your water bottle, please.' Anselm took
a deep gulp and wiped his mouth on the back of his hand. He
replaced the stopper and put the water bottle between his feet.
'Simon the sexton died for the same three reasons. Was he, too,
asking awkward questions? We found a scrap of parchment on
his chancery desk written in English, Norman French and Latin.
What did it say? "Now Lucifer was the friend of Saint
Michael's?" Lucifer, before he fell, was an archangel, too. Was
Simon openly hinting about you, Sir William? A friend of Saint
Michael's Church and yet, at the same time, Lucifer, the fallen
angel?' Higden just glared back. 'And of course, what a tale!
A story to reinforce your intentions, Sir William. The poor
sexton, driven to suicide, cutting his own throat in his own
church – nonsense!' Anselm sniffed. 'Simon was lured into this
nave. You cut his throat. You locked and bolted both the sacristy

door and the main door. As far as the ancient corpse door is concerned – well, it sticks and groans when it opens. You removed the key and, after the murder, Almaric, a carpenter, coated the side of the door with a heavy glue; the type wood-workers use when they fashion a casket. Enough glue to keep that heavy door firmly shut. I found small glue droppings on the path outside. I wondered, why? Now I know.' Anselm paused. 'Once inside the church, when we'd discovered Simon's corpse and became busy with your victim, one of you slipped shut the bolts on the corpse door and proclaimed the key was missing. Of course it wasn't – you had the keys and so you created a real mystery. A church where all three doors were locked and bolted yet a man within, all alone, had his throat cut. The work of demons, of ghosts. In a way people were right about your work, Higden, you and your two minions here.' Anselm paused to drink from the water bottle. He offered this to Stephen, who shook his head. The novice was tense, absorbed in the unfolding tale.

'Parson Smollat and Isolda also had to die. Perhaps the good parson had seen or heard something he shouldn't have. Perhaps Bardolph did confide in him, though I cannot prove that. Anyway, you and your kind paid the parson a visit late one evening. Smollat and Isolda must have been terrified. Gascelyn worked with the Inquisition before you turned him. He would know what to do. You forced Smollat to write that message, implicating himself in the destruction of his own church. You then forced him and his woman to drink cups of drugged wine. Once they had, you took them out to that yew tree and hanged them. You stained their hands with oil and saltpetre. Afterwards, you saturated the church with oil, cannon powder and saltpetre and turned it into a hellish inferno.'

'Parson Smollat bought the oil!'

'Of course he did – at your request, before you paid him that fatal visit. You'd explained to him how both Crown and Church wanted this building cleansed and razed.' Anselm took a deep breath. 'Parson Smollat may have even welcomed that. Finally, you decided on our deaths.' Anselm grabbed Stephen's shoulder and pressed hard. 'At Sir Miles' sumptuous dinner party, you whistled up your coven of killers. Sir Miles was murdered.

Thank God we escaped.' Anselm got wearily to his feet. 'You know, Higden, Sir Miles always suspected you were not what you claimed to be.'

'Proof, proof, proof!' Higden shouted. 'Evidence, apart from a casket full of tawdry items.'

'And the logic of my allegations?'

'Proof!'

'The casket and . . .' Anselm dug into his pouch and pulled out the script found in Parson Smollat's house.

'You can search my chambers!' Higden protested.

'We would find nothing. You have already proved you hide your footsteps well, except,' Anselm twirled the strip of parchment between his fingers, 'for Parson Smollat's last message. You should have studied your hornbook better, Higden. Sir Miles certainly did.'

'What do you mean?'

'*Habeo igne gladioque,*' Anselm read out loud, '*destruxi ecclesiam nostrum* – I have, with fire and sword, destroyed our church. In the Latin original,' Anselm whispered, 'if you take the first letter of each word, what do you get?'

'No,' Almaric protested, 'no, it cannot be!'

'But it is,' Anselm soothed. 'The word Higden is formed. Parson Smollat, whatever he was, knew he was going to die. For once he acted the brave priest. I think it is very appropriate, don't you? A message from the dead, from beyond the grave? Sir Miles certainly understood the message, as did I. We thought we would wait and get further proof – we certainly shall.' Anselm turned. 'Master Cutwolf, you have them?'

The clerk whistled into the darkness and the archers brought a sack forward. Cutwolf shook out the long white Carmelite robes. He and Bolingbrok swiftly dressed, both robes had rents at the side so swords and daggers could be drawn in an instant. They pulled up the cowls, had a murmured conversation with the captain and left the nave. Four of the archers followed at a discreet distance. Higden went to move. 'Stay!' the Captain of the Archers bellowed. 'Only the Carmelites may move.' Stephen watched the line of archers bring up their bows – ghostly hooded figures, their winged death merely a whisper away.

'Pray, Stephen.' Anselm touched the novice lightly on the

arm and went to kneel on the sanctuary steps. Stephen walked through that ominous line of bowmen to the ruins of the corpse door. He stared out across the night-shrouded cemetery. So much had happened there, and now a gathering was imminent.

'Dark night. A host of shadows cluster,' a voice whispered. 'They will snare the sin-drenched souls in their dizziness. Hem them in their own terror-filled madness.' Figures merged out of the blackness twisted in deformed infirmity. A faint rotten-ness teased Stephen's nostrils. 'Corruption lays siege,' a voice hissed, and the visions faded. Far out in the cemetery a light appeared, small but brilliantly white. Then abruptly a baby laughed cheerily. 'Christ's tiny voice!' The very air breathed the words. 'The Divine Child.'

'Blessed be he,' another voice thundered, 'who prepares my arms for war and my hands for battle.'

'The shield wall still holds.' The first voice spoke again. 'But will the armour fail, the heroes fall?'

Stephen broke from his reverie. Clear on the night air echoed the soul-chilling clash of steel. The ringing scrape of sword on sword, the vicious clatter of dagger blades. Shouts and cries trailed then lapsed into silence. Stephen stared in the direction of the lychgate. A light appeared – the hungry flames of a cresset torch, the murmur of voices, the groans and cries of wounded men. Cutwolf and Bolingbrok strode out of the night; behind them archers dragged two men garbed in black leather. Both were wounded: one had a bubbling cut to the side of his neck while the right leg of the second man simply trailed as a piece of useless, twisted flesh. Hoods and masks had been removed to reveal hard, lean, unshaven faces. Stephen stared closely. He was sure both men had, at some time, visited The Unicorn. He hurriedly stepped aside as the cortège swept into the church. Cutwolf was brutal. Seizing the prisoner with the broken leg and, despite his screams and protests, he forced him to kneel, yanking back his head, pressing the cutting edge of his dagger against the prisoner's pulsing throat.

'Who were you to kill?'

The man shook his head, crying to himself.

'Who?'

'Two Carmelites,' the man blurted out. 'We were told they would leave the church and take the lanes back to White Friars sometime after the Vespers bell sounded. We watched the church. We saw you leave so we withdrew and waited.'

'For the surprise of your life,' Bolingbrok jibed. 'And your orders? Come, man, let your tongue chatter.'

'We received a message.'

'From whom?'

'The tavern master of The Gates of Hell.'

'The Southwark tavern?'

'The same.'

'And?'

'We were told to visit a haberdasher's shop in the Mercery. To look for a message in a leather writing case, embroidered with the arms of Castile.'

'And payment?'

'To visit the church of Saint Frideswide as the bell for Terce sounded tomorrow, and look for six silver pieces in a pouch pushed into the old leper-squint in the wall.'

Cutwolf, ignoring the man's protests, pulled him to his feet and thrust him forward so the other prisoner had to catch him. Higden, Almaric and Gascelyn, subdued and watchful, clustered together.

'Who?' Anselm strode to stand in front of them. 'I ask you as the only people who knew that two Carmelites were here at this time, are now with us in this church, so who told these assassins?'

Cutwolf broke the brooding silence. He drew his sword with a rasp and held it up, fingers clutching the cross-hilt. 'I, Edmund Langley, commonly known as Cutwolf, clerk in the Secret Chancery of England, faithful retainer of Edward King of England, Scotland and France, by the power given to me, adjudge you, Sir William Higden, Squire Gascelyn, Curate Almaric and,' Cutwolf pointed at the two moaning prisoners, 'all your adherents, to be traitors taken in arms against the Crown.'

'We demand a fair trial,' Higden spluttered, face pale as he realized the full impact of what was happening.

'Taken in arms against the King.' Cutwolf stepped back. 'You murdered my master, a royal clerk. You pillaged the King's treasure. Your coven attacked the King's loyal servants. You murdered then revelled in your victims' blood. You have committed heinous treason, sacrilege and arson.'

'By what right?' Higden took a step forward.

'I am a cleric,' Almaric bleated.

'By this.' Cutwolf, still holding the sword up, dug into his wallet and handed Stephen a small script. 'Read it aloud, boy, read it so all can hear.'

Stephen, hands shaking, unrolled the stiff, cream-coloured parchment.

'Out loud!' Cutwolf repeated.

'What the bearer of this seal has done, he has done for the Crown, the realm and Holy Mother Church. All officers and loyal subjects of the Crown, on their duty of allegiance and on pain of treason, must give the bearer of this seal and all his work full sustenance and support.'

'And?' Cutwolf demanded. 'What else?'

'Given under the secret seal at our Palace of Sheen, on the fourth of May in the forty-seventh year of our reign, Edward the King.'

'And the seals?'

'Two,' Stephen replied. 'The signet seal of the King.' Stephen peered at the generous blob of purple wax. 'And that of the Secret Chancery at Westminster.'

'Taken in arms.' Cutwolf's words were full of menace. 'Adjudged traitors, sentenced to death, punishment immediate.' He stepped forward. 'Archers,' he lifted a gauntleted hand. 'Notch!'

Stephen shivered at the ominous rattle. Higden fell to his knees. Almaric turned, looking wildly for escape. Gascelyn drew his dagger.

'Loose!'

The air thrummed with a sombre twang, the hiss of feathered death as the arrow shafts, one volley after another, sped into the exposed group. The two failed assassins simply toppled over. Almaric, his back turned, was hit three times. One shaft pierced his neck, bursting through his gullet. Gascelyn was struck in both face and chest. Higden, caught on all fours, rolled in agony as the shafts pierced deep into his side and belly.

Stephen glanced at Anselm. The exorcist's face was as white
as snow, his lips crusted with blood. He could only sketch a
cross in the air. The condemned lay sprawled. Gascelyn and
Higden still jerked. Cutwolf, sword sheathed, misericorde dagger
in his hand, moved from corpse to corpse, slitting throats as
cleanly as a woman would clip a flower head. Once finished he
plucked the commission out of Stephen's icy fingers, winked at
the novice and walked away. 'Do not grieve for them,' he called
out over his shoulder. 'Hell has them and God's creation is richer
for it.' Cutwolf walked back, tears glittering in his hard eyes. 'I
loved Sir Miles,' he whispered, 'more than David loved Jonathan.
A good man, Stephen. In my eyes, God's own child. These
villains brought their death on themselves. God will judge them.'

'What now?' Anselm moved back to sit wearily on the sanctuary steps.

'We will burn the corpses,' Cutwolf replied, spittle wetting
his dry, cracked lips. 'We will have it rumoured abroad how
poor Sir William and his loyal servants were trapped in another
hideous blaze at Saint Michael's. The King will know the truth.
He will seize all of Higden's wealth, along with this treasure
hoard. He will embrace me as his friend and order chantry
priests to sing Masses every day for the repose of Sir Miles'
soul. And you, Brother?'

'I must finish what I first came here for,' Anselm replied.
'Now the root of all this evil has been pulled up – the sheer
human wickedness which nourished and sustained it – I must
finish the cleansing process.'

'Here?' Cutwolf asked.

'No, in the cemetery, on the burial pit. If you could set up
a makeshift altar . . .'

Anselm took Stephen deeper into the sanctuary, to the recess
where those who fled for protection used to shelter. Anselm
made them both as comfortable as possible; they sat with their
backs to the blackened wall while Cutwolf and Bolingbrok
became busy. The corpses were heaped in the centre of the nave
and a funeral pyre of dry wood, kindling and bracken was
swiftly built about them. Archers were despatched to find oil
and saltpetre. 'The King's business!' Cutwolf shouted after
them. 'Arouse anyone you want.'

'Do not light the fire,' Anselm called. 'Not yet, not until I say.' Cutwolf nodded in agreement. Stephen, cold and desperate, sat thinking about Alice. The more he did, any compassion or pity for Higden and his adherents ebbed away; their deaths had been shocking, sudden and cruel, but just. He watched as the archers worked. He could tell from the shouts and cries that the priest's house had been broken into and Anselm's altar was being raised on the place of slaughter. Stephen's eyes grew weary and he slept. He awoke to Anselm talking.

'I have waged war on you all my priestly life.' The exorcist was pointing at something or someone crouching before him. 'So this is our last confrontation?' Anselm paused, nodding as though listening to a reply. 'If necessary,' the exorcist murmured, 'if that is the price, I will pay.' Stephen could see nothing. No voices sounded, no visions swirled.

The funeral pyre was ready and it rose – a sinister hive of oil-drenched wood and kindling, the bitter smell of saltpetre tainting the air.

'All is ready, Brother!' Anselm, coughing and spluttering, clambered to his feet. They walked down to the corpse door.

'We found these in the priest's house.' Cutwolf gestured at the vestments heaped on a stool.

Anselm swiftly dressed in the alb, stole and amice. He crossed himself and walked out into the dark. The altar, a plain table, stood ready in the centre of the burial pit. Candles fluttered in their brass holdings either side of the black crucifix on its wooden stand. A dish of cruets and a plain brass paten and chalice were also there. Stephen placed the exorcist's pannier close to the altar, opened it and took out the sacred chrism, phial of salt, the small stoup of holy water and asperges rod as well as the exorcist's battered brown leather psalter. Anselm grasped the latter and, in the light of the lantern horns, placed either side of the altar, sifted through its yellowing pages. 'We will say the Mass of Michaelmas, Stephen, the Mass of Saint Michael, Lucifer's great opponent. Help me now!' Anselm crossed himself and intoned, 'I will go unto the altar of God, the God of my youth . . .'

The Mass began. Stephen was swept up by the power of Anselm's voice and his vigorous observance of the ritual. An

array of cowled archers circled the altar. Stephen was surprised.
The night had fallen quiet. There was a deathly calm – no sign
of anything, nothing but the wild grass and bramble bush
bending under a gentle breeze. Anselm moved to the consecration, bending over the wafer, the thin host Cutwolf had found
in the priest's house. He murmured the words of Christ and
was about to raise the paten when he staggered back.

'Get you gone, prattling, filthy, stupid priest!' The voice
cracked like a whip. Abruptly the air around them was filled
with trails of smoke, each formed into the ugly, sinister face of
that old woman. A stench like that of the filthiest cesspit swept
across, forcing both Carmelites to gag and retch. The candles
fluttered out. Red blotches appeared on the white altar clothes.
Above these swarmed a horde of black flies.

Stephen was aware of Cutwolf beside him. 'What is the
matter?' the clerk whispered.

'Can you see anything?' Stephen begged.

'Nothing,' Cutwolf hissed. 'The candles have gone out. This
stench, and the cold!'

'Leave us!' Anselm ordered. The exorcist stepped back to
the altar but he was caught by a coughing fit. A dark-feathered
bird of the night came swooping over the altar, wings wafting
threateningly. Stephen glimpsed its cruel jutting beak and curved
claws. A raven appeared as if out of nowhere; the bird sailed
slowly down, wings extended, through the gloom to perch on
the top of the cross and caw raucously. The archers became
agitated; their shouts and cries broke the silence. Shadow-tinged
shapes moved through the bristling gorse, long and sinister, as
if some wolf or wild dog pack circled ravenous for prey. Wraiths
danced around the altar. Anselm had returned to the Mass but
his words were drowned by a cacophony of voices hurling
blasphemous obscenities. 'Stephen,' Anselm declared, 'we
continue. Cutwolf, order your men to pray. Ignore what is
happening.' Anselm continued with the ritual. A horrid face
appeared above the altar; only half of this could be glimpsed,
a red eye glaring from a deathly pallor. Somewhere a drum
sounded the death beat of a tambour. A shape, like that of a
war horse caparisoned for battle, clattered through the cemetery,
hooves pounding, armour rattling. Anselm, who had finished

the consecration, now moved to the exorcism. Armed with the sacred chrism and holy water, he anointed the night air to the east, north, south and west, a circle of protection as he called on the powers of heaven.

'Bitter blasts!' a voice called. 'Look, they come! Shall we be destroyed?'

'Kill the priest,' a second voice urged. 'Shut the shaven pate's scrawny throat! Silence his tongue!'

Stephen watched as the faces of the night-prowlers, the juddering shapes, gathered around Anselm. The exorcist was now on his knees, leaning back on his heels. Blood dribbled from his mouth; his shroud-white face was drenched in sweat. The hideous sights and sounds faded, leaving the old priest throbbing with pain. Anselm began to cry; tears drenched his cheeks as he shook his head and breathed replies to his tormentors' questions. The cemetery lay silent; even the breeze had fallen. Anselm was sobbing like a child, praying fervently, striking his breast in an act of contrition. Stephen went to grab his hands and started in horror. Anselm's right hand was so cold while the left was too hot to even touch.

'Stay back, Stephen, stay back!' Anselm's feverish jerking grew worse. He coughed huge globules of blood and spittle, eyes half-closed he tried to pray. Cutwolf came and crouched beside him. Stephen gazed around helplessly; the night was proving to be a beautiful one. He caught the scent of wild flowers in his nostrils; the air was warm.

'Light the fire!' Anselm's bloodshot eyes opened, staring frantically. 'Light the fire!' he repeated. 'Now, burn the wicked ones.'

Cutwolf hurried to obey. Anselm stretched out a hand and Stephen helped him up. The exorcist insisted on finishing the Mass, mouthing the words quietly. He reached the kiss of peace. '*Pax vobiscum*,' he called.

'*Pax tecum*, Magister.' The phrase was repeated time and time again out of the darkness. '*Pax tecum, deo gratias* – Peace to you, thanks be to God.' Stephen heard a sound and whirled around. The funeral pyre had been lit, the flames roaring heavenwards. He turned back just in time to catch Anselm as the exorcist collapsed in a dead faint. Cutwolf came and knelt beside them. 'The fire is consuming them, Brother.'

'And they have consumed me.' The exorcist opened his eyes and smiled up at both of them. 'The final battle,' Anselm tapped the side of his head, 'was in here. The last great temptation. They taunted me, Stephen, with the sins of my youth but they were defeated, driven back. Now,' he coughed, and a trickle of blood seeped between his lips. 'My body's for the dark, my soul for the light. All is finished.' He paused. 'Do you hear that, Stephen?'

The novice, tears in his eyes, glanced up, then he heard it. Despite the dark and the raging flames, the liquid, beautiful song of a nightingale carried from somewhere deep in the cemetery.

'It is finished, completed, consummated.'

The exorcist jerked and fell back, staring blindly up into the star-filled sky.

ooOOoo

Words Amongst the Pilgrims

The physician finished his tale. One hand leaning on the mantle of the great fireplace, he turned, smiled at his fellow pilgrims and toasted them with his wine cup. 'No more,' he declared. 'My story is done and so am I.' His words were greeted with cries of applause and appreciation. The pilgrims, busy discussing both his story and their own encounters with the powers of evil, rose and began to leave the taproom. Chaucer remained, as did two others – the Wife of Bath and the summoner. Chaucer watched as they and the physician gathered at the head of the common table, heads together, whispering heatedly. Chaucer rose and sauntered towards them. Curious, yet he would not have stayed if the summoner hadn't grabbed his arm, indicating that he should join them on the bench. Once he did, Chaucer pointed to the physician. 'Tell me, sir, you are Stephen of Winchester?'

'I am.' The physician smiled. 'After Anselm's death, I no

longer heard the voices or saw the visions. I also realized I had no vocation for the religious life. Instead, I decided to follow my father's calling and so I have, to be the most skilled of physicians.'

'And also a very wealthy man?'

'Yes, Master Chaucer, he is,' the summoner replied.

'And who are you really – Cutwolf?'

The summoner laughed and shook his head.

'And you?' Chaucer turned to the Wife of Bath. 'You must be Marisa.'

'I am. My father returned to Bath and died of a broken heart. I took my dear departed sister's name, Alice. I, too, am a wealthy woman.'

'Because of me,' the summoner intervened. 'I am Bolingbrok, Master Chaucer. My life, my energy is dedicated to hunting down and executing every single blood-drinking member of the Midnight Man's coven. The physician and the Wife of Bath spend generously on achieving this both at home and abroad. Many years have passed but the hunt continues.'

'So your story is not finished?'

'No, Master Chaucer,' the physician replied. 'Sometimes, very rarely, the visions return. But this does not matter; our pursuit of justice does.'

'And Cutwolf?'

'Oh, Master Chaucer,' a mocking voice answered from the darkness of the deep window embrasure behind him. 'Do not turn master poet but, believe me, Cutwolf is very much alive and never far away!'

ooOOoo

Author's Note

The *Midnight Man* is, of course, a work of fiction, though one seamed with major themes of fourteenth-century society. Caesarius Von Heiserbach, the Cistercian, is one of my main sources for the visions, hauntings and exorcism. Other chroniclers such as Walter Map, Gerald of Wales and William of Malmesbury are also a thriving source for all kinds of hair-raising stories, be it hauntings or the work of Satan and his legions. We must remember that the medieval mind viewed the veil between the visible and invisible as very thin – sometimes non-existent. We have our own theories of physics; they certainly had theirs. According to them, Satan and his legions did ride the black winds and demons lurked in corners, jibbering and waiting. The dead spoke to the living and interfered in their affairs.

The Church's attitude to formal exorcism was very much as it is today. Hauntings, ghosts and possession were taken with more than a pinch of salt. It was only ready to officially move when it had the evidence. It adopted a similar attitude to witchcraft and the black arts, certainly frowning on men and women leaping naked about in forest glades and worshipping some idol. However, both Church and State would only act officially against witchcraft when it was linked to treason, murder or heresy. The great witch craze, especially in England, occurred only after the Reformation. Indeed, more women were burnt or hanged for witchcraft in Essex between 1603 and 1663 than in the entire kingdom during the medieval period. Accusations of witchcraft during the Middle Ages were usually introduced in the destruction of a political opponent – for example, the Gloucesters in the fifteenth century, Saint Joan of Arc a few decades later and, of course, Henry VIII levelled the same allegation against Anne Boleyn.

Glastonbury and the legends of Arthur dominated the Middle Ages. Glastonbury Abbey was, and undoubtedly still is, a spiritual and mystical place. Of course, the good monks there were not, as they say in Ireland, backwards in coming forwards. They portrayed their abbey as Arthur and Guinevere's last resting place, their tomb allegedly discovered in 1191. Successive English kings visited Glastonbury to celebrate this shrine so sacred to their monarchy. Certain artefacts mentioned in the story, such as the Merlin Stone, are fictitious, but Eleanor's Dagger and the Cross of Neath are genuine items.

The underworld of medieval London was both colourful and violent. Professional beggars and thieves flourished. There was no safety net and if you fell, the fall could be long and hard. Certain areas of London, such as Whitefriars and Southwark, were the nesting places of these undesirables. The problem was worsened by the presence of sanctuaries in London such as Westminster and St Paul's, where outlaws could shelter with impunity, protected by the Church, and be safe from arrest. However, the real danger of medieval London was, as it is today, organized professional gangs, who often had powerful patrons amongst the so-called respectable leading citizens of the City. These gangs or rifflers could prove very dangerous. For example, in 1326 the gangs actually took over London. They even killed the Chancellor of the Exchequer at the time, Walter Stapleton, the Bishop of Exeter, outside St Paul's, along with two of his squires. Many people think the Tower of London was built to protect the city. It wasn't! The Tower's main purpose was to overawe the city, which was why the constable was always a King's man, both body and soul.

Puddlicot's robbery did take place in the spring of 1303. A failed businessman, Puddlicot brought together all the undesirables in London. Outlaws, sanctuary men, defrocked priests, whores and thieves, as well those judged more worthy, such as aldermen and the sinister sheriff of the time, Hugh Pourte. The goldsmiths, the medieval bankers, handled stolen items, though of course they later protested that they were innocent and did not know the origin of the precious items which flooded the London markets. Puddlicot certainly suborned the leading monks, Alexander of Pershore and the sacristan in charge of security, Adam Warfield. Both these abbey luminaries enjoyed an unsavoury reputation with certain ladies of the town. They successfully managed to blackmail their abbot, Wenlock, over the latter's illegitimate daughter. Wenlock seemed to act like a man in a dream, claiming he had no knowledge of what was happening in his own abbey. Puddlicot did sow fast-growing hempen seed in the monks' cemetery, and used members of this gang to cordon it off. He hired the master mason, John St Albans, who forced open the crypt window. The robbers broke in on the eve of St Mark and helped themselves. The list of magnificent items stolen is given by Henry Cole in his 'Records published by the Records Commission' in 1836. A similar list of documents can be found in F. Palgrave's, *Kalendars and Inventories of the Exchequer.* Puddlicot's confession can still be read in the original (National Archives Kew: King's Remembrancer E/101/332/8). This document conveys Puddlicot's cool impudence and his clear assertion that he did it all his way, as well as the fact that he organized an earlier robbery of the abbot's silver to finance his great undertaking!

Puddlicot did have a leman, Joanne Picard, and took sanctuary in St Michael's, from which he was dragged and dispatched to the Tower. The clerk, John Drokensford, later Bishop of Bath and Wells, was Puddlicot's nemesis: a mailed Oxford clerk, utterly loyal to the King. Drokensford allowed nothing to get in his way; at one time he even carted off a hundred monks from Westminster and lodged them in the Tower.

The principal robber twisted and turned but eventually he was brought to judgement and sentenced to death. He was hanged in Tothill Lane just outside Westminster Abbey, after being taken to the gallows in a wheelbarrow. The route stretched the entire length of the north bank of the Thames, and the spectacle was both public and noisy. A contemporary chronicler, The *Annales Londinienses* describes it as follows: 'In that year, Puddlicot the clerk was led in a hand-cart from the Tower of London to Westminster, and there judged on the account of his violation of the King's treasury.' Others may have joined him there, including John Rippinghale, a defrocked priest whose confession also exists. For hundreds of years no one knew what Rippinghale was saying – it was a farrago of nonsense. In the end, I concluded that Rippinghale was simply buying time, leading Drokensford on a wild goose chase. Of course, no one escaped the gallows. There were further humiliations in store, probably for Puddlicot and his henchmen. Beneath the hinges on an ancient door leading to the chapter house at Westminster is what antiquarians have described as 'human skin'. There is every possibility that once he'd been hanged, Puddlicot's body was not only gibbeted but skinned; this was then dried, cured and hung on that door in the south cloister as a warning to the monks. The existence of this skin was first noticed by the antiquarian G. G. Scott in his book, *Gleanings from Westminster Abbey*, published in 1861. On page forty, Scott asserts: 'On the inner side of the door, I found hanging from beneath the hinges some pieces of white leather. They reminded me of the story of the skins of Danes. One theory was that marauding Danes in the eighth and ninth century had been captured and skinned. However, it is highly unlikely that the monks would have allowed this. Another theory was that the skins were hides used as draught excluders.' Scott continues: 'A friend to whom I'd shown them sent them to Mr Quekett of the College of Surgeons who, I regret to say, pronounced them to be human. It is clear that the entire door was covered with them, both within and without.' If this is true, Edward I may have had the corpses of all the robbers skinned and nailed to the door as a warning to the monks, a logical step of Puddlicot being hanged on the abbey's gallows in Tothill Lane.

I have been privileged to visit the crypt beneath the chapter house at Westminster Abbey. I have been down the ancient steps; you can still see where the wooden stairs were once used. In the crypt below I have examined the great pillar, bricks of which can still be taken away. I have seen the sixth crypt window without its sill, a reminder of John of St Albans' crafty skill in obtaining access to the King's treasure. The crypt is a brooding, gloomy place. I read in a modern account of the abbey how at night the security guards report all sorts of phenomena; having visited the abbey and researched Puddlicot's story, I can well believe it!